MERLIN
The Old Magic

Based on the television miniseries created by
Hallmark Entertainment Inc., starring Sam Neill as
Merlin, Helena Bonham Carter as Morgan Le Fay,
Sir John Gielgud as King Constant, Rutger Hauer as
King Vortigern, James Earl Jones as the Mountain
King, Miranda Richardson as Queen Mab, Isabella
Rossellini as Nimue and Martin Short as Frik.

Hallmark Entertainment Presents
Sam Neill Helena Bonham Carter
John Gielgud Rutger Hauer
James Earl Jones Miranda Richardson
Isabella Rosellini Martin Short
'Merlin'
Legend Advisor Loren Boothby
Music by Trevor Jones
Creature Effects by Jim Henson's Creature Shop
Executive Producer Robert Halmi, Sr.
Produced by Dyson Lovell
Teleplay by David Stevens and Peter Barnes
Story by Edward Khmara
Directed by Steve Barron

Original Soundtrack Available on
Verèse Sarabande Compact Discs

4 Hours   NBC

MERLIN
The Old Magic

JAMES MALLORY

Voyager

Voyager

An Imprint of HarperCollins*Publishers*
77-85 Fulham Palace Road,
Hammersmith, London W6 8JB

A Paperback Original 1998
1 3 5 7 9 8 6 4 2

A catalogue record for this book
is available from the British Library

ISBN 0 00 651289 5

Typeset by Palimpsest Book Production Limited,
Polmont, Stirlingshire
Printed and bound in Great Britain by
Caledonian International Book Manufacturing, Glasgow

MERLIN
The Old Magic

CONTENTS

THE COURTS OF SHADOWS

*S*he rode the winds of the upper air in search of a very special man. She did not remember how long it was since she had travelled this way, for her kind did not reckon the passing of Time in the same way as mortal men. Seasons spun over the face of the earth like shooting stars, but she paid little attention to their passing. She was the stuff of stars, not seasons, and the Old Magic ran in her veins, hot, fast and pure. She was Mab, Queen of the Old Ways.

But the Old Ways were dying.

It had started so insignificantly that she could not put her finger on exactly when the initial challenge to her power had come. Perhaps when the first Christian had come from Rome to preach his pernicious doctrine to the people of her land. She had been strong then, and arrogant in her power, and what did the trivial doings of men matter to her as she listened to the crystal music of the stars in their courses? She had thought the land would take them in and its magic change them, as it had so many others.

But the land had not changed the Christians. They had changed the land. When they began to lay waste to her people, cutting down the sacred groves and toppling the standing stones that marked her temples and sacred places of power, she had lashed out at them in a hundred furious battles, but it was already too late to win. These Christians were not content for their strange god to live in harmony with the other powers of Britain. They demanded that those powers be cast down and banished forever – and Mab's kind could not live without human believers.

So war came to a land that had never known it before. As the gentle spirits of field and wood were destroyed by cold iron and holy water, the people no longer lived in harmony with the land. Weeds grew among the scanty crops that had once grown lushly at the behest of the priestesses of the Old Ways. Trees that had once borne abundant fruit withered. Famine spread throughout the land, for man and beast alike, and now humankind laboured with incessant toil to bring crops from the barren soil and turned in ever greater offerings to the priests of the new religion for the certainty and security they promised.

As they did, Mab's people – the fairyfolk – began to die. When humans forgot them, they dwindled away into nothingness. Mab must save them, somehow. She must destroy the Christians and the Christian king who persecuted her people.

She needed allies, tools . . .

*   *   *

The mead-hall was lit by flickering torches whose smoke spiralled up to the age-darkened rafters of the Great Hall, decorated with carved dragon heads. The sightless wooden eyes appeared to gaze down on the feasting Saxons below as if hungry to join in their merriment.

The walls were hung with the painted round shields of the Saxon war band, the bright designs and snarling faces flanking the tables full of drunken and victorious men. Their enemies called them pirates; they called themselves warriors – landless men and younger sons who had no patrimony save a sword-blade and no skills save those of war. And so they sailed and raided up and down the Frisian coast, seeking the gold and glory that could take the place of a homeland.

The war leader looked out over his followers and wondered why he could not share in their merry-making. He was a young man, Saxon-fair and muscled like a young bull. He wore a great wolfskin cloak and gold glittered about his brow and upon his brawny arms, marks of success in countless previous attacks. The raid they celebrated here tonight had gone well – they'd sacked a village a few days' sail down the coast and came away well-laden with gold and glory and few men lost. Now he, as their leader, hosted a great feast for them, with bards to make songs of his prowess and valour in the battle. And by so much his glory increased.

But it wasn't enough. Gold was easily spent and glory faded. His eyes, the pale wintry blue of northern ice, looked out over the merriment of his companions with increasing restlessness. Only land was eternal, and you could not load land aboard a ship and sail away with it . . .

'But you could still take it,' a voice whispered in his ear.

The young warlord straightened in his chair and turned sharply toward the sound of the voice. What he saw made his eyes widen.

A woman stood beside his chair, but a woman like none he had ever seen. Her skin was white as moonmilk and her long black hair was dark as a raven's wings. It was twisted and braided and studded with jewels, but enough of it fell free to coil about her shoulders like glistening black snakes. Her face was painted into a harsh mask, her eyes rimmed with black that made their translucent fire glitter like moonlight on ice. She wore a trailing black gown that made the young warlord think of smoke and shadows and the dark and powerful undertow that could claim men and ships and drag them to the bottom of the sea in an instant.

'Who are you?' he asked, but in his heart he already knew. His people called her kind *svartaelfin* – the dark folk of the fairy. This one must be their queen, so rich and powerful did she look.

'One who can give you what you desire,' she answered. She put a hand on his arm, and at her touch he felt a mingling of alarm and desire that excited him. He had never felt so strong an emotion before, save in the heat of battle.

'And what do I desire?' he asked, angling his body toward her and looking over his shoulder to see who noticed. All were occupied at their drinking. No one saw her but him, he was sure of it now.

'Land. Power. A Kingdom. A name that will live forever.' Her voice was like the surf hissing over the rocks.

'All men desire that,' the warlord said. He was beginning to be irritated as well as wary, and his temper was not good at the best of times. 'Where are these lands?'

'West of here,' the woman said. She pointed in the direction of the sea. 'They are undefended and ripe for the taking, groaning beneath the tyranny of a Christian king.'

'Britain?' The young warlord was astonished. 'Britain is a Roman province; Constant rules there as their puppet and, if he should cry for help, the Legions will come to his aid. They'll slaughter my men by sheer force of numbers.'

'Rome will send no more legions to Britain,' the woman answered. Her eyes gleamed like those of a hunting cat. 'The Empire is falling – now is the time for strong men to carve out new empires. And I will help you.'

Rome falling? But the Roman Peace had lasted for as long as the Saxons could remember, the Roman Legions keeping them from raiding the soft, fat villages of Brittany, Armorica, and Gaul – all Roman provinces – and protecting Britain most of all, for the Romans valued the tin trade that flourished there.

His eyes narrowed as he studied his companion. Most men would fear her, but he was not most men. He had known from the cradle that he was different, that he was born to rule.

Now he would.

'And your price for this aid, Lady?' he asked levelly.

Her face twisted into a mask of hate. 'Kill the king! Kill Constant and every Christian in the land and I will help you rule in his place,' Mab hissed. 'You will have power and rich lands beyond imagining. You are pagan, and I do not care who rules there so long as the people return to the Old Ways.'

'Killing Christians. War. Sounds reasonable,' he said with satisfaction.

Let her think he served her, until he had his kingdom. He bowed down to no power on earth or beneath it – he cared not what gods or spirits existed or didn't so long as he ruled.

Prince Vortigern smiled.

CHAPTER ONE

THE
COURTS OF
WINTER

*T*he road to Anoeth was long and twisted. Only the dead travelled it easily. It was a land of grey mist and the blackened stumps of stark, twisted trees that reached out of the mist like hands from the grave. Even Mab felt its chill and she shivered as she groped her way among the standing stones that marked the path. This was not her own kingdom – this was the land of Death and Winter, ruled over by its own dark king, Idath.

Once they had been lovers, for Idath, grim and terrifying as he seemed to the souls he harvested, was as necessary to the Old Ways as Mab herself. When the Wheel of the Year turned, spinning the seasons from summer to winter, Idath was there to take up the weak who fell to winter's cruel sharpness. Without death and change, there could be no light and life.

But death must balance life, not overwhelm it. The war that had raged over Britain since Vortigern landed had sown death in its wake as a farmer sowed seed, until the land was awash in blood. King Constant was old and crafty, and his priests filled his armies with the terror of Hell and the death which has no rebirth. They fought like maddened wolves for their king, but Vortigern had allies in the Danelaw, and with their help he had slowly pushed the royal armies back across the face of Britain, but at a terrible cost to both sides in lives.

Now it ends, Mab told herself. Vortigern was camped outside the walls of London and her allies would open the gates to him. Before another dawn, the Christian rule in England would be over, washed away in blood.

But though Mab could see many things, the future was closed to her. For that she turned to Idath. His Cauldron of Rebirth showed the future of all lives that were reborn from it. He would tell her the outcome of today's battle.

The endless misty plain frustrated her and she howled her displeasure – a wailing, terrifying cry that had slain grown men on the battlefield. They had named her *bean sidh* – the banshee – for it, and Morrigan, Lady of the Ravens, those birds who were the only victors on any battlefield. They had loved her once.

The echoes of her cry died away in the mist and Mab snarled with rage at her memories.

'There's no need to shout,' Idath said mildly.

He appeared before her, tall and gaunt, his whole being cloaked in shadows. Beneath the heavy antler-crowned bronze helmet he wore, his eyes glowed a feral red. Yet he, just as she, was dwindling away through the force of the humans' disbelief.

'Don't play games with me,' Mab raged. 'You know what I've come for.'

'You've come to know what will be,' Idath answered. 'But are you sure that's what you truly want? The future holds only sorrow, for all things die.'

'Not us!' Mab answered quickly. 'We shall live forever – for as long as the hearts of the people beat in tune with the Old Ways.'

'And if they are all dead?' Idath answered inexorably. His cloak billowed and now Mab could see the glowing metal of the Cauldron of Rebirth, souls rising from it like steam as they returned to the world; the dead who filled it being transformed by Idath's powerful magic. 'You have made much work for me in these last years, with your Vortigern. His appetite for slaughter is endless.'

'He was necessary,' Mab answered. 'Constant and his Christians were destroying us. Vortigern is pagan. He will restore the Old Ways once he rules England.'

'Are you truly certain of that, my love? Gaze into my cauldron and tell me what you see here.' Idath stepped back.

Almost reluctantly, Mab came forward and gazed down into the mists. The pearls that studded the lip of the cauldron glowed like captive moons, turning the liquid within an eerie glowing emerald. The vapours that boiled up from the cauldron's depths veiled the surface.

'I can't see anything,' Mab complained.

'The future is always in motion,' Idath replied. 'Wait a moment and it will settle . . . there.'

Mab gazed down, fascinated by the mirrored scene the cauldron contained. She saw the gates of Pendragon Castle forced open by treachery, saw Vortigern's troops swarm through the breech, slaughtering everyone they could reach as the Red Dragon banner of King Constant was dragged down and trampled underfoot. She watched as the king, knowing his army was defeated, ordered all his prisoners slain, and she watched as Constant was slain in turn. His golden crown rolled across the floor, away from the spreading pool of blood.

Vortigern picked it up, a slow smile of satisfaction spreading across his heavy Saxon features as he placed it upon his head. He stepped up to the throne from which Constant had been dragged only moments before, and seated himself on it.

'Where is the boy?' Mab heard him ask.

'Your Grace, he has escaped to Normandy with Queen Lionors,' Kentigern told his brother. 'He's just a boy.' His voice shook a little with fear as the new king frowned.

'Boys grow up to be trouble,' Vortigern rumbled. He seemed to recover his triumphal feelings of a moment before with an effort. 'But meanwhile, there's work to do. Take as many knights as you need and ride through the kingdom. Slay everybody, pagan or Christian, who isn't loyal to me and won't pay my new taxes. The Queen of the Old Ways thinks I will rule as her puppet to bring back the Old Ways, but she's wrong. From now on, the supreme power in the land is me – and only me.'

'Yes, Your Grace,' Kentigern said, bowing and nearly stumbling with the relief of leaving the royal presence alive.

'No!' Mab's shriek of despair shattered the smooth surface of the cauldron, dissolving the image. 'No! I gave him Britain so that he would bring back the Old Ways! He has betrayed me! He has betrayed all of us!'

'He has been true to his own nature,' Idath said relentlessly. 'His symbol is the White Dragon, and the White Dragon cares for nothing but battle.'

'He will serve me in the end,' Mab vowed through gritted teeth. 'Whether he wills it or not. But the next champion I choose will not be able to betray me, ever – this I swear!'

'Gracious Lady, thrice-crowned Queen, hear the prayers of those who worship you, and come to our aid.' Ambrosia finished her morning prayers in a hasty rush and got to her feet.

Not that you'll help, she added cynically.

The hilltop shrine – no more than a tiny altar hidden at the end of a long passageway made up of bluestone menhirs – was one of the few on the Downs that still remained undefiled. But even it had not escaped without injury, for at the back wall the carven stone image of Mab in her three aspects – Morrigan the Warrior, Titania the Maiden, and Melusine the Mother – had been marred by some angry and disappointed petitioner until only the Warrior aspect was still whole. The Maiden and the Mother had been battered almost into invisibility, but between them, Mab-Morrigan – Raven-lady, sword-crowned Queen of Battles – looked down at Ambrosia with sightless, knowing eyes.

Ambrosia lingered, more from weariness than from any desire to commune with the Lady she still grudgingly served. On the crude stone altar a bronze lamp shone down on the meagre offerings: a barley cake, some flowers, water from the sacred well. Little enough to offer to the Queen of Air and Darkness, but her followers were starving.

'And it isn't as though you're going to come for them,' Ambrosia said with a sigh. Ambrosia had not seen Mab in the flesh since she was a child first serving at the great shrine of Sarum, when Constant's rule, though Christian, had not yet descended into its later madness. In those days the followers of the Old Ways had been persecuted and driven from their holy places, but they had not been hunted and slaughtered as Vortigern was doing now. It was scant consolation in these dark days to know that the Christians suffered equally from the new king's tyranny.

Ambrosia lifted the carved amber amulet that she wore about her neck and kissed it dutifully. Then she turned reluctantly away from the altar, back to the world and her duties. *There are times when I wonder if you ever cared for us at all*, she thought. Ambrosia only had her mother's tales of the golden time when the Old Ways reigned supreme, their magic setting in motion the stars and the seasons. Now everything was darker, grimmer.

She stepped out into the daylight again, blinking as her eyes adjusted to the light. All around the shrine and its sacred well there were crude shelters made of wicker and animal skins where refugees from Vortigern's end-less pogrom took shelter. Some of those hiding here were Christians, Ambrosia was almost certain of it, but in the old days the shrine of the Old Ways had been open to anyone who sought refuge there and Ambrosia intended to continue that custom.

'You look tired today, my dear,' Lailoken said. He was a Druid, and still wore the hooded white robe of his order and carried the golden boline hung at his belt, but his oak-grove had been cut down long ago. Since that time he had been a wanderer among the courts of those lords who clung to the Old Ways, but under Vortigern's rule no one dared harbour a prophet and seer any longer, lest they be accused of plotting against the king.

'I'm always tired,' Ambrosia said crossly. 'And hun-gry. But there's no use grumbling about it. There are hungry mouths to feed, and –'

She broke off, studying his lined and weathered face. 'Lailoken, you look as if you'd been eating green apples. Have you had a vision?'

'Yes, well . . . that is to say, I'm not quite sure.' The old Druid's voice quivered, both with age and with the fear of his own powers that had not diminished with the years of secrecy and hiding. Once he had been a great prophet, able to see into the future and advise men on what the fates held in store for them, but the years of persecution had taken their toll.

Ambrosia put a hand gently on his arm. 'Oh, well, never mind it now. We'll talk about it later over a nice cup of herbal tea,' she said reassuringly. At least they still had the herbs for that.

But later never came, and in later years she often wondered what Lailoken's vision had been, and whether knowing it would have done her any good at all.

The sun was overhead when the riders appeared upon the horizon. Ambrosia was standing beside the sacred well, overseeing the filling of buckets and waterskins that would provide water for cooking and cleaning for all the camp's inhabitants.

She squinted her eyes, peering into the distance, trying to see. Her heart sank as she counted the horsemen's numbers. There were too many of them to be anything but trouble. A trick of the wind stretched their banner smooth against the sky for a moment, and on its dark surface Ambrosia could see the White Dragon. These were Vortigern's men.

Lady, save us! Ambrosia breathed a terrified prayer, clutching the amulet she wore, as if Mab might truly come in answer to this prayer when she'd come to no other. For one long minute she stood frozen, transfixed by the horror she could envision so clearly.

Then she found her voice. 'Run!' she cried to the startled folk around her. 'The White Dragon is coming for us! Run!'

She dropped the bucket she'd been filling and ran down the hill to the huts to raise the alarm. By the time she got there, the panic had already spread, for the fastest of Vortigern's riders had reached the outskirts of the camp.

It was a slaughter. The refugees were given no chance to surrender and less to escape. Some of the men fought back, with quarterstaff and spear, but they were cut down like summer wheat. Vortigern's men rode among the women and children, slashing and stabbing like madmen and setting the torch to everything that could burn. Within moments, the encampment was a hell of smoke, fire, and blood, filled with the shouts of the butchers and the screams of the dying.

Ambrosia clutched a shrieking child in her arms – snatched up as she fled in panic from the riders – and looked around herself wildly for some direction that promised escape. Seeing a gap in the fighting she began to run toward it, clumsy with the burden in her arms.

She did not see the blow that knocked her from her feet and sent her spiralling down into blackness and silence.

The pain harried her back toward consciousness like a sheepdog nipping at the heels of its flock. Ambrosia grunted, opening her eyes and coughing from the smoke she breathed. The smell of blood was a sweetish sickly rot that overlay everything like the stench from a poisoned wound. She tried to move, but a great weight lay upon her back and legs, and even the motion of lifting her head brought a bright flame of agony alight behind her eyes. She groaned in pain and frustration, the memory of the attack coming back to her in mocking fragments. She froze for a moment, listening, but there was no more sound of slaughter . . . only the quiet of death.

It took her nearly an hour, wounded as she was, to struggle from beneath the body of the dead man whose corpse had concealed the fact that she still lived from Vortigern's marauders. At last she stood, bloody and aching and sick, in the middle of an ash-covered ruin that had once been a holy place. It was twilight and the sun was setting in a sky as red as the blood-soaked earth beneath her feet. The unburied dead lay all around her

– man, woman, and child, slain for no more reason than that they were here. She walked among them, searching, hoping to find someone who had survived as she had, but there was no one else alive. All were dead, butchered, their possessions looted or burned around them.

At last Ambrosia looked up the hill. Vortigern's men had been thorough. Some of the stones of the shrine had been pulled down and a fire set there too. Its smoke was still rising in an oily black column. There were bodies there as well, the bodies of those who had fled to the sanctuary in fear and hope, but they had received no answer to their prayers save the cold steel of a sword-blade. This place was a holy refuge no longer, merely another place that had been broken by the king's will.

And no one had stopped him.

No one had come to their aid.

No one had answered their prayers.

'Damn you, Mab.' Ambrosia's voice sounded harsh and rusty, like the cry of the ravens who already flocked here to feed on the dead. 'Do you hear me, you midnight hag? I said, damn you and all your heartless kind! Why didn't you help us? Don't we matter to you?'

She looked down at the amber talisman she wore,

the symbol of the triskelion spiral crowned by a horned moon that marked the covenant she had sworn to the Old Ways, and suddenly she could bear to wear that mark no longer. She jerked at it, breaking the leather cord, and flung the amulet as far from her as she could.

'Well, if we don't matter to you, Lady, then you don't matter to me – not you, nor any god under heaven. Never again. I'd rather worship a stone statue like the Christians do. It'd be more honest.'

With dragging steps Ambrosia began to walk slowly away from the scene of so much death and pain. She did not look back.

She did not know how long she wandered, weak and sick, across the war-torn land. No one bothered her, for who would interfere with a madwoman who wept and laughed and sang as she walked and ranted against unseen presences? She ate what she could beg or steal, and drank from streams and standing ponds, and mourned her dead and cursed her gods as she wandered.

Until at last she came to Avalon.

Avalon Abbey had been the first outpost of the new

religion in Britain. Kings had risen and fallen, but all had left Avalon alone, for it was known the length and breadth of the land that a new kind of magic ruled here and even kings were wary of what they did not understand. First a chapel, then a church, then a convent and hospital had been built upon the tiny outcropping of land in Britain's western shore, where Avalon endured from century to century, its green mist-shrouded heights rising up out of the tidal flats like the bulk of some primordial sea-beast.

And though all the world knew that the new king feared nothing under heaven or beneath the earth, even he did not disturb Avalon's peace, for the finest healers in all the land dwelt there, and even a king may some time need to be healed.

Elissa had first come to the Abbey as a tiny child in her mother's arms. Her mother had been Queen of Orkney, to the north, but King Constant's dream of a unified Britain had left no room for queens and northern kingdoms. The war he made sent Queen Morgause fleeing with her infant daughter to the sanctuary of Avalon, and she died there soon after – some said of a broken heart. Elissa had grown to womanhood within the sound of Avalon Abbey's tolling bells, a princess without a country. Though she had received offers of an honourable place in many a nobleman's house, in her heart, Elissa did not long for what was lost. With her thick dark hair, sparkling eyes and a tendency to freckle if she stayed too long in the sun, she was cheerful where her mother had been grand, pretty where Morgause had been beautiful. The peaceful life of the holy sisters suited her, and she asked no more than to be able to spend the rest of her days in Avalon.

But she was young, and it was summer, and even the most contented of Avalon's inhabitants could be forgiven for playing truant from an afternoon of weeding the garden to curl up against the sun-warmed wall of the apple orchard and dream. And after all, she was not yet one of the holy sisters, vowed to obedience, merely a young postulant who might some day become a novice.

It was while she was sitting in the shadow of the wall looking out over the land that she saw the old woman.

Elissa did not question how she could be so certain at this distance that the bundle of rags that lay upon the flats was a woman, or even alive. There was one thing that Elissa knew full well: the tide was coming in, and no amount of prayer could hold back the running sea. Without someone to help her, the woman would drown.

Elissa flung herself to her feet and ran through the trees. She reached the bottom of the orchard and lifted her skirts to leap over the wall, agile as any boy, and ran down the path that led to the mainland. The sea-washed stones were cold against her feet as she ran, and she tried to calculate how long it would be until the space between Avalon and the mainland was awash with the running sea. Not long enough to take the time to summon help; what she must do here she must do alone, and quickly.

Elissa reached the prostrate figure and knelt beside it, turning the body over gently. It was a woman, as she'd first thought. The woman's hair was streaked with grey and there were lines of pain etched around her mouth. Her clothes were ragged, but they had been of good quality once. Elissa saw the pagan signs embroidered on the tunic at wrist and hem and crossed herself hastily, though she did not think that one so injured could possibly do her harm.

'Who are you?' Elissa asked. There was no answer. In the distance she could see the shining line of the advancing sea. It seemed as if there was plenty of time, but Elissa knew from experience how fast the sea came in. She shook the old woman gently. 'Wake up, wake up – you cannot stay here.'

Elissa saw the old woman's eyelashes flutter. Her head tossed from side to side fretfully and she coughed.

'Le' me 'lone,' the old woman muttered, flinging up an arm over her face to shield her eyes from the sun.

'I can't do that,' Elissa said reasonably. 'I can't just go off and leave you here now that I've seen you. Besides, the tide's coming in. You'll drown.'

'I don't care,' the old woman said, but there was more life in her voice now and it seemed as if she'd resigned herself to living.

'I'm Elissa. What's your name?'

'Ambrosia.'

Elissa pondered this. 'It doesn't sound very much like a good Christian name,' she said tentatively.

'I'm not a very good Christian,' Ambrosia muttered. 'Look here, girl, if I get up will you shut your row and leave me alone?'

'Let me help you up,' Elissa said, evading the question. Between the two of them, they got Ambrosia to her feet.

She leaned heavily on Elissa, and Elissa could feel how thin and starved she was through her rags. When she coughed, her whole body shook. Elissa was a practical person, and began composing a mental list of all the things her patient would need once they reached the Abbey. Though it was only a short distance to the gates, she was all but carrying Ambrosia by the time they reached it.

'No more, girl. I can't walk another step. Let me die here,' Ambrosia gasped. Behind them, the sea foamed over the causeway, cutting Avalon off from the mainland.

Elissa looked around. There was no convenient place she could leave her patient to rest while she went to find the serving brothers and get a litter down to carry Ambrosia to the hospital. Only the chapel was near, and if Ambrosia were truly a worshipper of pagan gods, she might not be willing to go there.

But the whole isle is holy ground, and she is already here, Elissa thought reasonably. *There is no other place. The chapel will have to do*.

'Come on. It's only a little further,' she coaxed. She half-dragged Ambrosia to the open doorway of the chapel and carried her inside.

Once out of the sun, Ambrosia seemed to recover a little more of her strength. She straightened up and looked around, standing unsteadily upon her own feet.

'What's that?' she said in a surprised voice. 'By the Lady – it's glowing.'

'It's the Grail,' Elissa said proudly.

Avalon Abbey had been founded by Joseph of Arimathea, who had come from the lands east of Rome seeking a refuge, for in those days the followers of those whom the Greeks and Romans called The Anointed One were weak and few, and were heavily persecuted. Avalon had been their refuge, the land deeded to them by an ancient pagan king, and it was here that Joseph had brought the new religion's greatest treasure: the Cup that their Master had touched with his own hands, the Cup from which he had crafted their link to the Eternal.

It blazed with white radiance as it hovered above the altar; a great silver chalice, its lip edged with pearls. There was always someone keeping vigil before it day and night; when Ambrosia and Elissa had entered, the young brother who was watching the Grail stood and stared at them curiously.

'This is Ambrosia, Giraldus,' Elissa said to him. 'She's injured. She needs help.'

But when she turned back, Ambrosia was tottering unsteadily toward the Grail's radiance. Its pale light shone on her face, making her look again as she must have looked as a young girl. She reached out a hand as if to touch it, but before her fingers could brush it there was a great flair of light and Ambrosia squealed as she fell backward.

'Are you all right?' Elissa and the young brother asked in almost the same breath.

'I . . .' Ambrosia drew a deep breath without coughing. 'I'm more than all right. I haven't felt this good in years.' She got to her feet, and it did seem to Elissa that she looked sturdier than she had when she'd come into the chapel.

'The Grail healed her. It's a miracle,' Brother Giraldus said.

'Laddie, where I come from we have miracles with our morning tea,' Ambrosia said, fixing him with a glittering hawk-keen gaze. 'Still, I've got to admit that it was more use than any of Herself's tricks ever were. Now, who did you say you were?'

'I'm Elissa. This is Brother Giraldus. Welcome to Avalon.'

Elissa could see Giraldus puffing up to deliver one of his lectures on the wickedness of the pagans, but from all that Elissa had seen of them, they did not seem very different from Christians.

'Avalon?' The name seemed to mean something

to Ambrosia. She looked alarmed, as if she expected both of them to jump on her. 'Not the Christians' place?'

'She's a pagan,' Brother Giraldus said in disgust.

'Pagan or Christian, all are welcome here,' Elissa said firmly. 'Yes, we are Christians here, but the Grail's magic is for all.'

'Oh, aye, the way it was under the old king,' said Ambrosia, 'with the axe set to the root of every tree in every sacred grove.'

'The false gods must be swept away by the light of the true religion,' Giraldus said.

'If it's the true religion, it doesn't need our help to prevail,' Elissa said gently. 'You saw what the Grail did, Giraldus – can we choose to do less? Avalon's arts are free to all who ask. Our Lord would ask nothing less of us, for he taught that the love in the human heart is the greatest magic of all, and here, by the Grail's aid and example, we try to live that magic. Whoever you've been, whatever you've done, it does not matter within these walls,' she said to Ambrosia. 'Vortigern's war cannot penetrate here.'

Ambrosia studied Elissa with surprised respect. 'Eh, girl, you'll do. Pity there aren't more who think as you do.'

'There will be,' Elissa said, with a certainty that startled even her. 'The truth will prevail in the end.'

In the Hollow Hills deep at the heart of the earth, Mab had listened and heard and felt the outcries of her followers as the slaughter grew ever greater. With every murder of her folk she had felt the deathly cold of extinction strengthen its grip on her, leaching away her power, her very life – and the lives of all she ruled.

'No!' her scream of fury had struck sparks from the walls of her crystalline kingdom, and hot fury had banished the pangs of weakness.

In the long centuries of war between Christianity and the Old Ways, her heart had hardened. After so much loss, Mab could no longer love as she once had, and, after so many deaths, honest grief, too, was denied to her. All that was left was the need to fight back, to lash out against the tormentors. Weak as she had become, there must be something she could do before all was lost!

But when she reached the site of the battle that she had been summoned to, all that was left was crumbling bone and the embers of a battle long over. Victor and victims alike were gone – all that remained were the bones of the dead and the blackened stones of the defiled shrine.

'Gone . . . all gone,' Mab whispered.

But even if she had come in time, there was so little she could have done. Her powers lay in trickery and illusion, and Vortigern's men feared their master far more than they could ever fear any apparition of Mab's.

Vortigern.

She had thought it would be so simple, that once the Christian king was gone the people would return to the Old Ways. She had used Vortigern as a sword to cut off Constant's head, but her weapon had turned in her hand, and the new king slaughtered her people just as the old king had – and worse. Now more and more of Vortigern's subjects were abandoning the Old Ways in fear and despair, hoping that the new god could defend them against the White Dragon as Mab could not.

I have tried! she wailed silently. It was only that she had made the wrong choice. She had chosen a warlord, but her people needed a leader.

And that was what she would give them: a leader. She had learned her lesson well. She had made a bad choice in Vortigern – very well, she would not look for Britain's saviour among the people of the mortal world this time. She would create him. A prophet and wizard who could see what must be done to return Britain to the Old Ways, and who would do those things through the power of the magic that was his birthright.

Mab smiled, feeling the promise of victory beat through her veins like hot wine. It would take all the power she possessed, but she would weave the greatest spell of her existence. Through her magic she would create a warrior to humble Vortigern, a leader to lead her people back to the Old Ways. He would be no simple soldier, but a wizard, a true heir to the Old Ways, born of her magic. One who would be loyal to the land and to her, who would fight for not only the body but the soul of Britain.

She could do it. It would be hard, but she knew this plan would work. No foreign kings or alien usurpers – this would be a leader formed in the heart of Britain, made to rule and to serve the Old Ways.

The lake's surface was a flawless mirror in the morning sun, and the land around it was beautiful and wild. Mab stood upon the shore and called soundlessly to the power that dwelt here, summoning it forth.

Suddenly the surface of the still clear water began to churn and waves appeared as if lashed by a ferocious storm. A brightness flashed beneath the water and then broke into the air. Then all at once the surface of the lake was placid once more, as a shining figure swam through the air toward Mab.

She shone like the sunlight on the waves, and moved languidly through the air as if it were her own watery kingdom. Her gown seemed made of bright water, and, as a necklace, she wore a circlet of shimmering fish that swam back and forth around her throat. Her silvery hair floated on the air, moving slowly after her like a mermaid's tail. Where Mab was dark, she was bright. Where Mab was hard, she was supple. Where Mab was stone, she was water.

She was the Lady of the Lake, and she had ruled there since the first raindrops had gathered to form a pool in a hollow on the cooling earth.

'Sister . . .' she said, and her soft voice was the sound of water rushing over stones. 'I got your message.'

'I have come to a great decision,' Mab said. The fairy queen seemed out of place here in the Lady of the Lake's domain. Mab was a creature of night and shadow. Here in this shining green and silver land, she seemed like a scrap of glittering darkness dropped from some other world.

'I don't like the sound of your voice when you say that,' the Lady of the Lake said mournfully. Small circling motions of her hands allowed her to hold her place in the air before Mab. The bright silver fish flitted back and forth about her throat and she gazed sadly at her sister.

'I'm going to create a leader for the people,' Mab answered. 'A powerful wizard who will save Britain and bring the people back to us and to the Old Ways.'

But the approval – the interest – she had hoped to see on her sister's face did not appear. The Lady of the Lake was one of the strongest powers still left in the world, but she had not suffered as Mab had. She did not hate as Mab did.

The Lady of the Lake sighed, shaking her head slowly. Her pale hair swirled around her face. 'It will be too much for you, Mab. It will drain you of what power you still have.'

Don't you think I know that? Mab wanted to shout. But she held her tongue. What did the Lady of the Lake care for the fears that haunted Mab? 'If I don't do it, we'll die,' she said desperately. 'If people forget us we won't exist any longer. The new religion has already pushed us to the edge. Soon we'll be forgotten.' *I need your help*, she thought, but could not bring herself to say the words.

'All things change, sister,' the Lady of the Lake sighed. 'It's sad, but Heaven, Hell, and the world move on. It's our fate. Accept it.'

'I won't accept it!' Mab hissed in her snake's voice. 'I'll fight! Will you help me?'

Her sister shook her head slowly, gazing at Mab pityingly. 'You forget that I am the Lady of the Lake. I'm made of water, and now that the tide has turned away from us I accept it. I'm sorry, my dear.' With a last backward glance, the Lady of the Lake swam away, sinking again below the surface of the water.

Mab stared without seeing at the silvery plane of the lake. All along she had been fighting for survival, to reclaim what was hers. Now she realized that she was willing to die for it as well. Her sister had been right: to create and shape the leader who would save Britain would take every ounce of power that she possessed. In making him she might unmake herself, vanishing from the pleasant world of men forever. But, at last, Mab realized that it didn't matter. Her death didn't matter. No one's death mattered.

Winning was what mattered.

'Then I will do it myself.' The darkness swirled around her and she was gone.

Rather to her own surprise, Ambrosia was accepted easily into the community of lay brethren who lived side by side with the religious at Avalon in a tiny village called Glastonbury. She found that Elissa's views were far more widely represented than Brother Giraldus's, and she was valued here for what she could teach of herb craft and herb lore and the healing arts that were unaligned with pagan magic. Slowly her spirit began to heal as her body had been healed, and as summer died into autumn and the Wheel of the Year turned, Ambrosia began to wonder what the future held. She had renounced her allegiance to Mab and the Old Ways, but she could not find it within her heart to follow Elissa into the new faith.

Trouble isn't in the gods, it's in ourselves, she thought to herself. *We make the gods over in our own image and then wonder why they're always quarrelling and scrapping. And their followers are worse – look at young Giraldus, all puffed up with pride just because he's spent some hours kneeling on a cold stone floor. No, I'm through with gods of any stripe, pagan or Christian. King Vortigern, Queen Mab ... it's all one in the end.*

But in the end, it did not matter whether Ambrosia had renounced the Old Ways, for the Old Ways were magic, and magic would find her eventually.

'Frik? Frik! Where are you?' Mab shouted as she swirled into the enchanted sanctuary at the heart of her power.

This was where she crafted her strongest magics, and being here was like being in the heart of a jewelled rainbow. In the centre of the spherical chamber was a great crystal altar that seemed to have risen up out of the living rock. The floor surrounding it was as smooth and polished as a mirror, and around the edge of the circle, row after row of concentric rings of crystals stretched as far as the eye could see, crystals that glittered with magical fire in every colour of the spectrum. The whole sanctuary glowed with a complex shimmering fire; deep in the heart of the earth, the chamber was awash in a dark unearthly radiance, a light never meant for mortal eyes to see.

'Frik!' Mab shouted again, and her servant came running.

He was dark and misshapen, as grotesque as Mab was beautiful. His long pointed ears and goggling eyes made him look as if someone had tried to create a parody of a human being and hadn't got it quite right. He had been her servant and companion for so long that Mab herself could not remember when the relationship had begun. Had she captured him? Had she created him? Neither of them remembered, but while Mab preferred always to remain herself, Frik was in love with the powers of illusion, taking a thousand different guises purely for his own amusement and rarely appearing before Mab in the same form twice.

Today the gnome bowed low before her, dressed in a pair of grey-striped trousers and a black coat that hung down in two tails behind. The costume seemed to amuse him greatly.

It did not amuse Mab.

'You saw it all. You were eavesdropping again, weren't you?' Mab demanded.

'Madam?' Frik said, trying to look innocent.

'She denied me!' She closed her eyes in fury, clenching her fists. 'The Lady of the Lake denied me!'

'I'm afraid your sister is rather indecisive when it comes to making decisions, madam,' Frik said obsequiously. 'She never gives you the support you deserve.'

'She deserves to be forgotten – but I don't! We're on our own, Frik. You know what I mean to do, and now I must do it alone. I'd better get started.'

At this her gnomish servant actually looked alarmed. 'Don't you think you should at least wait a few days?' he asked, trying to be assertive and servile all at once. 'To build up your strength?'

'There's no time,' Mab snapped. 'Our world is dying.'

She knew in her bones that Frik was mistaken. To rest would not restore her strength. Only the destruction of the new religion could do that. Every moment she delayed was another moment in which it grew stronger and she grew weaker.

She sensed Frik backing away as she closed her eyes, drawing upon all of her power. A wizard, a leader, a saviour for Britain. She concentrated upon that image, shaping it with her will, as all about her the crystals of her sanctuary glowed with enchantment, pulsing with colour and light.

A figure began to form, reflected a thousand times in the hearts of the glowing crystals. Mab opened her eyes, unable not to look. She saw the image of a beautiful young man with light brown hair and piercing dark eyes.

He was perfect.

'Merlin . . .' Almost reverently Mab breathed his name. She would name him for the merlin falcon, the swift and nimble bird that soared through Britain's skies. Merlin. A great weight of frustration and sorrow – even guilt – seemed to lift from her shoulders. She had been wrong in choosing Vortigern. One who could not wield the magic would never be the saviour the Old Ways needed. But her Merlin, her wizard-prince, would be a creature of the magic itself. He could never betray the magic, any more than he could betray himself. He was not yet born, but already Mab tasted the sweet joy of victory.

But thus far all she had cast was illusion, enchantment. Now she must give him life.

To make true creations was the hardest thing for any of her kind to do. Her power and that of her kindred lay in the realm of illusion and dreams, not the material world. It was said that the most ancient of her kind had sung that whole world into existence where before there had been nothing but the Void, but if that were true it had been long ago, in the morning of the world when the powers of the fairyfolk were at their height. Now, weakened by centuries of battles and losses, Mab struggled to reach beyond herself, to draw upon the very power that kept her alive in order to give life to her illusion, to make her Merlin real.

My champion – child of magic – protector of the Old Ways – the thoughts in her mind scattered like a shower of sparks from the Beltane fires that marked the turning of the year, but the image of Merlin stayed bright and true within her. Only she could give him life. Only she could save them all.

I cannot do this alone!

She could not do what she had first intended and instantly create the grown man of her vision. She was too weak for that, and so Merlin must begin as a spark in a mortal woman's belly and grow to manhood the way the mortal kind did. Frantically, the power growing in her moment by moment, she cast about for a suitable vessel.

He must be born a prince and the son of princes. An image of her Merlin raised within the walls of a noble house, wearing the golden coronet of rank upon his head and dressed in furs and velvets, filled her mind for an instant. Yes. That was as it should be. Let the mortal kind bow down to him from the first instant of his life.

Suddenly her whole being was jarred by the clangorous sound of iron bells – Christian bells, ringing out their holy music over the land that Mab was fighting to reclaim for her own. Avalon. Her search had brought her to Avalon.

Mab knew that the nobility often sent its soft pretty daughters there to be schooled in safety. So be it. She would find the vessel for her Merlin here and, at the same time, strike a blow against the powers she so hated. She would enjoy the irony of planting the saviour of the Old Ways within the walls of a Christian stronghold. With a sigh almost of relief, Mab freed the burgeoning power she had summoned. It welled up and through her, power drawn from the very fabric of the earth itself. She held nothing back – if it cost her everything she was, still she would do this thing. Her very bones tingled as she summoned all her arts, drew power from every source and shaped it to her will. For Merlin – for Britain – for the Old Magic –

For Mab. At last it rushed from her grasp, taking everything that she was – her fire, her heart, all the best of her – with it. Out there in the world, on the isle of Avalon, her Merlin took form, took life, took wing like the owl upon the wind.

And only darkness remained in the cavern beneath the Hollow Hills.

Elissa heard the church bells chiming on the wintery air, ringing out the glory of the blessed Nativity. When midnight came, the doors of the Grail chapel would open, and all who could manage to fit inside would crowd in to hear mass in the presence of the blessed

Cup. But until that time, Elissa watched before the altar in the Grail chapel alone.

She had become a novice only last month, but the Father Abbot said that if she studied and prayed hard she might become a professed nun as early as the spring. The thought made her wriggle with excitement, though she tried hard not to succumb to the distraction of idle thoughts. It was a great honour to be chosen to watch over the Grail, especially on this holiest of nights.

Though preparations for a great Christmas feast were going on everywhere throughout the Abbey, Elissa did not feel left out. It was wonderful beyond imagining to be able to spend this time alone in the presence of the Grail, its soft radiance shining down upon her alone and mingling with the light of the dozens of candles lit in the sanctuary. If Giraldus got his way, these wonderful hours would end.

Since the summer the Grail had healed Ambrosia, there had been dissension in Avalon. Brother Giraldus, and others who sided with him, thought that the Grail should be kept locked safely away like the great treasure it was, so that no pagans could profane it by their touch or presence. This was the faction that thought as the old king had, that their mission must be to convert the heathen to the new religion by any means – or, failing that, execute them so that they could work no more wickedness. Fortunately the Father Abbot who ruled over their small community believed as their founder St Joseph of Arimathea had: that the Grail's magic should be free to all who sought it and that love must be their ultimate law.

Elissa sighed faintly, keeping her eyes fixed upon the shining Cup. People made everything so complicated, when surely there was one simple truth that bound them all together, pagan and Christian. Perhaps when she became one of the healing sisters she would be able to work toward its discovery, so that they could all live together in peace. It must be possible, for Elissa knew that Ambrosia was a good woman, nothing like the pagans Giraldus preached of when he'd had a little too much wine. She wondered how many pagans Giraldus had actually seen, for he had come to Avalon as a small child, just as she had.

Suddenly, as if it were a divine punishment for her irreverent, uncharitable thoughts, the doors to the chapel burst inward with a sound like the rushing of great wings, and a black wind blew out all the candles.

'Who's there?' Her voice was cracked and high with fear.

The darkness seemed to pluck at her with a thousand tiny hands. She shrunk away from the touch, whimpering with terror. The chapel, so welcoming and friendly moments before, was now as cold as the wind blowing in from over the sea, filled with a presence whose rage and triumph filled Elissa with agonized despair. She wanted to scream for help, but the presence of the malign spirit that had somehow entered this holy place seemed to stifle her cry stillborn. There was no light anywhere – she could not see the Grail – and as she sprang to her feet and tried to run, the long full skirts of her novice's habit tripped her and sent her sprawling across the cold stone.

This is my fault! It's because I made fun of Giraldus . . .

But she could not complete that thought, for suddenly her whole body was pierced with a spear of pure liquid agony. It was as if she had been struck by a bolt of black lightning that meant to burn her to ash and remake her as some creature of the darkness. She drummed her fists against the cold stone of the chapel floor but could not feel the blows. Every nerve in her body sang with the vengeful power that had come upon her in the holiest place in all Christendom.

Because of her. It must be because of her. Hers the guilt and hers the blame.

At last the agony passed, and her body was her own again. She screamed as loud as she could, a keening wail of pain and loss and guilt that took the last of her strength with it.

The next thing she knew she was being shaken roughly. Elissa opened her eyes, for a moment not knowing where she was or how she'd come here, and gazed up into the angry face of Brother Giraldus.

'Where . . . ?' she began, but he did not give her a chance to ask the question.

'Fool! Strumpet! What have you done!' Giraldus shouted at her, dragging her to her feet.

Her head ached and the chapel seemed to spin about her. With dazed miserable eyes Elissa looked around herself. The only light came from half a dozen torches carried by the crowd that filled the chapel. The candles were all quenched, and the high altar was empty.

'I – I – I . . .' Elissa stammered, but she knew there were no words that could do any good in the face of this disaster. No comforting presence glowed there to heal and encourage. The Grail was gone.

And, with a terrible, impossible certainty, Elissa – Princess Elissa, daughter of Queen Morgause of Orkney – knew that she was with child.

CHAPTER TWO

THE COURTS OF THE GREENWOOD

*I*t was late September and the leaves on the trees were beginning to turn the yellows and reds of autumn. All the forest creatures, from squirrels to deer, were preparing for winter, and the Witch of Barnstable Forest was preparing too.

She'd been living in the north for the better part of a year and had settled at last into a new life after the months of wandering north and east. Her nearest neighbours were Border Celts, red deer and a few peaceful farmers. Many of the country people felt as she did: not yet ready to accept the new religion, but disenchanted with the Old Ways. Together they walked a third path: acknowledging the great forces that shaped their lives but not blindly idolizing them. She had made a place for herself here, providing the populace with the herb craft and small charms that eased the harshness of a life that seemed drearier with every passing year.

We're none of us as young as we used to be, Ambrosia grumbled to herself, straightening up to ease a kink in her back. She'd spent most of the morning fetching water from the nearby spring and the result of her labour was now steaming away in a large cauldron hung over the firepit in the centre of the clearing.

Elissa did what she could to help, poor child, but these days the heavy lifting fell to Ambrosia's lot.

If only that poxy Giraldus hadn't been so full of himself, Ambrosia sighed. There was no denying that she'd rather have the warm stone walls of Avalon Abbey around both of them than shiver here in this forest hut with winter on its way. But the loss of the Grail had shaken the small religious community badly, and too many there at Avalon had been willing to believe Giraldus's accusations that it had vanished because Elissa had trafficked with the Dark One. The little community had cast Elissa out, and Ambrosia, infuriated by their intolerance, had gone with her.

The only Dark One Ambrosia knew was Idath, Lord of the Wild Hunt, and while no one particularly wanted to meet him and journey to Caer Anoeth, the Land of the Dead, he was as much a normal part of life as springtime and the harvest.

But the Christians' Dark One was a different matter altogether. They called him the Lord of Lies and feared him passionately. Once Giraldus had accused Elissa of being in league with such a monstrous creature, people had stopped thinking altogether.

I suppose we're both lucky they didn't burn her as a sorceress, and me beside her, Ambrosia thought with a sigh. At least all they had done at Avalon was cast Elissa out. When Ambrosia heard about it, she'd left the nearby village to go after the girl and bring her here, to make a home in the lonely forest. By then Elissa was great with child, which only confirmed Ambrosia's secret fears. She knew of only one force vindictive enough to lash out at the heart of the Christians' power at the Yuletide.

Mab.

Ambrosia was willing to bet anything that Mab had been behind the trouble, and she fretted in her heart over what sort of fairy-begotten child Elissa would give birth to. Would it take after its mortal mother, or resemble more closely the eldritch force that had kindled the spark of its life?

In the distance, a twig snapped. Someone was coming up the path to her cottage. Instantly Ambrosia was on the alert. There was little in this wilderness to attract Vortigern's attention, but that did not mean the forest was without dangers of its own. Barnstable Forest had become the haunt of the outlaws and landless men that Vortigern's reign had created. It was part of Lord Ardent's lands, but he was an absentee landlord, since most of the time Vortigern kept him at court.

'Ambrosia!' a familiar voice called out, and she relaxed.

'Herne, you scamp! You scared the life out of me,' she scolded.

Herne stepped into the clearing, a slain deer slung over his shoulders. He was a young man little older than Elissa, dressed all in green leather from his boots to his tunic. His long fair hair was tied back with a strip of buckskin, and he carried a bow in his hand.

'Now, how could a poor country lad like me put something over on the most feared and respected sorceress in the whole forest?' He slung the deer to the ground. 'Fresh venison,' he said.

Once, like her, Herne had been a cleric of the Old Ways: Herne had served Idath in his aspect as Lord of the Wild Things. But as the Old Ways had dwindled and Vortigern's oppression had grown, Herne had set aside his priestly horned crown. The people needed more than rituals and homilies in those dark days – they needed a champion. Herne could not protect them officiating in a woodland shrine, and so he had made a difficult choice. Now he poached the king's deer and stole the king's gold to feed the hungry people of the shire, and lived the life of an outlaw in the greenwood with a price upon his head.

'And where did that come from?' she asked chidingly. 'I suppose it got up and walked out of Lord Ardent's larder?'

'I swear to you, Ambrosia, that's exactly what happened.' Herne grinned at her, then sobered. 'I've been to Nottingham Market. There's fresh news of the true king.'

Ambrosia frowned. Vortigern held the land in an uneasy grip while Queen Lionors and Prince Uther were free in Norman lands. 'And which king would that be? I suppose it isn't good news either way?' she said.

'Depends on how you think of it. The queen is safe in Normandy at the court of the French king, raising an army to get Uther's throne back.'

'Vortigern won't like that,' Ambrosia observed.

'Uther is yet a child,' Herne answered. 'He won't trouble the high king this year or next. But it won't be long before he's a man grown, ready to lead his army right down Vortigern's throat. And Vortigern will be that many years older.'

True enough. Vortigern was at the peak of his manly strength now. In ten years, or fifteen, he would be past his prime, weary with years of kingship and fighting, and Uther would be young and fresh and ready to fight him.

'One king or another, what does it matter to us? Uther's a Christian, just as his father was before him. He won't love us any better than Constant did.'

'He can hardly be more trouble to us than Vortigern,' Herne pointed out reasonably. 'How fares the Lady Elissa today?' he asked, changing the subject. Over the months that they had been here, he had grown fond of the young girl, and Ambrosia thought he would marry her if he could.

'Well enough,' Ambrosia said. 'The child should be born before the first snow.'

Herne hesitated. Ambrosia hadn't publicized the turn of events that had led to Elissa's expulsion from Avalon, but scandal travelled the length and breadth of Britain on the wings of the wind. All the land knew that the Christian Grail had vanished through some fault of Elissa's, and Herne could see with his own eyes that the girl was with child. It did not take a great leap of intellect to guess that the Old Ways were somehow involved – and Herne, like Ambrosia, walked warily where such matters were concerned.

'Ambrosia!'

The frightened cry came from within the hut in the middle of the clearing. Ambrosia turned toward the sound, and saw Elissa standing in the doorway, one hand clinging to it for support, the other clutching at her swollen belly.

'The baby – I think it's coming now,' Elissa gasped.

She was not dead, but she was less than she had been. Seasons spun through their courses as Mab lay unmoving upon a bed made of crystal, tended carefully by a nervous Frik. The magic that was in her guttered faintly, a black flame that might be extinguished at any moment. But, carefully tended, and slowly, she recovered her strength. One thought sustained her: that she had succeeded. She had brought Merlin into the world. Her loneliness, her struggle for bare survival, were ended. The Old Ways would triumph, her people would no longer be persecuted, and her power was assured.

And finally, one day she opened her eyes, threw back the covering of silvery cobweb lace that Frik had placed over her and rose from her bed.

A cloud of sprites, their wings all the colours of a springtime garden, flew into the air and hovered like startled butterflies as she moved. Once the tiny creatures had been of mortal size. In those days humankind had called them the *sidhe*, the bright elves, and had gone in fear of their powers and their wrath. But as the world of men had ceased to believe in them, they had dwindled away to these silly fluttering things that could barely tie knots in a horse's mane or sour milk in a jug. Mab could hear the high squeaky sounds of their voices as they called back and forth to each other, proclaiming the self-evident news that their mistress was awake once more.

Fear not, my subjects, Mab thought, watching the rainbow cloud of sprites flutter about the room. *Soon you will be as you once were. Soon all will be as it once was.*

This I swear.

As she expected, Frik appeared almost immediately. He was dressed all in white, with tiny glasses perched on the end of his nose and a stethoscope looped around his neck. The black bag that he carried had a large red cross in a white circle painted on its side. Templars? Mab wondered, sorting through all of Time to try to make sense of that strange symbol. Frik looked ridiculous in this costume, but then, her servant always looked ridiculous to her. She despised him, and sometimes she despised herself for having him. But that, too, would change once Merlin came into his power.

'There now. And how are we feeling today?' Frik asked ingratiatingly.

'Don't try my patience,' Mab answered. She strode from the bedchamber. Frik dropped his black bag and rushed after her, holding a cloak.

'You mustn't risk a chill,' he said self-importantly, tucking it about her shoulders when she stopped.

Her head whipped around and Mab regarded her assistant with blazing eyes.

'That is . . . that is to say, unless you wish to catch a chill, of course, madam. Very much your own choice to make, of course,' Frik said hurriedly. 'Only . . . that is to say . . .' He stopped, obviously at a loss as to how to proceed without arousing his mistress's volatile temper. 'I mean, of course –' He gave up. 'It was a success, was it not, madam?' he asked plaintively. Then Frik closed his eyes tightly and waited for whatever would come.

But Mab was in a mood to be forgiving. She patted his cheek with a jewelled hand and her long black fingernails glittered.

'Of course it was a success! But you're wondering, aren't you, where he is?' she purred.

Frik gulped, his eyes still closed, obviously unable to decide whether to agree with her or deny that he'd ever doubted her success.

'I thought of creating a full-grown champion, but I decided not to. This way is better. My Merlin will be half-human, half-fairy. He will not have to rely only upon fairy illusion for his magic, because he will also be human. And since he will live amongst them, the mortals will love him and follow him – but he will also be a wizard, bound to the Old Ways, and so he will follow me!'

'Oh, I say, madam, how frightfully clever,' Frik said in relief. 'He'll be a much better champion of the Old Ways than Vorti – I mean, than that other fellow that we just won't mention.'

'He will save us all. You and I, Frik, will teach him everything he needs to know to rule Britain and bring back the Old Ways!'

'We will? I mean, of course we will,' Frik said, recovering gamely. He looked around. 'But – just a trifling matter, my own mistake, certainly – where is he?'

Normally Mab would have made Frik spend several days as a rock for annoying her so, but today she could not be annoyed. Today victory was in her hands. She smiled at Frik, a truly terrifying sight.

'He is in the mortal world, being born.'

The labour was long and difficult, and almost from the beginning Ambrosia grimly realized that Elissa would not survive it. She hid that knowledge from the girl as well as she could through the long gruelling hours of the night, hoping that she was wrong. She had been wrong occasionally in her long career as a midwife. Mothers were tougher than they looked, and the will to live could work miracles.

But not this time. The child drained Elissa's strength as it struggled to be born, but somehow Ambrosia could not grudge it that strength. The poor babe would need all the strength he could muster to face the world as it was.

Elissa had gone into labour at mid-morning, but it was dawn by the time Ambrosia was able to pull at last the child from the girl's pain-racked body.

'A boy,' she said with relief. 'It's a beautiful boy.' With no mark of the Old Magic anywhere on his red wrinkled body, to Ambrosia's great relief. Whatever force had begotten him had left no surface marks. She tucked the child into its mother's arms. Elissa's face was shiny with sweat, her eyes great sunken wells of pain and suffering. She touched her baby's face with trembling fingers, then held the tiny squalling bundle out to Ambrosia once more.

'I'm dying,' Elissa whispered.

'No, no,' Ambrosia said soothingly, though she feared the girl was only telling the truth.

'You've done so much for me, Ambrosia. You took me in when good Christian souls cast me out to die – now I ask you to do one thing more.' She paused, gasping for breath, her face grey with effort.

'Rest, child, rest – there will be time for this,' Ambrosia said soothingly. She began to move away to lay the baby in the cradle Herne had made for him, but Elissa grabbed a fold of her skirt in a deathly grip.

'No! You must . . . you must look after my baby, Ambrosia. Teach him about the Grail – the magic of the loving heart. I beg you – I beg you, Ambrosia!' As she struggled to pull herself upright the bleeding began again, fresh blood staining the bed linens a deep crimson. 'Swear it! Swear!'

Words were power; it was the first thing every acolyte of the Old Ways was taught. Ambrosia hesitated only a fraction of an instant, knowing that the words she spoke here would bind her spirit as unyieldingly as iron shackles could bind her body. 'I swear,' she said, and took the infant's life into her keeping. 'Now sleep,' she added, as Elissa's desperate grip on her skirts relaxed. 'I'll take care of the child.'

Elissa fell back on the bed, her eyes closing. Ambrosia turned away, the child in her arms. When she glanced up, she gasped in astonishment.

The Queen of the Old Ways stood in the centre of the hut, dark and jewelled, with her misshapen servant cringing behind her. Her face twisted in a dreadful parody of a fond smile as she saw the baby, and she held out her arms. Ambrosia stared incredulously at Queen Mab, the warm living weight of the child in her arms, and all she could think was, *I loved you once. Loved you, hated you, wanted you to come back . . . it's all gone now, burned away to cinders.*

'Let me see the child!' Mab hissed in her hoarse raven's voice. Her voice had been beautiful once. Mab herself had been beautiful and loving, once. But that was a long time ago, before Constant had begun his persecutions of her people. And now, despite the imperious tone, it was obvious that Mab was attempting to be ingratiating. Slowly Ambrosia held out the child.

Mab took him in her arms and gazed down at him, her painted face showing honest emotion. Ambrosia could see that as much as it was still possible for her to love anything, Mab adored the baby.

So it really was you at Avalon, was it, Queen of Air and Darkness? I thought I recognized the stamp of your handiwork. This trouble is your doing.

Mab raised the child in her arms and held it up

toward the roof of the hut. 'I name this child Merlin!' she cried, her voice a harsh cry of victory.

'Well, while you're making gestures,' Ambrosia snapped, losing patience, 'save the mother. She's dying.'

Mab glanced past Ambrosia to the bed. 'No, she isn't,' Mab said smugly, handing the baby to Frik. 'She's dead!' She smiled triumphantly at Ambrosia.

Poor child. A pawn in a chess-game of queens and kings. Ambrosia walked slowly over to the bed and pulled the coverlet up over Elissa's face. 'Sleep easy, child,' she whispered sadly. 'May angels fly thee home.'

She rounded on Mab. 'What's your excuse! Why didn't you save her?' Ambrosia demanded.

Mab stared at her with wide cat's eyes, her expression smooth and unmarred by guilt – or even by the under- standing that she ought to feel any. 'She'd served her purpose,' Mab said, shrugging dismissively.

'*Served her purpose?*' Suddenly, Ambrosia could feel seething within her all the anger that she had been unable to feel on that long-ago day when Vortigern's riders had overrun Mab's shrine. 'Served her purpose? You're so cold, Lady, that if I punched you in the heart I'd break my fist!' Ambrosia turned to the basin beside the bed to wash her hands. 'And to think that I once served you in the Old Ways!'

'Until you changed and became a Christian!' Mab sneered.

'Who told you that?' Ambrosia demanded. She looked past Mab to Frik and nodded to herself. 'That snooping smiling blatherskite! Well, he's wrong. I'm not pagan or Christian. I follow my own heart, that's religion enough for me.' She glared at Mab, ready to fight for little Merlin.

'Why do you allow her to talk to you like that, madam?' Frik blustered. He held the squirming newborn child as if he might drop it at any moment.

'Because she needs me, idiot.' Ambrosia crossed the floor and took Merlin carefully from Frik.

Mab was pacing like a black leopard deciding when to spring. 'Why do I need you, Ambrosia?' she asked, with as much sweetness as she could summon into her viperish hiss.

'To take care of this child,' Ambrosia answered levelly. She supposed she ought to do Mab the courtesy of being afraid of her; diminished as she was, the Queen of the Old Ways still wielded vast power. But on the day the shrine had been destroyed, the Old Ways had lost their power to frighten or overawe her.

'I can take care of him!' Mab retorted.

She gestured, and instantly the hut was filled with

a cloud of colourful winged sprites. Before Ambrosia's astonished eyes they began to build a cradle of rowan twigs lined with soft river moss and birds' down.

Outside the window, Ambrosia could see that another cloud of sprites hovered around her old nanny-goat while a brownie milked it into a tiny wooden bucket. The inside of the hut began to sparkle, decorated with out-of-season flowers and the bright feathers of tropical birds. An empty jug on the table began to fill with flower nectar, gathered by an army of pixies.

'Tricks,' Ambrosia sneered.

At Ambrosia's remark Mab stopped, her head tilted to one side like some great bird of prey as she regarded the old priestess. Ambrosia braced herself for a fight.

'You need more than tricks to bring up a child, you know. You don't know the first thing about it, do you? You need patience, understanding, and love.' Ambrosia sighed, suddenly sad for everything they had all lost. 'Above all, you need love. That's something you had once, but no more.'

She could tell that no one had spoken so plainly to Queen Mab in a long time. Frik cowered back against the wall of the hut, trying desperately to become invisible. Mab drew herself up, seeming to grow taller in her fury.

'He won't need love,' Mab snapped. 'He'll have power. Give him to me!' Mab glowered and raised her hand as if she would strike.

Ambrosia held the baby closer. *I do this for you, little Merlin. You have the right to know both sides of your heritage – and who will teach you about humankind if I don't?*

'You want him to grow up, don't you?' Ambrosia countered, taking a step backward. 'You want him to become a man?'

Mab hesitated, watching her with the intensity of a hungry wolf.

'Nothing grows in the Land of Magic,' Ambrosia said. 'Time stands still there, Queen Mab. We all know that. If you want this child to grow to be a man, you have to leave him here with me to grow.'

'I wouldn't trust her if I were you, madam,' Frik said officiously, overcoming his earlier alarm.

Mab turned on him, Ambrosia momentarily forgotten. 'When I want your opinion, Frik, I'll give it to you! The witch has always had a sharp tongue, but she's always spoken the truth . . . unlike some at my court.'

She turned back to Ambrosia, but all of her attention was fixed on the baby in Ambrosia's arms. Mab regarded Merlin with such a look of longing, almost of love, that it nearly softened the heart of her former priestess.

But Ambrosia knew too well what Mab had become.

'Very well,' Mab finally said. 'The boy stays with you – but don't you try to turn him against the Old Ways, Ambrosia, or you'll answer to me! He belongs to me: he's my son. You can keep him only until his wizard nature awakens within him. On the day that the power of the Old Ways rouses in him, I will send for him.'

May that day never come! Ambrosia thought fiercely. She nodded slowly. 'That's fair, Queen Mab.'

'Fair or not, it's my ruling!' Mab spat. She flung up her arms and vanished in a flicker of light.

Frik remained behind. He and Ambrosia stared at each other for a frozen moment.

'Scat, you bumblewit!' Ambrosia spat, shifting the baby to one arm and reaching for the hearth-broom.

Frik hastily disappeared as well.

Ambrosia looked around the empty hut, still littered with glittering fairy trash. There was an empty basket on the hearth, laid ready last night for the child to come. Ambrosia picked it up, setting it atop the table beside the fairy cradle. When she bumped it, the cradle fell from the table and exploded into a pile of leaves on the floor.

'Pretty things,' Ambrosia muttered, 'but they don't last.'

She set the baby in the basket and tucked him up warmly, then picked up the broom and began to clean the leaves and flowers and cobwebs the sprites had brought out of the little hut. It took her several hours, but she wasn't willing to stop until everything that Mab had brought with her was gone.

She'd dumped the last bushel of leaves at the edge of the clearing, when she looked up to see Herne standing in front of her, in the shadow of a large oak.

'I didn't see you there,' Ambrosia said brusquely. She could see by his face that there was no need to tell him the news.

'I've only just come,' Herne said quietly. He indicated the spade leaning against the tree. 'I thought that at least I might dig her grave.'

'You do that, lad,' Ambrosia said. The tears she had held back for so long welled up in her old eyes, and she scrubbed them roughly away, turning back into the hut.

She picked up the jug on the table – still half-full with nectar – and went out to finish filling it with fresh goat's milk. When it was full, she poured the mixture into a bottle, and then sat down on a stool before the hearth and set about the business of giving little Merlin his first meal.

She looked down into his crumpled newborn's face, already beginning to smooth out into infant roundness. He was a beautiful baby, and he'd grow to be a handsome man – if nobody meddled too much.

She'd been reluctant to make the promise to Elissa, but now she was glad she had. With Mab's blood running in his veins, Merlin had as great a potential in him for harm as for good. But Ambrosia would love him, and pray that her love would awaken the heart-magic of the lost Grail in him. At Avalon they taught that love was the greatest power in the world, and Ambrosia hoped fervently that they were right.

'Poor little babe,' she said, rocking him gently in her arms. 'No father and three mothers . . . whatever are we going to do with you, young Master Merlin?'

CHAPTER THREE

THE
COURTS OF
MIRRORS

*S*pring followed winter, melted into summer, withered into autumn, and became winter again as the Wheel of the Year spun onward. The boy learned to walk, and, soon, to run. He ruled over his forest kingdom like a young prince, roaming wherever he chose, confident and unafraid. It was the greatest gift of all those his foster-mother Ambrosia gave him; although she worried constantly about his safety, Merlin never knew.

The morning air was cool and dew still glistened on spiders' webs and leaves as Merlin made his way along the forest path.

He was a gawky teenager – at that awkward age, his foster-mother said, all knees and elbows and good intentions. His wide-set eyes were the vivid green of the trees, peering out from a fox-sharp face he had yet to grow into. His long unruly brown hair collected more than its fair share of twigs and tangles and bird-feathers in the course of each day; Ambrosia scolded him as she combed them free each night. He wore the same simple homespun that the farmers did, and in his greens and browns he could blend into the trees nearly as well as his friend Herne, but his sunny open nature saw little need for concealment. He had never experienced any unkindness or disappointment in all his seventeen years. He was kind to everyone he met, and received kindness in return, and in his innocence, Merlin thought that was the way the world ran.

The basket under his arm creaked as the heavy contents shifted, but the boy simply hugged it tighter. Nestled in the basket beneath the rough cloth were a crock of his foster-mother's apple preserves with brandy, two loaves of fresh brown bread and a ramekin of sweet butter – a tempting assortment for an always-hungry boy, but Merlin resisted determinedly. These provisions were for a friend of his – the hermit Blaise, who lived deep in the heart of the forest.

Blaise was a follower of the new religion, but Merlin found nothing odd in that. He had many friends who believed in many different things. For all people to believe the same thing, Herne said, would be as strange as expecting wolves to eat acorns or red squirrels to chase mice. Each beast of the forest was true to its own nature, and so it was for every man.

'Merlin – Merlin – Merlin – where are you going this morning?' a voice called over his head.

I could reach out my hand and blast you into a ball of feathers.

The cold angry thought appeared in his mind like

a hostile stranger, and Merlin recoiled from it in dismay. He did not understand the source of such black thoughts, or the suspicion – almost a premonition – that he really did have the ability to act on these cruel thoughts. Sometimes it was as if he shared his body with a stranger – a stranger he never wanted to meet.

He took a deep breath and peered up at his friend. 'I'm going to see Blaise,' Merlin said. He held out his free hand, and the speaker floated down through the air to perch on his hand.

'Are you bringing him food?' the raven asked eagerly. 'Do you think he might share?'

'You're always hungry, Bran,' Merlin said with amusement. The impulse of cruelty had vanished as quickly as it had appeared. 'Well, hop aboard. We'll see.'

The raven hopped up his arm and perched on Merlin's shoulder. Merlin reached up and stroked its feathers with one finger, and the bird preened its enjoyment.

'Oh, Merlin! Don't listen to him. Bran never tells the truth!' a pair of red squirrels chattered. They stopped halfway up a tree to regard Merlin with bright black eyes.

'Oh, you can believe Bran when he says he's hungry, because it's almost always true. Hello, Rufus. Hello, Rusty,' Merlin said, waving as he continued along his way. The squirrels chased each other, scolding and chattering, up into the high branches of the ancient oak.

He did not find it odd to be able to talk to the animals, since no one had ever told him that most people didn't do things like that. In his seventeen years, Merlin had seen very few people other than Blaise, Herne, and his Aunt Ambrosia, and those he had met were mostly taciturn shire folk who came to see Ambrosia for herbs and medicines. If he had not had the birds and beasts of the forest for company, Merlin would have been very lonely indeed.

But until recently he had never been tempted to leave the wood to seek out others of his own kind. While he knew that there was a whole world beyond the forest edge, until lately he'd been content to confine his explorations to the forest itself. But for the last several months a new restlessness had been growing in him, something for which he had no name. Part of him feared that this nameless feeling was linked to the ugly thoughts appearing in his head, and part of him longed to understand it. It seemed to him as if this peculiar new uneasiness was like a cluster of bright berries that hung just out of reach – you'd never be able to know if they were sweet or sour, edible or poisonous, until you found some way of reaching them.

'Ow!'

Bran pecked him sharply on the ear and Merlin realized that he was standing still, stopped at the place where the little forest path crossed the wide track of the main road that passed through Barnstable Forest. Ambrosia had forbidden him ever to follow the road to see what lay beyond the forest, and as it was the only thing she'd ever forbidden him, Merlin had always assumed the prohibition was for his own good. He'd never questioned it – until now.

'Hurry up!' the greedy raven demanded.

Merlin stepped out of the bushes and stood in the middle of the road, peering down its length. There was a whole world out there – wonders he'd never glimpsed, let alone imagined. How dangerous could it be to follow the road and find them? *You have the power to do just as you please, and no one can stop you*, the inner voice wheedled. Merlin tried to ignore it.

'Bran, do you ever wonder what's out there?'

'No!' the raven said positively. 'Don't think about such things, young Merlin – it only leads to trouble.'

'I suppose you're right,' Merlin sighed, and crossed the road. He knew enough to stick to the path in this area, because the forest was filled with treacherous mud holes wide and deep enough to suck down a horse and cart in seconds. All the forest animals knew enough to avoid the mud holes, and they had taught Merlin the location of all of them over the years.

A few minutes more brought him to Blaise's forest dwelling. Blaise lived in a hut much smaller than the one that Merlin shared with Ambrosia. When Merlin had befriended him, the hermit had been hardly more than skin and bones, living entirely on eggs and mushrooms and whatever he could gather in the forest. Now, with the help of years of Ambrosia's cooking, the old hermit was decidedly plump.

'Blaise!' Merlin shouted, as he entered the clearing. 'Blaise, where are you?'

'Here, young Merlin.' Blaise crawled out through the low door of his hut and stood up.

The old hermit's hair and beard were long and white, and winter and summer he wore nothing more than a simple tunic of deerskin, going barefoot and cloakless no matter how deep the snow on the ground. When

Merlin had been much younger, he'd asked Blaise why.

'So that I can pay more attention to what's important in this life. It's the only one we have, young Merlin, so we have to pay attention while we can,' the hermit said.

Merlin laughed, not understanding. 'I've had many lives before this one, and I'll have many more,' he answered.

'Perhaps you will,' Blaise told him. 'But it's to your advantage to live each life as if it were your only one, so that you can be proud of it.'

Merlin had not known what Blaise meant at the time, but more and more these days, his mind turned back to those words. How did you live a good life, one you could be proud of? He'd asked the deer and the wolves and the ravens, but none of them had understood his question.

'Is that a basket I see?' the old hermit asked, smacking his lips in anticipation. Merlin held it out to him.

'Aunt A baked yesterday. She sent me to bring you some bread and butter – and the last of the apple preserves she put up last winter.'

Bran flew up off Merlin's shoulder and settled on a low tree branch, watching the food closely.

'It will be berrying season soon,' Blaise said, coming to take the basket and peering inside. 'I'm looking forward to another pot of Ambrosia's blackberry jam. But come, lad, sit down. I was just making tea, and I've got a nice large honeycomb for you to take back to Ambrosia.'

Merlin sat down on a stone beside the door of Blaise's hut. Bran fluttered from his shoulder to the roof of the hut, where he could get a better look at the basket.

'You stay out of that,' Merlin warned.

'Eh?' the hermit said. He lifted the steaming kettle from the fire and carefully poured its contents into two thick clay cups.

'Oh, I was just talking to Bran. He's hoping for a hand-out,' Merlin said.

'Charity is always a virtue, unless it is motivated by conceit,' Blaise said. 'Then it ceases to be charity, and becomes cruelty.' He handed Merlin his cup, then reached into the basket and broke off a chunk of bread. He held it out to the bird, who seized it eagerly in his beak and flew up into a tree to enjoy his feast.

'How can charity be cruel?' Merlin asked, puzzled. In the years they'd known each other, Blaise had told Merlin many things – from the names of the trees in the forest to the names of the stars in the sky. His talks with Blaise always challenged his mind, filling it with questions that lasted for weeks. Whatever Ambrosia did not know, Blaise did, and Merlin had always assumed that, between the two of them, they knew everything there was to know. But lately, Merlin had begun to realize that there was something outside their vast store of knowledge, something that he had to discover for himself. He listened closely to Blaise's reply, still hoping to find his answers there.

'When charity is given only to impress its recipient with how superior the giver is, then its purpose is to sow anger and despair. The charity of princes leads to wars, more often than not, because only the truly humble and good can dispense true charity.'

'Can't a king ever be humble and good?' Merlin asked.

Blaise smiled. 'Have you ever known one who was?'

'I've never known any kings,' Merlin admitted, sipping his sweet herb tea. 'Everyone says we have two – Vortigern and Uther – and that Uther is our true king, because he's the son of King Constant. But if Uther's our rightful king, why isn't he here? And if Vortigern isn't our true king, how does he rule?'

Blaise sighed. 'You ask deep questions, Master Merlin, and I have no easy answers for you. All the answers to that sort of question lie outside this forest – and the world out there is a cold and wicked place.'

'It's because the king is wicked,' Merlin said dreamily, staring at the dancing dust-motes in a beam of sunlight. Sometimes the new inner voice told him interesting things, and this was one of them. 'Because the land follows the king, and the king serves the land. If I were king, I'd be humble and good, and teach others to be good also.'

'You cannot teach goodness,' Blaise said tartly. 'It comes from the heart – it isn't something you can slap on like a coat of whitewash.'

Merlin sighed, shrugging himself out of his daydream. There were so many voices, both inside and out, that at times it was hard to know which to listen to. 'I have so much to learn, Blaise. There's something I need to know – only I don't know what it is. But it's as if there's something inside me, and it's a part of me, but not like me at all. I want to be good, and fair, and just – but how can I tell if I'm being good, when I'm not sure what being good is?'

The old hermit sighed. He reached out and patted Merlin's knee reassuringly. 'Patience, young sir. Have patience. You'll know all the answers to your questions in time. But be wary in your search for truth. You tread a dangerous path.'

'I know,' Merlin said, although he didn't. It seemed these days that more and more of his talks with Blaise ended in warnings. It was frustrating to be warned about something, but not to be told what that something was.

His Aunt Ambrosia knew, Merlin was sure of it. But no one could get Aunt A to talk about something if she didn't want to.

Perhaps he could find his answers outside the forest. But everyone told him that the outside world was a big place – if he went in search of answers there, how would he even know where to begin looking?

They talked for a while longer, and Blaise gave him the honeycomb wrapped in oiled muslin – 'And mind you don't eat it all before you get home, young sir!'

But somehow Merlin didn't feel like going straight home today. When he left the hermit's hut, Merlin wandered aimlessly through the forest, but none of his usual diversions had the power to distract him from his brooding that day.

It was springtime. The birds were building nests for their eggs; the young bucks, their antlers still covered in velvet, locked horns over the does in contests that were still half in play; the she-wolves in their dens guarded new litters of downy cubs with the help of the proud fathers.

All the animals of the forest had families – except him. Aunt Ambrosia was all the family he had, and Merlin sensed that there was something missing. He could not share this confused feeling with his foster-mother, and that saddened him. Once he had shared his every thought with her, but more and more these days, Merlin found himself brimming over with thoughts and ideas and questions he could not even form into words.

Disconsolately, he kicked at a stone in his path and watched it skitter off into the bushes, disturbing a colony of hares. The sentry-hare drummed at him angrily with its powerful feet before following the others in flight. Merlin sighed, leaning against a tree. Even hares had families. *I'm all alone*, he realized with surprise. He'd never thought about it before; somehow it had never mattered. But now it did. It mattered very much.

'Why isn't there anyone like me?' he demanded plaintively. He wanted companions of his own kind. He couldn't be the only one like himself in all the world. The world was huge – Blaise had said so.

But what if he was? What if he was going to be alone forever?

Herne watched Merlin. Though he was only a few feet away, Merlin did not see him – nor would he, unless Herne wished it. He shook his head sadly at Merlin's words. Both he and Ambrosia had known this time would come. The boy was lonely without knowing what he longed for.

Herne knew. Merlin was not a child any longer. The boy was nearly a man. The same restlessness that drove all the creatures of the springtime forest drove him as well. Soon he would want to claim his rightful heritage – but what was it? Did Merlin belong to Mab and the Old Ways? To Avalon and the faith of his dead mother Elissa? Or was there a third path that Merlin must find for himself, if he could?

Perhaps I can help him find his answers – and perhaps give him something that will shield him from the harm that may come.

Herne made a cryptic gesture with his right hand. Like Ambrosia, he had given up much when he had forsaken the Old Ways, but, just as she retained her knowledge of herbs and healing, some small magics were left to him.

A shining figure appeared in the distance, stepping grandly out of concealment and into Merlin's sight. It was a great silver stag, its branching antlers shining like fire in the spring sunlight. Its white coat shone with the soft pale brilliance of the full moon, and it gazed at Merlin with wide knowing eyes.

Run, boy. And find only the good that the world holds, Herne commanded silently. A flick of his fingers sent the stag leaping away, with Merlin running after it.

When it ran, Merlin chased it almost without thought. The glorious creature was like nothing he'd seen in all his life and he wanted to get close enough to touch it. In the thick undergrowth of the forest, Merlin was as fast as any deer, but somehow no matter how hard he tried, he never seemed to gain on it. The beast ran tirelessly ahead of him, just out of reach, and the longer he chased it, the more determined Merlin was to catch it.

It seemed as if he ran for hours at its heels without it tiring or slowing. He was breathing hard, with the sweat running in salty trickles down his face and into his eyes, but just as he was about to give up, he realized that he'd been gaining on it at last. Victory was within his grasp, and Merlin gathered all his strength and made a wild leap for the stag's back.

But as he jumped, his foot caught in a tree root, and instead of landing on the stag's back, Merlin crashed full-length to the forest floor. As he lay gasping for breath, he heard a distant crackling of branches. By the time he scrambled to his feet, he couldn't even see in which direction the creature had fled.

He shook his head, pushing the hair back out of his eyes, and ruefully assessed the damage. He'd lost the honeycomb somewhere back at the beginning of the chase. His skin was scratched and his clothes were berry-stained and bramble-torn. Aunt A would not be pleased. Maybe some wildflowers or rare herbs would appease her, although frankly Merlin doubted it. The effort was worth making, though. He looked around to see where he was and gauge what might be growing nearby.

Funny. I don't remember ever seeing this place before.

Since he'd been old enough to venture away from his own front door, Merlin had roamed the forest. He was sure he knew every inch of it as well as Aunt Ambrosia knew her own kitchen.

He'd never been here.

It was later than he'd realized at first – almost suppertime. The evening light shone down upon a forest pool that welled up out of a cleft in the rock behind it. He was hot and thirsty from his long run; kneeling beside the water, he cupped his hands to take a drink.

Another face stared up at him from out of the water.

'Yah!' With a startled cry, Merlin jumped backward and fell sprawling. Common sense reasserted itself a moment later, and he advanced warily on the spring. This time, when he looked down, he could see that the face that had gazed up at him was a carving, not a living thing. He drank thirstily, and then carefully cleared away the debris and leaves that had fallen into the pool over the years until he could see the carving clearly.

It was a carving depicting the faces of three women, cut into the granite at the bottom of the pool by some long-forgotten master craftsman, as perfect and beautiful as the day that unknown artist had laid down his chisel. Two of the faces were shown in profile – one facing left, one facing right – with the third one gazing straight ahead. The three faces shared a certain resemblance, but each was subtly different. He did not know how he knew them, but somehow he did – a secret knowledge that emanated from some hidden place within. Once, before the Christians, even before the Romans, these had been the gods of Britain.

Mab-Morrigan the Warrior – Lady of Ravens, Queen of Battles; Titania the Maiden – Bright Enchantress; and Melusine the Mother, Mistress of the Silver Wheel . . .

The one facing left was a young woman: Titania. The Maiden's cheeks were full with youth and dimpled with a hidden smile. Her hair was long and flowing, braided with wildflowers, the blossoms carved in such loving detail that Merlin fancied he could almost reach into the pool and pluck them from her hair.

The one gazing straight ahead was older, a grown woman, sombre and purposeful. This was the Lady in her Warrior aspect: her mouth was set with solemn determination, and there was justice but no mercy in her expression. Her eyes gazed steadfastly into his. She wore the coronet of rulership upon her brow, and clusters of raven's feathers were braided into her hair.

The third of the three faces turned toward the right: Melusine, the Mother. It was the face of an older woman, her features marked with lines of both joy and pain. The Mother's hair was braided and coiled upon her head, and held in place with jewelled hairpins depicting the moon and the stars.

Carved into the stone above the centre face, Merlin could see the crescent moon and triple spiral that marked a shrine of the Old Ways – Ambrosia had told him how to recognize such places, though she'd told him little else about the Old Ways. From what people had said in his hearing, Merlin had got the idea that all the shrines to the Old Ways had been smashed, either by Constant or by Vortigern. But if that were true, they seemed to have missed this one.

Nobody knows this place is here but me. Delighted with his secret knowledge, Merlin flopped onto his belly and gazed down into the pool.

The Warrior aspect disturbed him obliquely, and the Mother-self reminded him of his Aunt Ambrosia. But the Maiden, her eyes downcast and a secret smile upon her face, seemed to him in that moment to be all that Merlin had dreamed of in his unfocused dreams. Gazing at her, all the vague longing he had felt for so long crystallized with a sharpness that bordered on pain.

Come to me, he thought to the beautiful image. *I'm all alone. Aunt Ambrosia has her work, and Blaise has his god, but what is there for me? You are all there is of love; I can see it. Come to me, come to me – I need you . . .*

But the power he called to with all the passion of an untutored young wizard had long since lost the ability to feel the love that filled young Merlin's heart. Ages ago the Queen of the Old Ways had lost that gentle loving part of herself – Time and War had cut away her maiden and mother selves, leaving behind only the Warrior, Mab-Morrigan of the Ravens. Mab could not hear the cry of a young lover's heart any longer, let alone respond to it.

But such a call could not go unanswered. Somewhere in all the world, there must be someone to hear. Merlin gazed into the water and saw the reflection of his face shimmering over the stone carving, giving the features the illusion of warm-blooded life. But when he reached out his hand to touch her face, the ripples his fingers made as they brushed the surface of the water shattered the image into a thousand bright dancing rings . . .

The candle flame cast bright rings of light on the mellow stone walls of the Abbey. The sound of the bells tolling for evensong drifted in through her window, and Nimue wondered what life would be like when she could no longer hear them each evening. Would church bells ring in the shadow of her father's castle? Or would she join her father at King Vortigern's pagan court and never hear the church bells again?

Nimue could not suppress a small shudder. Vortigern had been the bogeyman of her childhood, the threat that had commanded her obedience. Her family had always been loyal to King Constant, but things had grown so bad in the last years of the mad old king's reign that Ardent had welcomed the new usurper even as he helped to smuggle Uther and Lionors to safety in Normandy.

But Vortigern had swiftly proved to be as bad a king as Constant, and so Ardent had sent his only child to the holy sisters of Avalon for safekeeping. Nimue had grown from gawky child to poised young woman safely behind the walls of Avalon, isolated from the troubles of the world.

But not unaware of them. Each messenger from her father had brought fresh – and often disturbing – news from outside. Vortigern trusted no one, and kept his barons close about him at his court rather than leaving them at liberty upon their own lands as Constant had. He had abandoned Constant's royal city at Londinium to begin building an enormous city in the western hills, a city that would be dominated by a fortress named for the White Dragon that was his emblem: Pendragon. He taxed the people of Britain heavily to pay for all his building, and many were turned out of their homes for the inability to pay. Destitute and starving, the people cried out for help and no one listened. Every year it seemed that things could be no worse, and every year things managed to become more terrible than the year before.

This was the world that her father had summoned Nimue back to. The messenger had come early this morning, entering the moment the gates of the Abbey were opened. As soon as an escort could be gathered for her, Nimue would head north to her father's castle, and from there to Vortigern's court.

What will happen to me? What will I become? she wondered. There was a marriage in her future almost certainly – a loveless marriage of duty to whichever noble her father commanded her to wed. Nimue sighed. She had learned love in her years at Avalon, but she had learned duty as well, and it was her duty to marry whoever her father ordered, to strengthen the web of political alliances that kept the land from plunging once more into civil war.

But what if Uther comes back? They said he has begun to gather troops in Normandy to invade Britain and retake the throne. When that day comes, which side will our family be on? Who will my husband support?

Who will I support?

The question was a startling one: in all her sixteen years, Lady Nimue had never considered the possibility that her opinions might differ from her father's. But now, as she faced the possibility for the first time, Nimue realized that she had very strong opinions – and she did not want to marry some nobleman who was blindly loyal to Vortigern while there was a possibility of another civil war. War meant a new king, and the chessboard of politics tipped over yet again.

What shall I do? she wondered. She could not defy her father – nor did she wish to. But perhaps she could persuade him to wait – to wait for the saviour of Britain to appear at last.

I feel as if I already know him somehow, she thought, staring absently into the candle flame – and as she did, the flame seemed to swell and swell until all the world was filled with light and her eyes were filled with visions.

At first she saw only familiar sights: green meadows and a young spring lamb bleating lustily for its mother. But in the very instant that she recognized the peaceful scene, it changed.

A white dragon swooped down from the sky like a hunting hawk. Its scales glittered like hoarfrost and its breath left grey ice everywhere it touched. It pounced upon the lamb, its cruel claws digging deep into the young flesh, and carried it off into the sky.

But then a red dragon, with scales that shone like fresh blood and a hot breath that withered the grass upon the ground, dived out of the sun to attack the white dragon, fighting for its prize. As the two battled, the lamb fell to the ground, too injured and terrified to run. Whichever dragon won could easily devour it.

Nimue stared, transfixed with horror as the two dragons fought on until it began to seem that the whole world would be destroyed by their war of fire and ice. But just when she began to despair, a shining falcon, with feathers as gold as the sun, appeared out of nowhere to attack both dragons. Its piercing cries drowned out the roaring of the dragons, and its shining ivory talons left long bloody gouges in the scales of both beasts. It seemed as if only moments passed before both dragons fell lifeless to the ground, and the falcon folded its wings and followed them groundward.

But the poor lamb. It seemed that the lamb's fate was to be devoured no matter who triumphed, but just as the bird's talons touched the earth it shimmered and became a golden young man wearing a great feathered cloak.

Who are you? Nimue cried silently.

He picked up the lamb and cradled it tenderly against his chest, and then looked up as if he could see Nimue watching him. His eyes were the deep green of the forest, and as their gazes met she felt his look pierce through her, and in that instant it was as if he knew her. He smiled, and her heart beat faster in response.

Nimue wrenched herself free of the vision with a gasp, her heart beating as wildly as a caged bird's. The bells still rang for evensong – what had seemed to take hours had in fact taken only seconds.

She got to her feet and began to pace in agitation, the face of the golden young man still before her mind's eye. What did the vision mean? Was it an angel she had seen? The words she had heard in her heart when he had looked at her still echoed through her mind: 'You are all there is of love. Come to me, come to me – I need you . . .'

He was late for supper and Aunt A scolded him severely, but even that could not drive the image he had seen from Merlin's mind. For a moment he had seen a flesh-and-blood woman in the pool – a woman with dark eyes and soft brown hair and a mischievous smile. Seeing her had made him aware of an emptiness where no emptiness had been before, an ache he did not know how to heal.

His foster-mother remarked on his absent-mindedness in the following days. He knew it worried her, but he could not find the words to allay her fears. There was something he had to do, something he had to find. He did not know whether it lay within him or outside him, but there was something he needed to know, to learn.

The milk jug crashed to the floor with a loud thud, spewing milk all over the floor. Merlin stared at it as if he'd never seen it before, startled out of his daydream.

'Out!' Ambrosia lifted the hearth-broom menacingly. 'A wild boar would be more use in the house than you are! What's got into you, Merlin?'

'I don't know.' The boy hung his head, staring at the jug. 'Sometimes I just –'

Ambrosia reached out and hugged him, ruffling his hair. 'I know, Merlin. It isn't easy for you. But this is a difficult time. You have to be careful.'

Why does everyone keep telling me that? It seemed to Merlin as if he was always being warned about something these days, but still no one would tell him what it was. Once again he felt the flash of cold selfishness, as if some other self were struggling inside him, striving to be born. Again he pushed it away, but each time he felt it, it seemed to be stronger.

'Why don't you just run along, then, Merlin. It's such a beautiful day it seems a shame to be indoors. I can finish up the spring cleaning by myself,' Ambrosia said. 'But be sure you're back in time for dinner. I'm making your favourite: buttered parsnips.'

Merlin smiled in anticipation of the feast. He backed carefully toward the door, alert for any more milk jugs lying in wait. By the time he'd reached the edge of the clearing, he was running, his vague preoccupation forgotten.

If he had known that this was to be his last day as a boy running free in the forest, Merlin could not have chosen a better way to spend it. He visited all his old friends and favourite places, feasted on fresh honeycomb and raspberries, and idled through the afternoon with nothing more pressing on his mind than the need to get home in time for supper.

Late in the afternoon, he crossed the main road, but even that did not have its usual power to disturb him. He found a warm place near it, in the shade of a hollow tree, and curled up to rest for a moment. Basking in the sunlight, he was asleep before he knew it.

He dreamed that he was a merlin, like his namesake, a shining falcon that rode the wind. Below him he could see the tops of the trees, and beyond the edge of the forest he could see castles and hills and rolling meadows. The landscape seemed vividly real but somehow mysterious, as if everything he saw was both itself and standing in for something else. But that was less important to him than the fact that he was free, soaring above the world.

Then, far below him, movement caught his eye. He looked down and saw two dragons fighting. The land all around them was devastated by their battle; the trees had been burned to ash and the grass had been frozen, and nothing grew or lived as far as his falcon's eyes could see, save for one small lamb that lay upon the ground, bleating in terror and pain.

I must stop this, Merlin thought, and dived at the two dragons, shrieking defiance.

They were far larger and more powerful than he was, armed with claws and fangs and their deadly breath, but somehow that did not matter to him. He battered at them with his wings and tore at them with his talons, as a flock of sparrows will harry a crow, and at last the two monsters fled, abandoning their battle and their prey. Folding his wings, Merlin dived for the ground, but when he landed, the lamb was gone, and there was a young girl in her place. It was her face he'd seen in the forest pool – her face that haunted his dreams. He reached out to take her hand . . .

When laughter woke him.

CHAPTER FOUR

THE COURTS OF LOVE

$\mathcal{N}$imue had experienced no more visions after that first one, and she was grateful – she feared and mistrusted such things as traps sent by the Old Magic to seduce her away from the new religion. But as the days passed without incident she allowed herself to be distracted by her departure back to her father's estate. Lord Ardent had sent a party of courtiers and ladies in waiting to fetch her, and for once in her life, Nimue was surrounded by people her own age. As they laughed and chattered on their journey, relating tales of life at Vortigern's court, Nimue allowed herself to hope that the future was not as bleak as she'd feared.

The party had stopped the previous night at an inn outside the village of Nottingham, and it was late afternoon by the time the travellers reached the edge of Barnstable Forest, which lay between them and the castle where they would spend the night.

'They say it's haunted,' young Lord Aneirin said, staring at the thick woods with gloomy relish.

'Haunted or not,' Mistress Ragnell answered him stoutly, 'it will be slow going to get through such a tangle. We shall have to lead the horses.'

'Then let us begin,' Nimue said firmly. She vaulted down from her horse's back, took its reins and began to lead it along the path into the forest. Reluctantly, the others followed.

She felt very cross, and was doing her best not to show it. Aneirin was the younger son of Lord Lambert, and this morning over breakfast he'd let it slip that his older brother, Bercilak, was a hostage at court. He hadn't seemed very worried about it, but all of Nimue's buried fears about her future had resurfaced, and she'd become reluctant to finish her journey and discover her fate. But the holy sisters at Avalon had taught her not to shrink from unpleasant tasks, so she held her misgivings in check and tried to make good time on the homeward journey.

But as she walked along through the warm summer afternoon leading her horse, her mind wandered from what might be to what ought to be. She imagined a dashing young knight ready to fight for her hand, the embodiment of all that was noble and good . . .

'I think we're lost,' Drust the page said.

Nimue stopped and looked up, roused out of her daydream. She frowned at the tree. Hadn't they passed one very much like it an hour ago? She looked around, and realized that there were trees all around them and the path had dwindled to a narrow deer track.

'We're doomed. We'll be devoured by wolves and

no one will ever know what's become of us,' Aneirin said.

'Don't be foolish,' Nimue answered. 'Someone must live here, and when we find them, we can ask our way.'

There was no sign of habitation, but a few minutes later, as if in answer to her prayers, Nimue spotted a sleeping figure curled up at the side of the path.

He was dressed in rustic homespun garments. His tattered breeches came only to his knees and he wore leather buskins on his feet. His tunic was woad-dyed hempen cloth, with twigs and feathers caught in its coarse weave, the seams fraying at elbow and hem. For a moment she wondered if she had stumbled across one of the pagan forest-spirits who belonged to the Old Ways. But Brother Giraldus swore they had all been banished from the land by the prayers of good Christian souls.

'How funny he looks!' Ragnell giggled. The other girls joined her, giggling and whispering.

At the sound, the young man roused from sleep and looked up. His eyes were a vivid green, as clear as water, and his expression of dumbfounded amazement at the sight of all these grandly-dressed lords and ladies standing in front of him made Nimue smile as well.

*   *   *

The sound of laughter like the twittering of forest birds woke Merlin from his strange dream. He opened his eyes and saw an angel standing before him, glowing with light.

He blinked, and the angel became a mortal woman . . . the most beautiful he had ever seen. She was wearing a rich gown of ivory and cream and a golden circlet about her forehead. Her soft brown hair flowed freely over her shoulders and her mouth was the rich red of fresh raspberries. Merlin scrambled to his feet.

'Please excuse their rudeness,' she said softly. 'We're travelling to Lord Lambert's castle and we've lost our way.'

Behind her he could see several other young women and men, whispering together and laughing as they stared at him. They all wore rich gowns and tunics, and their horses' saddles and bridles were splendidly decorated, but none of them was as wonderful to look upon as the woman who stood directly before him.

'It's about a mile,' he said, pointing. Though he'd never gone there, he'd listened closely when the travellers who visited Ambrosia's hut spoke of their journeys. 'Take the right fork when you reach it. But don't try any short cuts. It's dangerous and you can get lost.'

The beautiful woman smiled and glanced toward the path he had pointed out. 'Thank you, sir.' She spoke with simple dignity, as if she saw no difference between them, though he was dressed in tattered homespun and she in velvet and silk. 'What can we offer you as a reward?'

'A kiss,' Merlin answered. He'd wanted nothing else from the moment he'd seen her face.

The women standing with the horses broke out into scandalized whispers. 'Do you know who you're talking to?' one of them demanded.

'This is the Lady Nimue,' another said.

'Who?' Merlin was honestly puzzled.

'Lord Ardent's daughter,' came the huffy reply from the one who had spoken first.

'She asked me what I wanted and I told the truth,' Merlin said simply. He recognized Ardent's name – he was the lord who was rumoured to have helped Uther and his mother to escape to France, although he now gave every appearance of being a faithful lackey to the tyrannical king.

Nimue smiled at him. 'And I think it's a fair price,' she said, laughter in her voice. She held out her hand to him.

Her white skin was soft against his hand. He raised

her hand to his lips and kissed it – and then pulled her to him and kissed her on the lips.

I love her, said something inside him. *I will always love her. Somehow we'll be together.*

'My name's Merlin,' he whispered.

'Mine's Nimue,' she answered, her face still close to his. Then she pulled away and spoke loudly for the benefit of the others. 'And I think you're a very rude young man!'

She walked back to the others, and they began to move off almost at once.

'I'll never forget you, Nimue! We'll meet again – I can see it!' Merlin shouted.

She looked back at him as he spoke, and for a moment her face lit with a hope and a promise that matched his own. Then her expression changed to sorrow, and it was as if the sun had gone behind a cloud.

'I don't think so, Master Merlin,' she answered sadly.

Merlin scrambled up into the branches of a nearby tree so that he could see her for as long as possible. He watched until the horses were invisible through the trees.

Nimue . . .

*   *   *

If only life were as simple as that, Nimue thought to herself as she followed Aneirin and the others through the forest. *If only I could just run away with some simple woodcutter like Merlin, and spend the rest of my life far away from kings and crowns!* But it was foolishness even to think such a thing. Her life had been all set out for her from the moment she was born; there was no use wishing for adventure or excitement.

Or love.

She smiled at the memory of their impulsive kiss. Merlin had been so honest, so direct. His manner had none of the cringing deference that had become typical of the peasantry in Vortigern's Britain. There was a kind of goodness that radiated from him . . . it reminded her of the holy brethren of Avalon, yet different from what she had felt there.

If I go on thinking this way, I'll go running back to him and forget my duty! She had dropped behind the others; laughing and talking together, they didn't notice. *There must be a quicker way out of this stupid forest!* Angry, and afraid of her new feelings, Nimue spotted a path that seemed to run straighter than the broad winding path the others were following. Forgetting Merlin's warning, she tugged her horse after her, leading it along this new path at a right angle to the rest of the party. In a few minutes, even the sound of their voices was gone.

Merlin lay in the fork of the tree, turning over his meeting with Nimue in his mind. Ardent's castle lay not too far from here – if he went there, perhaps he could see her again. She'd looked so sad when she'd walked away, and Merlin wondered why. Perhaps he could help her. Boyish daydreams of ladies and knights filled his head. He could go on a quest for her – he could rescue her from a dragon. He closed his eyes, the better to concentrate on his dreams . . .

Merlin! Help me!

Suddenly he could hear Nimue's voice inside his mind. She'd left the path. She was in danger.

He flung himself down out of the tree and ran toward the sound of the screams that echoed in his mind.

She lost the trail almost immediately, but she'd been sure she could find it again. She was no longer certain where she was, and the rest of her companions were nowhere to be seen or heard. At last Nimue began to worry. She needed to return to them. But before she had taken a dozen steps in what she hoped was the right direction, the ground gave way beneath her feet. She stumbled, letting go of the horse's reins, and found herself sinking into a mud hole that had been hidden beneath a fall of leaves. Her elaborate gown clung to her like a shroud, and no matter what she did, her struggles only pulled her deeper into the mud. She realized that there was no bottom to the mire; she would not stop sinking. The mud would pull her down beneath its surface and she would drown.

Nimue began to scream, then she tried to pray, so that she could go to God with a pure heart, but all the prayers she knew had been driven from her mind by terror. She would die here on a warm summer day, and never see her home or Avalon again.

At that moment, Merlin raced into the clearing. 'I'm here!'

'Help me!' Nimue screamed, terrified.

'Don't struggle,' he said quickly. 'You'll only sink deeper. Stay calm.' On hands and knees he felt for the edge of the sinkhole. When he found it, he reached out to her, but her struggles had carried her too far from the edge for him to be able to reach her.

Frantically he cast about for something she could hold on to. If he only had a rope! But by the time he could return with one, Nimue would have been sucked beneath the surface. So he grabbed the longest thing he could see – an old branch – and, lying full-length on the ground, held it out to her.

It was still too short.

Only her head and arms were above the surface now. In moments she would be gone. And he would have to live the rest of his life without her.

You have to be long enough. You have to!

'Grow!' he said desperately. 'Grow – grow!'

Suddenly, as if his words had been the spark, the power kindled within him, fuelled by his desperate desire. He felt it tingle in the pit of his stomach, then rush down his arms and through his hands into the branch. The dry, brittle wood darkened, becoming the collar of a living branch. It seemed to vibrate in his hands, as though he could feel the heartbeat of the mother tree. And then leaves appeared upon its twigs and it began to grow . . . longer . . . longer . . . until it was long enough to reach Nimue.

She grabbed it with both hands; Merlin rolled to his feet and began dragging her from the mud. Soon she was close enough to grasp his hands, and he threw the branch aside and lifted her out of the mud.

She collapsed against him, gasping and laughing with relief, and the combined weight of her and the mud on her clothes sent both of them sprawling on the ground once more.

'I told you we'd meet again,' Merlin said, holding her tightly.

'How did you do that – with the branch?' Nimue gasped.

'I don't know.' He'd been as surprised as Nimue when the branch had begun to grow. He glanced toward it. 'I don't know. What did I do?'

'Well, whatever it was, it saved my life,' Nimue said. 'You deserve one more kiss for that.' Boldly, she pressed her lips to his.

'Only one?' Merlin said, laughing, and Nimue kissed him again.

But the moment could not last, and Nimue pushed herself to her feet, staggering with the weight of her mud-encrusted skirts.

'I have to get back to the others. They'll be looking for me.'

'I'll take you,' Merlin answered. He ran to catch her horse, and led it back for her to mount. 'Now that I've found you, I don't want you to get lost again.'

Once they were gone, a small shrub at the edge of the clearing took a few cautious steps forward.

The leaves shimmered as it turned from a shrub to a crouching gnome. Frik straightened up, groaning as he stretched.

'I'm getting too old for this,' he muttered, plucking a sprig of greenery from behind his ear and tossing it away, then brushing himself off. Leaves and bits of twig fell to the ground.

Glancing around once more to see that he was not observed, Frik stepped cautiously over to the branch that Merlin had tossed aside. Picking it up, he held it under his nose and sniffed it thoroughly, then bit it cautiously.

'Yes, indeed,' he said aloud. Whatever he had discovered from his examination of the branch pleased him, because he tossed it back to the ground and rubbed his hands together.

'Young Merlin is using magic at last. Won't Her Majesty be pleased? I must tell her at once.'

There was a shimmer, and Frik vanished.

Merlin led Nimue's horse through the forest. She was seated on its back, her skirts still dripping mud. She smiled down at Merlin. 'You must come and visit me at my father's castle. I can't wait to tell him how brave you were.'

Merlin smiled, but his thoughts were elsewhere. He knew he'd done the right thing by saving Nimue, but at the same time he felt guilty, as if he'd done something terribly wrong. What he could do frightened as well as elated him. The magic seemed to bubble through his veins, daring him to use it again. He suspected that this was what Ambrosia had warned him about, but why wouldn't she want him to do something that was so clearly a part of him?

'Merlin?' Nimue said, and his brooding thoughts vanished. He smiled up at her.

'Tell me about yourself,' Nimue urged.

'Oh,' Merlin said, suddenly shy. 'I'm not very interesting. I'd rather hear about you.'

'Well, I'm not very interesting,' Nimue teased. 'I grew up at Avalon Abbey among the holy sisters there. This is the first time I've been away from it since I went there as a little girl.'

'Well, I've never left the forest at all,' Merlin said. 'I was born here and I've lived all my life here. I can't imagine living anywhere else.'

'That sounds nice,' said Nimue. She leaned forward to touch his hair, but just then they heard the sound of voices calling her name. 'Oh,' she said, sounding a little disappointed. 'They've found me.'

'I should go,' Merlin said, stopping. He looked around. It was later than he'd thought – Aunt A would have dinner on the table and be wondering where he was.

'No!' Nimue said.

She reached for him, but he stepped back, shaking his head. Her companions had laughed at his clothes before – the next time he saw them he wanted to make a grand impression, and be seen as worthy of Nimue.

'No,' he said. 'They'd just ask a hundred questions and not believe any of the answers. It's better this way. Don't tell them about me – about the magic.' He handed her the reins. He wasn't sure why it was so important to keep the magic a secret, but his heart told him this was the right choice.

'But where are you going? Merlin!' Nimue cried.

'Home – I'm late for dinner,' Merlin called over his shoulder. 'But don't worry. I'll see you again – soon.'

'I know you will,' Nimue said, smiling. 'I've seen it.'

Queen Mab sat on a throne made of darkness in the centre of her palace in the Hollow Hills. She could sense the years passing in the world outside, but here it was no time at all. It seemed only moments since she'd relinquished the baby Merlin into Ambrosia's care, and she still suspected that the priestess had tricked her somehow.

But no matter. Today, the day she had waited for from the moment she had first conceived her plan, had come at last. Merlin had used his magic.

Mab hugged herself in triumph, then gazed upward, toward the World of Men. She had sensed it the moment it had happened. The echoes of his act had swept through the living rock and made Mab's crystal cave ring with the sound of fairy bells. She felt a wild excitement rising in her blood. The eve of her people's deliverance was at hand. In the moment Merlin had called upon the magical power that was her gift to him, he had set foot upon the path that led to his destiny and bound him to her forever.

'He's mine now – and he'll never leave me!' she whispered.

'Madam!' Frik bustled in, breathless. He was wearing fringed buckskins with a coonskin cap and carried a rifle in his hand. Another of his ridiculous masquerades. Mab flicked her fingers and the rifle turned into a snake.

'Eek!' Frik squealed, startled into dropping it. The snake slithered across the floor and then turned into a length of rope. Frik stared at it forlornly.

'Well?' Mab demanded. 'Now that you've disturbed me: what?'

'Great news, madam,' Frik said. 'News that you've been waiting for. I've been spying on Ambrosia, just as you directed. Well, today I thought that just for a change I'd follow young Master Merlin about – for a bit of diversion, you know – and what do you think I found? Master Merlin has used his magic!'

Mab rose to her feet, fists clenched. Her green eyes burned into Frik's until his face lost its pleased expression. 'Don't you think I know that? Do you think that my child – *mine* – could embrace his birthright without my knowledge? I am the Queen of the Old Ways, the mistress of all magic!

'Go! Bring my son to me!' she commanded.

Merlin ran through the woods toward Ambrosia's hut. He stopped along the way to try to wash the worst of the mud off, but the attempt wasn't very successful. Water was still dripping from his tunic and breeches when he reached the hut, bursting with news.

'I've seen her!' he said as he came through the door. 'The most beautiful girl in the world, the only girl I'll ever love, I know it. And she loves me, and we'll love each other always.'

Ambrosia looked up and smiled as she saw him, then her expression sharpened into one of motherly concern. 'What are you babbling about, young Merlin?' she scolded affectionately. 'And you're dripping wet! Off with those clothes!'

He pulled his tunic off over his head as Ambrosia went to get a towel out of the linen chest. She carried it over and began to vigorously dry his hair. 'You'll catch your death,' she chided, but Merlin was still thinking about Nimue.

'I'm a hero, too; I saved her.'

'Saved who?' asked Ambrosia. 'From what?'

'Nimue – Nimue – Nimue –' Merlin sang. 'She's the daughter of some lord. She fell into a mud hole and I saved her.'

'Very brave of you, dear,' Ambrosia said, draping the towel about his shoulders. But Merlin could tell her attention was wandering, and he was determined to regain it.

'But the extraordinary thing was how I saved her. I took this branch, and I somehow made it grow.'

Caught up in his own retelling, Merlin did not see the expression on his foster-mother's face. Her face had gone grim, and she took a step backwards.

'I know it sounds impossible,' Merlin went on, 'but I

said, "Grow! Grow!" and somehow, that made it grow, and . . . what's the matter, Aunt A?'

He grabbed her as she swayed dizzily. Her face had gone pale and suddenly all the laugh-lines in it had disappeared.

'Tell me what's the matter!' Merlin demanded.

'It's the moment I've been dreading all these years . . . since the very day you were born. Merlin, it's time for you to leave.'

'Leave?' Merlin said, confused. 'I don't understand.'

Ambrosia sighed heavily as she settled into the chair beside the hearth. She stared into the flames for a long moment before she spoke, to gather her strength. 'I've never told you how you came to be born – nor much about the Old Ways. Was that a mistake? I don't know. If it was, it's too late to mend it now. But long before you were born, I served the Queen of the Old Ways, until . . . well, let's just say until we agreed to differ. I left off being a priestess, and I wandered until I came to Avalon. There I met your mother, Elissa.'

Merlin knelt beside her chair. He was fascinated. Ambrosia had never been willing to talk about his past before. 'And my father?' he asked eagerly.

'Let me tell this in my own way,' Ambrosia said,

patting his hand. 'In those days, the Holy Grail of the new religion was still at Avalon, and Elissa was training to be one of those who watched over it. When the Grail vanished and she was cast out of Avalon, I brought her here to the forest to live with me, and soon you were born. I raised you and loved you, because you were a very special child.'

'But –' Merlin began.

'You have no father, you see,' Ambrosia said. 'There's magic at work here. You were created by Queen Mab to be her champion, and that's why Elissa died giving birth to you. When you were born, Mab claimed you as her son, but I made her leave you with me, so you could grow up in your mother's world. But you are half Mab's as well, so she proclaimed that you could stay here only until you called upon the magic of the Old Ways. Now you have, and she wants you to join her.'

'I won't go!' Merlin said. 'I'll defy her.'

Ambrosia reached out and ruffled Merlin's damp hair. 'You have no choice, my dear. You cannot fight her – not yet.' She lifted his chin and made him look at her. 'You must be brave. Your time will come.'

'I don't want to leave you,' Merlin said. He buried his face in her lap.

Suddenly there was a sizzling sound, like bacon being dropped onto a hot skillet. A bright light like the noonday sun shone through the open door of the hut. Ambrosia gasped, and Merlin raised his head.

Come with me, Master Merlin.

For a moment Merlin thought it was the white stag come back again, but this magic was far more powerful. A white horse stood at the edge of the clearing, glowing as brightly as a candle flame. He was standing above the ground, his silver hooves not even touching the earth.

You're to come with me. I will take you to the Land of Magic.

The horse tossed his head, and Merlin could see that he wore a saddle and bridle of gleaming gold.

'He's talking to me,' Merlin said slowly. He got to his feet and stood, staring at the horse. His heart beat with excitement and fear. The magic was part of him. It was his destiny. But at the same time, it was a giant step into the unknown, and one he was reluctant to take. 'He says I have to go with him. I don't, do I, Aunt A?'

Behind him, Ambrosia was rummaging through a clothes chest. She pulled out his best tunic, and a warm cloak of new wool that she'd spent the whole summer making. She came up beside Merlin and handed him the tunic. Once he'd struggled into it, she wrapped the cloak around his shoulders.

'This will keep you warm on cold nights,' she said, not answering his question.

Merlin searched her face, beginning to be more afraid than excited. The only mother he'd ever known was sending him away to live with the mysterious and powerful Queen of the Old Ways. Merlin wrapped the cloak about himself, looking from the shining stallion to Ambrosia.

'Aunt A –' he began.

'Now, now,' she said, interrupting him. 'Remember what Herne and Blaise and I have told you. Magic has no power over the human heart, and in her way, as far as she can, I suppose Mab does love you. Just don't forget what I taught you. Never stop trying to be good and fighting for what's right.'

'I won't. I love you, Aunt A,' Merlin said.

Ambrosia hugged him fiercely, as if for the last time. 'And tell Her Royal High and Mighty Queen Mab that, magic or no magic, if she hurts you in any way, I'll have her guts for bootlaces!' She kissed him firmly on the forehead.

Merlin stepped back. His eye fell on the pieces of the

milk jug he'd broken, waiting on a shelf for someone to mend them. Had it only been this morning that he'd broken it? It seemed as if he'd lived a lifetime since then.

'Go on,' Ambrosia whispered, smiling.

Merlin raised his hand in a half-wave, then turned and began to trudge toward the white horse which was waiting impatiently. By the time he was halfway across the clearing, the light-hearted optimism of youth had reasserted itself, and he was running to embrace his destiny.

Ambrosia watched Merlin mount the white horse and ride away. When she was sure he could no longer see her, her face crumpled into tears, and she raised her apron to cover her eyes.

The hardest thing she had ever done in her life was to let Merlin ride to Mab without a single word of warning.

The horse beneath him ran like the wind, and instead of hoofbeats, Merlin heard the sound of silver bells. All around him, the familiar forest was subtly different, as if he saw it through different eyes. Tiny winged people flitted through the air, their voices as high and shrill as bats. At the roots of trees were diminutive figures wearing pointed red caps and bright green coats. Perched on a tree branch, a griffin watched him hungrily, fanning its golden wings.

'Where are we going?' Merlin shouted to his mount. Though he'd never ridden before, he had no trouble staying on the animal's back. It was as if anything involving magic was somehow familiar to him.

To the Enchanted Lake that leads to the Land of Magic, Master Merlin, the horse responded.

Though Merlin thought the horse was already running at top speed, he began to run even faster, so that Merlin had to cling tightly to the saddle and speech became impossible.

They reached the edge of the forest and crossed it, and now Merlin was riding through a land he'd never even seen before. The green and rolling hills of open countryside passed almost in a blur. Only a few distant huts and cart-tracks were visible, and it occurred to Merlin fleetingly that no matter how much wickedness King Vortigern had been responsible for, it had not affected the land itself.

Then even those few signs of habitation were gone, and the landscape was as wild and untouched as it had been since it was created. In the distance, Merlin could see a silvery gleam, which slowly grew and broadened until Merlin knew he was staring at the Enchanted Lake. The horse began to slow by small degrees until he was trotting, then walking, then stopped completely. Merlin slid from his back and stared out over the lake. A boat was coming toward them, gliding silently over the calm surface of the Enchanted Lake.

'Is the Land of Magic on the other shore?' Merlin asked.

No. What lies across the Enchanted Lake depends on who seeks it, and what they seek.

Merlin shook his head in puzzlement, and when he looked up the boat had reached the shore.

It was made of a rich silvery wood, with a band of runes carved about its hull. The prow and the stern tapered to high points, and there were neither oars nor sails aboard it. Inside the boat, Merlin could see a couple of benches covered in purple velvet for the passengers to sit on.

'Thank you,' Merlin said to the horse. He shook his silvery mane at him and did not answer. 'I suppose I'm supposed to get into the boat?' he said reluctantly.

The horse backed away, watching Merlin with wary eyes. Merlin glanced from him to the boat. This was it. He could probably still find his way back to the forest from here, but once he boarded the boat he would have no choice but to go where it took him. There'd be no turning back.

But if he thought he could turn back now, Merlin realized, he was fooling only himself. He was only half-human. The other half of himself – whatever it was – lay at the boat's destination.

Taking a deep breath, he steeled himself and climbed into the boat. It began to move off at once, as though some invisible force was drawing it along. He stumbled backward at the motion, and sat down hard on one of the velvet benches.

This was it, then. There was nothing to do but wait.

CHAPTER FIVE

THE COURTS OF FAIRY

L ooking behind him, Merlin saw the shore and the shining white spark of the magic horse dwindle and vanish in the distance, but the opposite shore of the lake still did not appear. He felt excited and uneasy about what was to come; even now he was quickly coming to realize what a haven the forest had been for him, and how sheltered from the real world he'd been as he grew up there. Everything that had happened to him since this morning was so strange and new, and yet he wasn't frightened by any of it. In a sense, it was as if he were coming home. He knew very little about Mab and the Old Ways . . .

But now all that will change, he thought to himself.

How it would change was something Merlin did not stop to consider.

As the boat travelled across the glassy lake, a mist began to rise up off the water almost like steam from a pot of soup. He did not notice it at first, but as the light dimmed, Merlin glanced behind him to see how far away the shore was, and saw that in those scant moments the mist had veiled the shoreline and the very water itself from his sight. When he looked back toward the bow, he marvelled to see that a great stone crag was rising out of the mists of the lake where a moment before there had been nothing but still waters.

As the boat sailed closer, Merlin could spy the opening to a cave in the base of the knoll, an opening that gaped as black and threatening as a dragon's maw.

Then he realized that they were about to sail inside.

It was the first time that it had occurred to Merlin that his journey might take him underground, and he was unprepared for the sharp pang of pure panic that possessed him. He clutched at the side of the boat until his knuckles ached, and after a few seconds he realized that he was calculating the best way to jump into the lake and swim back to a shore he could no longer see!

Don't be foolish, Merlin told himself chidingly. *The only things there are in a cave are bats and bears, and no bear will harm you if you do not harm it first. The boat wouldn't be sailing into it if it weren't safe! And Mab is waiting for you.*

And no sooner had he thought this than his apprehension faded and curiosity got the better of him. When he met Queen Mab, he would understand the other half of his heritage, and that was something he longed to do.

The boat was close enough now to the cave for Merlin to feel the wind that blew from its mouth. It was colder than the surrounding air, but instead of the lifeless odour Merlin associated with caves, this breeze smelled of something he could not put a name to.

Magic?

The prow of the boat passed with slow majesty through the cave opening. Looking up, Merlin saw the rock seem to rise up and crest over him like a breaking wave. A shudder of excitement passed through his body as he passed from light into shadow. Now the roof of the cave was his sky, and when he looked back, his view of the Enchanted Lake was framed by rock.

The sound of the water slapping against the sides of his boat was loud now as it echoed from the walls, and the boat jostled gently in the choppy water as it continued through the cave-turned-tunnel. A faint light seemed to radiate from everywhere at once, so that he could still see what ought to have been dark, and it seemed to Merlin as if every sense he possessed was being tantalized by some essence he could not yet sense. He had the feeling that there was music he could not hear, sights he could not see, just out of the reach of his mortal senses. He was beginning a great adventure.

This was magic.

Frik ran down the path to the boat landing, trying to

run and dress and gather his thoughts all at once. The great day had come, when the second stage of Mab's plan would come to fruition. Merlin was coming home to them.

Frik did hope the boy's arrival would put Her Majesty into a better temper. She been very touchy since Julius Caesar had invaded Britain, but the divine Julius hadn't been one tenth the trouble that Constant and his new religion had been. Once the mortals had started pulling down her shrines instead of stuffing them full of Roman gods, she'd been quite impossible. And of course, Vortigern simply made things worse. And he'd been all Mab's idea.

Oh, well, the gnome thought to himself, *least said, soonest mended.* At least having Merlin to teach would take Mab's mind off him for a while. Frik hadn't at all liked living under the constant threat of being turned to rock. What if Mab forgot about him and just left him to be a rock forever? It gave a chap the collywobbles just thinking about it.

And he did have to admit that he was interested in getting to know this Merlin. Of course, Her Highness was always bringing home these seven-year stands, like that Thomas Whatsisname who'd wanted to be a poet. Remarkably bad verse, if Frik remembered, and eventually Mab had become so tired of him that she'd put a curse on him to tell nothing but the truth. *That* had sent the fellow packing! But that sort of interlude wasn't like getting to know a mortal. Merlin would be – was – different. Although Frik had kept a weather eye on Merlin throughout the lad's childhood, he'd been spying from a distance. This would be a chance to get to know the young mortal on his own terms.

But young Merlin *wasn't* quite mortal, Frik reminded himself. He was Mab's child, half-fairy. He belonged as much in the Land of Magic as he belonged upon earth.

And what if – now that she has Merlin – she doesn't need you at all?

The thought gave Frik a momentary pause, but he brushed it aside. Merlin was to be Mab's champion, not a member of her household. No matter what, she would continue to need someone of Frik's calibre to manage her establishment.

Frik came to a stop, peering into the bank of mist that hid the mouth of the cave. The newcomer should be here any minute. He'd been supposed to go with the boat to greet Merlin, but to be perfectly frank, Frik and the Lady of the Lake weren't on the best of terms, and he'd been just as glad to miss it. So to speak.

Only now, as he waited for the magic barge to come back, his mind was filled with all the things that could have gone wrong in the mortal world. He wasn't sure he could find any place secluded enough to wait out Mab's displeasure if any of them had actually happened.

'Oh dear, oh dear,' Frik murmured to himself, checking the time with a large gold pocket watch; but just as he was about to despair, a dark shape appeared in the mist, and the prow of the barge emerged. There was a figure seated amidships.

Frik heaved a sigh of relief.

Merlin.

'Sorry I'm late,' Frik said briskly. 'The ship left without me. Coming aboard –' Quickly converting his pocket watch to a bosun's whistle, he piped himself aboard and leaped into the boat.

Merlin stared at the strange being. The new arrival had long pointed ears, strangely protruding eyes, and was dressed in the most peculiar clothes Merlin had ever seen – a bright red coat trimmed with lots of gold braid and large brass buttons – and was wearing a strange sort of three-cornered hat on his head.

'Who are you?' Merlin asked after some hesitation.

'Arr, Jim me lad, them as sails with Long John Frik must resign themselves to a life of adventure,' Frik said.

'But –'

'Shhh . . . I has to focus, I does. These is treacherous waters, strong currents, unseen rocks . . .' the creature's voice trailed off as it muttered to itself.

Merlin shook his head, confused. Why was this fellow talking so oddly? He would have welcomed some conversation, but now 'Long John Frik' was steering them through the cave system, his brow wrinkled in concentration. As soon as the ship had sailed into the tunnel Merlin had felt oppressed, as if the ceiling might collapse upon him at any moment. Now, even though the roof of the tunnel was several feet above the top of his head, Merlin imagined he could feel the weight of all the rock above him as though it were pressing on his chest. It wasn't a pleasant feeling.

But he forgot about all his problems when Master Frik piloted the boat out of the tunnel and into what proved to be the first in a series of large underground lagoons.

Merlin ducked as a sprite whizzed by overhead. Its

wings and body glowed faintly, so that it looked as if the air were full of thousands of multi-coloured fireflies all moving in different directions at once. His jaw dropped as he realized they had entered a vast cavern full of these tiny creatures.

There was a splash in the water near the boat, and Merlin glanced over to see a beautiful golden-haired woman clinging to the side of the ship.

'Scat, you!' Frik said, raising his barge-pole menacingly.

The woman laughed and slipped back into the water.

As she turned away, Merlin saw that at the waist her body became a gleaming emerald fish-tail with long transparent fins.

She was a mermaid!

He stared after her in amazement, and as he stared, he could see other rainbow gleams, far beneath the surface of the black water.

The boat crossed the lagoon, and entered another chamber where the walls were completely encrusted with enormous crystals in many different colours. Each of them gave off a soft glow like the bodies of the sprites in the previous cavern, some of which had followed the boat. Their radiance glittered off the glowing crystals, making the whole chamber seem to be in constant sparkling motion. The effect was like travelling through the heart of a rainbow.

'Here we are,' Frik said at last. 'Look lively, Master Merlin.'

Merlin stared hard. In the distance he could just make out an enormous flight of white marble steps leading up to an elaborate portico with tall pillars framing the doorway. The skiff glided over the black water with amazing speed, until Merlin could see a figure standing on the steps awaiting him.

Queen Mab.

The Queen of the Old Ways glittered more dazzlingly than the crystal-covered walls. She wore a flashing crescent-moon tiara of amethysts and black diamonds, and her long sleeveless violet gown was oversewn with the same jewels. On her arms, coiling from shoulder to wrist, she wore diamond-studded bracelets in the shape of poisonous snakes.

Suddenly Merlin felt shy, just as he had when he'd encountered Nimue and her party earlier in the day. Mab was so grand, so beautiful. How could she have any interest in him?

But she was the one who'd created him. Aunt Ambrosia had said so, and his foster-mother had never lied to him. He was Mab's child as much as he was his real mother's.

Seeing the Land of Magic glittering all around him, for the first time his own fairy heritage began to seem real to Merlin. He'd always thought of himself as a normal person, but now he had to accept that he was only half-human; a boy without a mortal father. The other half was magic; sorcerous, inhuman.

The boat bumped against the dock, wrenching Merlin out of his reverie. When he glanced toward Frik, the red velvet coat and the plumed hat were gone. Frik stood upon the dock, wearing a long blue satin robe that sparkled with embroidery, and sporting a small round hat on his head. His hands were tucked into his sleeves. He bowed, smiling.

'Follow me, follow me – don't get lost, don't get lost,' he chanted in a sing-song voice. He had long drooping moustaches, and his half-closed eyes were slanted like a cat's.

As he turned to go, Merlin saw with astonishment that yet another Frik was now facing him – a goggle-eyed gnome dressed in black tight-fitting clothes. He stared, unable to believe his eyes.

Frik bowed again – in a different style – and began marching up the long sweeping stair.

Merlin scrambled out of the boat and hurried after Frik.

'Your Majesty,' Frik began, as soon as Merlin reached the top of the stairs, 'may I present . . .'

But Mab was too impatient to wait upon protocol. 'Merlin, Merlin,' she whispered lovingly. 'You've come at last. Do you know who I am?'

'Queen Mab,' Merlin said uneasily.

He was not certain what he'd expected the Queen of the Old Ways to be like, but he found Mab oddly disturbing in a fashion he could not put a name to. He knew so little about her – it was only hours since Ambrosia had told him that Mab had created him, and he was still reeling from the knowledge. He wasn't even sure what the Old Ways were – he knew that they were important, and involved magic, but beyond that he was ignorant. Deliberately *kept* ignorant, he realized suddenly. Ambrosia and Herne and even Blaise had certainly known about them, but they'd always steered the conversation away from any discussion of these matters . . . or Mab.

Why?

Mab held out her hands to him. 'Yes–s–s . . .' she hissed. 'I've waited so long. You've grown handsome and true. I did well when I created you.'

Urged on by Frik, Merlin stepped forward. Though the words were fond, the way Mab had said them only increased his discomfort. She made him sound like a basket or a pot of jam, just an object instead of a person.

Mab spread her arms wide and shouted to the thousands of watchers – visible and invisible – that filled the air: 'This is Merlin who comes to save us! He is the great leader who will bring the people back to the Old Ways!'

Her words echoed unnaturally through the cavern.

Instead of dwindling away, the echoes got louder and louder, until it was as if a thousand voices shouted his name at once: *Merlin – Merlin – Merlin –*

Come to save us – save us – save us . . .

Merlin gazed around himself and felt a sudden flash of blind panic. If he knew nothing about Mab, he knew even less about the Old Ways – how could he save them?

I can't save them – I can't be what she wants me to be!

'But come,' Mab said, putting a long be-ringed hand on his arm. 'It is time to begin your training.'

Merlin followed Mab through dozens of rooms, each weirder and more colourful than the last. The strange sights he saw ought to have frightened Merlin, and a day or so ago they would have done, but he'd seen too much strangeness since then. Now the oddities he saw only excited and interested him.

It seemed as if they walked for hours through the splendour of Mab's palace before Mab stopped at a door. This door had a face carved into the centre of it, its eyes closed and mouth hanging open as if it were asleep.

'Well?' Mab demanded.

To Merlin's astonishment the eyes of the carved figure popped open and the mouth smiled ingratiatingly.

'Yes, madam. At once, madam,' the door said, and swung inward.

Inside was a room that, after all the wonders Merlin had seen, looked almost normal. It had a large fireplace on the left side, with a cheerful fire burning in the grate, and beside the fire, an enormous wooden chair, with a large red velvet cushion on its seat. The entire chair was carved and gilded into the shape of lions and dragons and snakes, and the name 'Mab' was engraved into the large gold crown that topped its back.

The room was filled with shelves packed with enormous old books, some of which overflowed onto the tables, and some were even stacked in piles on the floor. The room looked as if it were dusty and disused, but when he peered more closely he could see that, instead of dust, the corners of the room were heaped with drifts of crystals, each sparkling nugget larger than a lump of coal.

Merlin forgot his momentary panic in his curiosity about all the new things to look at. As Mab did not stop him, Merlin began to wander about the room, inspecting things which caught his fancy.

There was a great crystal ball, clear as water. Inside it there was a city of golden towers. As Merlin looked closer at it, he could see people moving on the streets, birds flying about the towers, and the bells inside the towers moving back and forth silently as they tolled.

Next to it was a cap with long ear-flaps woven of golden mesh with a band of diamonds and rubies around the bottom edge. There were words engraved on the inside, and Merlin felt the magic tingle over his fingers as he touched it. He drew his hand back in surprise, and then turned away from it as his attention was caught by a movement in a cage hanging from the ceiling. When he looked closely, he saw that the cage did not contain a bird, but a tiny white winged horse.

On the table beneath the cage there was a wide

jewelled belt, so small it must have been made for a gnome, and a strange long skull with a single spiral horn jutting from its brow.

Next to that was a large box carved of green stone and covered with golden letters in a language Merlin could not read.

On the shelf beyond the table was a crystal dome covering a single perfect blue rose, and next to that a pair of tiny slippers, barely as long as his hand, studded all over with glittering rubies.

He picked up one of the crystals that shared the shelving with the books. It was as large as his fist, a deep ruddy golden colour. When he touched it, he could feel the power resonating into him, a tingling warmth through his arms and body.

He glanced up and saw Mab smiling at him. She'd seated herself in the enormous carved, thronelike chair before the fire and was gazing over the room as if she owned everything in it.

Still carrying the crystal, Merlin walked back to her, stopping a respectful distance away.

'Why am I here?' he asked hesitantly.

'To learn,' Mab crooned. 'I'll teach you to become the most powerful wizard the world has ever known.'

'Why?' Merlin asked.

His dreams of the future had never involved magic. If anything, he had wanted to be a knight, a hero, doing great deeds and righting wrongs through the power of his sword. But those had been daydreams, nothing more. He'd never expected to achieve them. And now Mab was offering him something that was both greater than and profoundly different from those half-formed imaginings. He gazed at her, fascinated, delighted, and wary, all at the same time.

Mab smiled at him proprietorially. 'To lead mortals back to us . . . to the Old Ways.'

This was the second time Mab had spoken of his becoming the champion of the Land of Magic, and Merlin wasn't sure that either King Vortigern or his Aunt Ambrosia would approve of the plan. There couldn't be two kings in Britain – Merlin knew that very well – and Aunt Ambrosia said you had to live in the realities of the present, not the glories of the past.

'What if I don't want to be a wizard?' Merlin said warily.

'It's your destiny,' Mab said unequivocally. 'Remember that branch and how you made it grow?'

The memory was so vivid that for a moment Merlin was back at the sinkhole, the smell of wet earth strong in his nostrils as he frantically tried to reach Nimue.

Nimue.

He'd promised he'd come to visit her tomorrow. In the excitement of discovering the truth about his heritage and travelling to the Land of Magic, he'd forgotten all about his promise. Remembering so abruptly and at such a time made him upset and relieved all at once. What if Nimue'd found out the truth about him – that he was the child of no mortal father? He couldn't bear the thought of her looking at him with loathing and disdain. Perhaps it was better if he never saw her again. He looked back at Mab.

'I don't know how I made the branch grow,' he admitted.

She smiled as if he'd given her the answer she wanted. 'That's why you're here – to learn. Oh, Merlin, you'll soon know the power that's in you.'

She held up her left hand, and with amazement, Merlin saw his own arm rise to copy her gesture.

'And once it's unleashed, you'll hold this world in the hollow of your hand!'

Mab clenched her hand into a fist, and Merlin's fist clenched, too, of its own volition, grinding the crystal he held within his fist into glittering powder.

Merlin stared at his hand – not frightened, really, because no one he'd ever known had been unkind to him, but unsettled and worried, the way the forest animals were before a storm. Mab's gesture seemed to have such anger in it, yet he wasn't quite sure who she was angry with. He brushed away the residue of the shattered crystal, but before he had the chance to analyse his feelings further, Frik entered, grunting beneath the weight of another huge stack of books.

'Here we are,' said the gnome. 'All set for our first lesson.' He'd changed his costume again. Now he was wearing a flat black tasselled cap and a long black robe. He carried a long bamboo cane. Unruly tufts of gingery hair protruded from beneath the edge of the mortarboard, and a pair of wire-rimmed spectacles was perched upon the end of his nose.

Merlin moved toward him to help with the books, but before he reached Frik, the gnome had set the pile down on another table, making a place for them amid the scrolls and other manuscripts. He reached up and pulled down out of nowhere a chart covered with strange and cryptic symbols, then tapped it experimentally with his cane.

Merlin glanced from Frik to the chart to the pile of books, then gingerly opened the top volume. The page was covered with very small print. It looked like a very long, very dull book.

'All the magic of the universe and all the spells you'll

ever need are in these books, Merlin,' Mab said, with a gesture that encompassed the entire room.

'I'll need a lifetime to read all these!' Merlin said desperately, staring around the room in horror.

'You'll have a very long life,' Mab answered.

And I'll be spending all of it in here, Merlin thought despondently.

A thought occurred to him suddenly.

'If I'm half-mortal, will I die?'

His question was prompted more by curiosity than any real fear; at seventeen, the thought of his death was a remote and unreal thing.

'In the fullness of time.' Mab shook her head sadly, and when she spoke again it was almost with reluctance. 'We can't change that. But we can change form,' she offered, as though attempting to distract Merlin from this bitter truth.

She reached out a hand and grabbed the edge of Frik's mortarboard. When she pulled it off, Frik's whole face came with it.

Merlin gasped, appalled.

The face revealed beneath was completely different: handsome and dissipated, yet faintly cruel. It was painted and rouged, and its thick black hair was worn in tight curls that cascaded down over its shoulders.

Stuck to the face at the corner of the mouth was a small black patch in the shape of a star. The new face peeped slyly at Merlin.

Affecting a look of haughty surprise, the new Frik conjured a rose out of nowhere and, holding the blossom to his nose, smiled.

'But it is only an illusion – particularly in his case,' Mab said scornfully. She yanked at the top of Frik's head, and the new face came off just as the old one had, leaving Frik in his schoolmaster persona beneath.

Merlin thought that Frik looked a little disgruntled at being returned to his normal grotesque self.

'We can hurt,' Mab continued, 'but we cannot use our magic to kill – though humans hardly need any help with that from us. Sometimes we can see into the future –'

As before, Mab balanced a disadvantage with something she thought of as a reward. She waved her hand, and the wall of the library seemed to recede swiftly into the distance. Now, sitting on a stool before the fire, was an ancient, white-haired old man, stooped with age. He was older even than Blaise, his body twisted and gnarled until he almost resembled one of the ancient oaks of Barnstable Forest.

'This is you as you will be,' Mab said.

'Me?' Merlin stammered, shocked. 'Will I grow that old?'

'Have a care, young Merlin!' The ancient greybeard before the fire roused himself and glared at the boy.

'I'm sorry, sir,' young Merlin said humbly.

His elderly self relented. 'The years batter us as storms batter the trees of the forest, and sometimes we forget what's important. Try always to stay as young inside as you are now. And that's another thing,' the ancient wizard said, raising one gnarled finger for emphasis. 'Don't start giving advice,' he said in a confidential whisper. 'It always ends badly.'

'What –' young Merlin began, but with a wave of her hand, Mab banished his older self.

The fireplace shot forward into its proper place and the room was normal once more.

'Will I be able to do that?' Merlin asked, enchanted. The thought of always knowing what the future held was beguiling.

'Perhaps,' Mab said evasively. 'But you will have to develop your powers, and listen to all that Frik tells you.'

Mab gazed at Frik pointedly until he drew himself up to his full height and began to lecture in fussy, pedantic tones.

'Master Merlin, there are three classes of magic; three stages of progression to full wizard status. The first and lowest stage is Wizard by Incantation, or Voice Wizard; those who do spells and invocations through the power of magic words.' Frik struck a dramatic pose. '*Abra-cadabra dev and chort!*' he intoned, holding out his hand.

A silver goblet with a red rose in it appeared in his hand. Frik sniffed the flower appreciatively and then set the goblet aside. With all the wonders he had seen thus far today, Merlin was barely surprised.

'The second stage of wizardry is magic invoked through gestures of the hands and fingers: the Hand Wizard.'

Frik passed his left hand over the goblet, and the rose curled, withered, and crumbled to dust. Frik set the goblet aside.

'The third – and highest – stage of wizardry, whose exponents are the supreme embodiment of the mystic arts, are Thought Wizards, who need no words or gestures but by their will alone pierce the heavens and draw back the veil.'

Mab gestured – Hand Wizardry, Merlin noted with pleasure at his own cleverness – and the goblet full of water leaped into the air to dash its contents into

Frik's face. To Merlin's delighted amazement, the water stopped, hanging motionless in mid-air.

'Of course,' Frik said smugly, 'only the most supremely gifted personages become wizards of the third stage.' He preened.

'Get on with it,' Mab snapped, impatient. She snapped her fingers, and the water resumed its interrupted journey, drenching Frik thoroughly and even spraying Merlin with a few icy-cold droplets.

Frik bowed. 'Your Majesty,' he said. Mab flickered and vanished.

Merlin gaped at the place where she'd been.

'And now, Master Merlin, we will begin with a few simple drills,' Frik said. 'Raise your right hand . . .'

After a couple of hours of Frik's lecturing, Merlin found it impossible to keep his mind on what Frik was saying. To his dismay, it appeared that Frik intended that he learn everything about becoming a wizard tonight.

'What on earth – or under Hill – is the matter with you, young sir?' Frik demanded in exasperation after yet another attempt to gain Merlin's attention.

'I'm hungry,' Merlin said simply. 'The white horse

took me away before I had my supper – and Auntie A was making my favourite, buttered parsnips –'

He stopped, as Frik made apprehensive shushing motions.

'A word to the wise, young sir. It's just as well not to mention, well, *difficult* subjects where madam can hear. It could be quite *awkward*, if you take my meaning.'

Merlin didn't. He was an active young man used to regular meals, and the fact that there was bad blood between his foster-mother and the Queen of the Old Ways did not occur to him. He regarded Frik hopefully.

'Oh, very well, dinner it is,' the gnome grumbled. He gestured, and the work table changed its shape and became covered with a checked red-and-white cloth.

'Would m'sieur care to see the wine list?'

Frik too had changed his form and dress. He bowed low, offering Merlin an enormous book of parchment with a red tassel and cord holding the pages together.

'No, of course not,' Frik said, whisking the card away just as Merlin's fingers closed on it. 'I have it. We shall leave the matter to Gaston, and allow inspiration to take its course – if that meets with m'sieur's approval?'

Merlin wasn't quite sure what Frik had said. 'Thank you for your kindness,' he answered doubtfully.

To his relief, the meal appeared almost at once. It was a strange and delightful phenomenon, completely different from the simple home-cooking Merlin had been used to. Dish after dish was presented to him on silver and crystal platters carried in by swarms of sprites.

When he picked up the chicken with his hands, Frik *tsked* sadly.

'I'm afraid we must teach you more than magic, Master Merlin,' the gnome said.

Merlin stared at him blankly, a chicken leg in one hand and a piece of bread in the other.

'Oh, go on, go on. Camelot wasn't built in a day – or won't be,' Frik said, waving permission at Merlin. 'Or Pendragon either. You'll see, I'm sure. But everything in its own good time.'

Merlin ate until he felt he could not hold another bite of the wonderful, unfamiliar food. If things like this were what magic was all about, he thought he was going to like it.

'And now,' Frik said, whisking the dishes out of existence, 'we can return to first principles. Repeat after me, Master Merlin, *eko, eko, azarak . . .*'

After several more hours of lecturing by the tireless

Frik, Merlin began to nod off over his books, unable to keep his eyes open any longer no matter how hard he tried. Though Frik had remembered (when prompted) to feed Merlin, it had not occurred to the gnome that Merlin needed to sleep, since neither Mab nor Frik needed to sleep or eat as mortals did.

'Master Merlin!' Frik shook him by the shoulder anxiously. 'Master Merlin, is something wrong?'

Merlin yawned, squinting up at Frik through sleep-blurred eyes. 'Ohhh . . . What time is it?' he asked.

'Time?' the gnome echoed blankly. 'What has that got to do with . . .' his voice trailed off as comprehension dawned. 'Oh, I say! You were *asleep*! It must be that touch of mortal in the woodshed; you know, I've heard it often comes out in the most amazing ways. Very well then, come with me if you would, Master Merlin.'

Still half-asleep, Merlin followed Frik out of the schoolroom and down a long corridor where hands of living stone came out of the wall, passing between them the pair of flaming torches that lit Frik and Merlin's way.

Groggy and disoriented, Merlin did not even note this latest wonder.

'Here you are, sir, our best rooms, with hot and cold running water nymphs and a lovely view out over the mermaids' lagoon . . .' Frik said in round, plummy accents. He'd shed his schoolmaster's costume for a tight red jacket with several rows of gold buttons down the front and a pillbox hat trimmed with golden braid.

The walls were encrusted with clumps of crystals, as though they'd grown there. The furnishings consisted of a large wardrobe and a bed that Frik had plucked out of the time-stream because it had looked so inviting, all gleaming brass and bed-knobs and patchwork quilts. It was completely strange to Merlin, but not so much so that he didn't recognize it as a bed. He staggered toward it and was asleep before he lay down.

Frik tugged off his shoes and tucked him beneath the covers. When he was finished, he gazed down at the sleeping boy.

'What strange little creatures you mortals be,' Frik said.

'But how did you get all that mud on your skirts?' Mistress Ragnell demanded. 'I think the dress is quite ruined, My Lady.'

'I fell into a sinkhole,' Nimue admitted, before she

thought. She was determined to keep her promise to Merlin, but she hadn't realized how difficult it would be.

Aneirin and all the rest of her party stared at her with expressions of shock and disbelief. 'And how did you get out again?' Aneirin asked. He handed his cloak up to her and Nimue wrapped it around herself, grateful for the warmth. Her gown was wet and the day had turned cold, and she already missed Merlin's company.

'A hermit,' Nimue said quickly.

It was not quite a lie. She did not know for sure that Merlin was not a hermit, and such creatures were commonly known to live in woodlands such as Barnstable Forest.

'Praise God that you were delivered from such a terrible fate!' Mistress Olwen said, crossing herself piously. The others – including Nimue – echoed her gesture out of habit.

But Nimue suspected somehow that it was not God she had to thank for her rescue, but an older, darker power that the new church wished very much to forget.

A hour later the little party stood before the gates

of Lord Lambert's castle. Nimue was relieved that they had reached their destination before the sun set. The forest that had been welcoming in daylight had become dark and forbidding with the onset of twilight.

Lord Lambert was very solicitous once he heard of Nimue's misadventure, and soon she was soaking in a hot tub of perfumed water, sipping mulled wine as her servants did what they could to repair her muddy gown.

She wished she had not let Merlin leave. She was a noblewoman – she should have *commanded* him to stay beside her. She would have liked to present him to stuffy old Lord Lambert and seen the elderly man's eyes pop with shock, especially when Merlin did more of his magic.

Nimue shook her head, smiling at her own foolishness. As well order the tide not to ebb as to order Merlin. Even having known him for only a few scant hours, Nimue already thought of Merlin as embodying the same untamed spirit of freedom that filled the forest and other wild and lonely places.

She wished she had that sort of bold courage, but she suspected she did not. The rebellion, the defiance that others talked of so easily was something Nimue could not easily imagine in herself. The years she had spent at the Abbey had made her hate the thought of setting her will against someone else's, of the wilfulness and argument that led to open conflict; and between nobles, to skirmishing and worse.

Yet in Britain today, it seemed as if everyone must rebel in the end.

When Merlin awoke again, he barely had time to remember where he was before Frik bustled in with a large tray covered with food. The gnome rushed Merlin through his meal, and then hustled him back to the library to resume his studies of first stage wizardry.

'Why is there such a hurry?' Merlin wanted to know.

'You must master every facet of the Art Magical before you can become Mab's champion,' Frik answered. 'We've no time for idle questions.'

'But –' Merlin began.

Frik hushed him and pointed to a stool at the end of the table. Today the table had been swept clean of books, and all that stood upon it was a large white candle in a heavy squat silver holder in the shape of a gargoyle. Merlin sat down at the foot of the table as he had been ordered, and Frik took his usual place at the head.

Merlin wished Frik were willing to talk about things

he wanted to know, and not just about the things Frik wanted him to know. What did they mean about him becoming Mab's champion? Would that be like being a knight? What would he have to do?

Frik rapped his cane on the end of the table, and Merlin, caught woolgathering, jumped guiltily.

'Now, Master Merlin,' Frik said, 'kindly light the candle.'

Merlin looked around, but there was nothing in sight with which to light the candle. He looked back at his teacher.

Frik rattled off a quick sentence, and suddenly the candle was alight.

He let it burn for a moment, and then snuffed it out.

'Now you try, Master Merlin,' Frik said. 'Just do what I did.'

Merlin reached out and concentrated on the candle.

'*Alika-nick-ka-nock-ka-nick, fire light and candlestick,*' he chanted.

At first Merlin felt slightly silly, but then he felt the same tingle he had on the day he'd made the branch grow, as if he were a jug and magic was some bubbling effervescent liquid that rushed up to fill him and then spill over into the world.

A spark leaped from his pointing finger to the candle-wick, and the candle was alight.

Frik carefully blew it out.

'Now again, Master Merlin,' he said.

'But I just –'

'If you please, young sir,' Frik said severely.

Sighing, Merlin did it again.

They practised for hours. Merlin lit one candle, then several candles all at once, then several candles one after the other, then candles he couldn't see, candles in glass jars, candles in clay vases. The novelty of his new ability was wearing off fast, and Merlin wished that Frik would go on to something else, even it whatever it was would probably be just as boring. If he were going to be a wizard, Merlin wanted to do useful magic, magic that people could use – not just magic that did what people could do for themselves anyway, like light fires.

He was about to suggest that to Frik when Queen Mab appeared, flickering into existence like a black flame. She looked expectantly at Frik.

'Ah.' The gnome got to his feet. 'Master Merlin and I were just about to . . . that is to say, he's not quite ready yet to, ah –'

'Go ahead, Merlin,' Mab cooed dotingly. 'Show him what you can do.'

Merlin gaped at Frik in consternation, and stared at the fat silver candlestick upon the table, but there was no help to be found there. Suddenly everything he'd learned that morning had gone right out of his head.

Frik looked as nervous as Merlin felt, but he motioned him on.

'*Alika* – Um . . . *Alika* –' Merlin stammered. What were the words? Five minutes ago he'd have sworn he'd never forget them! He stared at Frik in horror.

'Go on, Master Merlin,' Frik said desperately.

Merlin didn't dare look at Mab. He clenched his fists and concentrated as hard as he could: light, light, light the candle . . .

'*Fire light and candle* – oh, *thorns and weeds*!' he shouted desperately, forgetting the end of the spell in his agitation.

The candle remained unlit, but flowers of all description began to rain down from the ceiling: nasturtiums, daffodils, roses, daisies, ragwort and dandelions. They fell into the fireplace and burned with a hiss. They fell into the torches and the other candles and put them out. They landed on the table and the floor and the shelves with soft plopping sounds. And they showed no sign of stopping. They rained down especially hard over Frik, who soon found himself buried in flowers.

'No, no,' Frik said irritably. '*Alika-nick-ka-nock-ka-zam*! That's *flowers*, not *flames*!'

The flowers rained down harder.

'I'll fix it,' Merlin said hastily.

'*No!*' Frik howled, but it was too late.

'*Alika-nick-ka-nock-ka-zound!*' Merlin yelled.

An enormous alligator fell from the ceiling and landed directly upon Frik, flopping and snapping.

'*Removal*, not *reptiles*!' Frik sputtered.

The alligator vanished in a puff of smoke, only to be replaced by a gentle rain of salamanders, newts and garter snakes.

Merlin looked around to see how Mab was taking this, but the Queen of the Old Ways had vanished.

After that, Merlin never caught Mab watching him at his lessons again, though Frik assured him that Her Majesty was pleased with his progress. The training continued. Merlin's day was portioned out in measures marked by the turning of the enormous hourglass that Frik kept on the mantel in the library, and his entire world narrowed to the Great Hall where he took his meals, the bedroom where he slept, and the library where he studied.

He began to feel trapped, like a wild animal that dies when confined to a cage. Though Mab's underground domain was vast, there was no *outdoors* to it. Even when he did manage to steal a moment to leave the palace itself, there was no sun nor moon nor stars above his head – only the vaulted roof of the cavern.

When he'd asked about going outside, Frik had feigned puzzlement until Merlin had realized the gnome was deliberately refusing to give him an answer.

Was there truly no way back to the world he'd left? What good was being a wizard if it meant he had to give up the feel of the wind and the smell of the long grass in the summer?

Three turns of the hourglass to lunch. Six turns to dinner. Three more turns to bed-time, then start again. Each day was exactly like the last, until Merlin's head felt stuffed to bursting with the knowledge it now contained.

'Why do I have to memorize all these incantations if I'll never have to use them?' Merlin grumbled. He gazed at Frik mutinously.

By now he'd graduated to lighting torches on the

walls and fires in the fireplace with a single command, and he was tired of all of it. The Land Under Hill had lost its novelty value, and Merlin had begun to miss the freedom of the forest and his animal friends with a distracting intensity. He wanted to be *out* – back in the world in which he'd grown up.

'We cannot always guarantee how far we will proceed in our studies,' Frik said pompously, 'try as we may. Therefore, every step along the path leading to the exalted heights of the Wizardry of Pure Thought must be scaled. You're doing quite well in Unnatural History and Technical Hermetics. As soon as you become proficient in summoning fire, we can proceed to memorizing the Twenty-Seven Basic Incantations for Most Purposes.'

'What fun,' Merlin said, sighing.

Every evening now, Merlin went to the Great Hall for his dinner.

The Great Hall was a daunting place. Its silvery walls soared hundreds of feet into the air, toward a ceiling lost in shadows. High narrow windows of stained glass glittered with deep rich colours, flaring to brightness when sprites outside flew past them. Between the windows, the walls were hung with banners, each of which glowed with complex and unfamiliar heraldry. One was bright gold, with three hearts and three lions marching across it. Another was blue with a single golden lion. One had thirteen gold crowns on a blue field, another a bright golden woven star on a red field, and another, whimsically, had three silver mice on a black field, a speckled chevron dividing them. The walls of the great hall were bright with griffins and leopards and hawks, suns and moons and stars.

'All the devices which you see were borne by knights in my service,' Mab told him proudly.

Merlin was seated at Mab's right hand at the long refectory table that filled the hall. This table was formed of a single sheet of black glass, yards long, that hung in mid-air without any visible means of support. Merlin was not able to count the number of chairs around it. Every time he tried he lost count. But no matter how many chairs there were, the only ones that were ever occupied were his and Mab's. Frik did not join them; at mealtimes the gnome transformed himself into the perfect servant, and waited obsequiously on the pupil he usually badgered. His behaviour puzzled Merlin, but it didn't seem possible for him to ask Frik about it.

'What happened to them?' Merlin asked.

'They died,' Mab said in her husky serpent's voice. 'And left me all alone.'

I won't leave you, Merlin thought, but somehow he could not bring himself to say the words aloud. It was almost as if they weren't true, though he believed they were. The idea of becoming Mab's champion was one that disturbed him more and more in a way he could not quite explain.

'Tell me more about the Old Ways,' he asked instead.

Both Mab and Frik were quite willing to tell him that becoming a great wizard meant bringing back the Old Ways. They spoke of them as if everyone knew what they were, but Merlin had little idea of what the Old Ways involved save having the magical powers to do precisely as one chose. He was beginning to realize that neither Blaise nor Ambrosia had ever discussed the Old Ways in any detail, and he did not feel comfortable exposing his ignorance to the Queen of Fairy.

'In the old days we were worshipped,' Mab whispered dreamily, staring down into her cup of wine. 'No king ruled save with our consent – and in return we saw to it that there was no lack. Everywhere there was plenty and contentment . . .'

But Mab's stories of a golden age of plenty and

contentment only confused Merlin further. If everything had been so wonderful in those days, why had anybody turned away from the Old Ways to follow the new religion?

Time passed, and Merlin became more involved in his studies. He reluctantly mastered the Twenty-Seven Basic Incantations for Most Purposes. He learned about Atlantis and Lemuria and drowned Lyonesse, about how to use mandrake root and unicorn horn, about reading palms and reading minds.

For a while he was even able to forget the peculiarities of the Land Under Hill, but if half of him thought of it as his home, the other half was equally homesick for the forest.

It's just the way it was before, except in reverse, Merlin thought sadly.

When he'd lived in the forest, he'd longed for the Land of Magic, even though he hadn't known that was what he wanted. And now, in the Land of Magic, he longed to be back in the woods again.

It just isn't fair, Merlin thought, sighing.

Wasn't there any place where *all* of him would feel at home?

*   *   *

'Frik?' Merlin asked one day. 'How do you know if you're living a good life?'

'Good?' the gnome asked blankly.

'You know,' Merlin prompted. 'How do you know if you are doing good? Living the right sort of life and acting with justice and mercy toward everyone?'

Frik removed his bifocals and polished them briskly on the tail of his gown.

'What does justice have to do with anything?' Frik demanded irritably. 'Oh, Master Merlin, I do hope you're not too attached to those sorts of ideas about good and justice and right. They're for humans, not for wizards.'

'But Aunt A –'

Frik whisked around the table in an eyeblink and covered Merlin's mouth before he could utter the fatal words.

'Mmmph!' Merlin said.

'I really do think it would be so much better if we just didn't mention that name, don't you?' Frik said hastily. 'And as you've been such a particularly good pupil, I've arranged a very special treat for you. A sort of a field trip. You'll like it.'

'Where are we going?' Merlin asked eagerly, willing to drop the ticklish subject for the moment. Frik might well have made up this field trip on the spur of the moment to distract him, but after the length of time he'd spent in Mab's palace, the chance to see anything else was intoxicating.

'Come with me,' Frik said mysteriously.

With a shimmer Frik changed from his cap and gown to a new costume that included shorts, a butterfly net, and a tan-coloured hat shaped a little like a mushroom cap, and led Merlin out of the library and down a long hallway lined with dark gilt-framed pictures of various notables wearing crowns and dour expressions.

Eventually they stopped before a large carved door.

'What's in there?' Merlin asked.

'Open it,' Frik said.

Merlin pushed the door open. Despite all that he had seen here so far, he gasped in awe.

Through the door lay the trees of an enormous forest. The trees grew right up to within feet of the open door. Outside, the day was dim and misty, and each tree was so tall that Merlin could not see the tops, for they soared into the mist and were lost.

'This,' said Frik importantly, 'is the Forest of the Night.'

'But it isn't night,' Merlin pointed out.

'Well, of course it isn't night,' Frik said fussily. 'It's

never night here – not without sun nor moon it isn't. *Night* is just a sort of expression. A metaphor, you might say, for the deeper reaches of the human mind.'

'The forest is in my mind?' Merlin asked, becoming more confused by the moment.

'No, of course it isn't! It's in *everybody's* mind. Imposs-ible boy,' Frik muttered to himself, striding through the doorway.

Merlin followed, and was soon caught up in the smells and sounds of the forest. He hadn't realized how much he'd missed the woodland until he'd come here. Mab's palace was lavish beyond his wildest imagina-tion, but it was all indoors, and something deep inside him chafed at the confinement. It was as if he couldn't breathe freely except in the wilds.

Merlin wandered along happily through the trees for some time until he saw a flicker of brighter light up ahead. Though it wasn't night here, beneath the trees the light was so dim that the light ahead was quite distinct. He looked for Frik, to ask him what it was, and realized he hadn't seen his tutor for quite some time.

'Frik?' Merlin whispered. 'Where are you?'

'Oh, don't mind him,' a soft voice advised. 'I'm sure he's around somewhere. Don't you want to go and see what that light is?'

Merlin looked up in surprise, and saw a small wild-cat perched on a tree branch above him, watching him with glowing green eyes. Its soft thick fur was striped and speckled until it seemed to blend into the tree trunk. Its ears were tufted, and its long plumy tail was ringed with black bands. Herne had told him about such creatures, but Merlin had never seen one until now. They lived in forests far away to the north, where snow fell heavily all winter.

'Who are you?' Merlin asked.

'I'm the Cath Palug,' the cat replied. 'I'm extremely well known in some circles.'

Merlin looked back toward the light.

'Is Frik there?' he asked.

'Why don't we go and see?' the cat suggested.

It backed down the tree, its claws scrabbling on the rough bark, then turned and sprang into Merlin's arms.

It was heavier than it looked, and its fur tickled Merlin's nose. He shook his head and tried not to sneeze as the Cath Palug climbed up onto his shoulder, balancing there by digging its heavy claws into his shirt.

'Let's go that way,' the cat suggested, nipping at his right ear.

Without Frik to guide him, one direction was as good as another, Merlin supposed. Putting one hand up to balance the cat, he began walking toward the light.

When he got closer, he could see that the bright light came from a ring of torches set around the edge of a large forest clearing. He stopped, some instinct warning him of peril. As he crouched down, the Cath Palug jumped off his shoulder and padded off. Carefully, Merlin peered through the bushes.

He was looking out into a wide forest clearing filled with people and baggage carts. The men in the clearing seemed to be soldiers from two different armies. One group were tall, fair-haired men wearing heavy studded leather corselets over wolfskins and leggings. They were bearded and wore their hair twisted into long plaits. They carried axes and long spears, and wore gold neckrings and armlets.

The other group of men seemed to be their prisoners. They were shorter and darker, wearing elaborate bronze armour with kilts and high sandals and long red cloaks. None of them was armed, and only a few of them still had their crested helmets. Their hands were tied behind them with strips of leather, and many of them were battered and bloody.

'I know these men,' Merlin whispered excitedly to the cat.

The men in the bronze armour were *Romans* – but according to Blaise, the last of the Imperial Legions had left Britain long before Merlin had been born. How could he be seeing them here?

The bearded men seemed to be arguing with each other in a language Merlin didn't understand. The argument stopped when a tall grey-haired, bearded man in a long white sleeveless hooded robe walked into the clearing. The old man had coiled snakes tattooed on his arms from shoulder to wrist, and he was barefoot. His robe was tied at the waist with a braided red wool cord, and from the cord hung a golden sickle.

He must be a Druid, Merlin thought excitedly. Long before he was born there had been many Druids in Britain and on the mainland, but most of them had died off long before Merlin's birth. This must be why Frik had brought him here to the Forest of the Night – to see the Old Ways for himself. He parted the bushes, striving for a better view.

The old Druid turned toward the sound, and perhaps would even have investigated if one of the bound Romans had not chosen that moment to make an attempt to gain his freedom.

Instantly all attention was diverted toward him, with the bearded men gathering around and clubbing the helpless captive with their spear-ends until he lay still.

Merlin froze as well, as still as any deer in the forest. He was beginning to realize that he would be in a very awkward and dangerous position if they happened to see him.

As he watched, the Druid selected several of the captives, including the one who had tried to escape. These were separated from the rest, and remained in the clearing. The others were yoked together with wooden collars and leather ropes and herded off behind the wagons until Merlin could no longer see them.

All this had taken place directly in front of Merlin, so he had not been paying much attention to things on the periphery of his vision. But now, at the Druid's command, several of the warriors began dragging a large wooden platform upon which stood a most peculiar object.

It was almost twenty feet tall, and carefully constructed from branches woven together. It was vaguely man-shaped, and in that it resembled the scarecrows the farmers around Barnstable put out in their fields to drive thieves like Bran away from their grain. But this wicker man seemed to have a far more sinister purpose.

Its sturdy legs and the lower portion of its belly were filled with wood and brush, and its arms and head were filled with livestock: pigs, chickens, goats and rabbits. There was a rugged door in the central chest cavity, which was pegged open. The bearded warriors brought a ladder, and by means of threats and spear-points induced three of the Romans, carrying their unconscious comrade, to enter the enormous basket that made up the chest area of the wicker man. Then they tied the door shut.

In the distance, Merlin heard a faint mellow sound, like a hunting horn blowing. Another answered it, and slowly a chair decked with pine boughs and coloured berries and borne upon the backs of several younger Druids, made its way into the clearing. Sitting in the chair was a woman dressed in white, wearing a golden crown set with amber and carved with the spiral and crescent symbol of the Old Ways.

It was Mab, but not as Merlin had come to know her. The ageless Queen of the Old Ways looked younger now. Her hair was not coiled in the elaborate designs in which she wore it as he knew her; instead it flowed freely down her back, blowing a little in the wind. She smiled and laughed in response to remarks the warriors shouted out at her, and accepted gifts – posies of flowers, or twisted knots of grain, or tiny dolls carved and painted to resemble her.

The young Druids carried her chair into the centre of the clearing, and stopped, still holding it, so that Mab was high above everyone save the Romans imprisoned in the wicker man.

One of them was shouting down at the bearded men in what sounded like their own language; the other two crouched on the openweave floor, supporting their injured comrade.

Surely she is going to order them to set the Romans free! Merlin thought wildly. But he didn't really expect it of her. Something inside him already understood that Mab loved and hated with all the fiery fury of her pagan heart, and restraint was foreign to her nature. The bearded blond warriors were her people, and therefore Mab fought for them to the limit of her strength.

'Who are they?' Merlin breathed. He was not really expecting an answer, but he got one.

'Germanii and Varengi mostly, with a few Saxons thrown in,' the cat said, bumping its head beneath his elbow. 'Part of the western Celtic migration. The Romans are one of Quintilius Varus's legions – see the

Roman standard propped up against that cart? Scratch my ears. Ooh, they're going to set it on fire now. I always like this part. Look at those birds.'

'But why?' Merlin asked despairingly, doing as he was bid.

The Cath Palug arched its back and closed its eyes, purring as he stroked it.

'Because it's always been done this way. This is the Forest of the Night,' the cat said proudly. 'We follow the Old Ways here.'

While Merlin had been looking at the cat, the chief Druid had taken one of the torches and thrust it into the brushwood that filled the legs of the wicker man. The tinder caught immediately with a bright, almost smokeless fire. Inside the figure's torso, the Romans were praying.

Merlin glanced toward Mab. She was seated in her chair, watching the spectacle with every evidence of satisfaction. The chief Druid stepped back from the flames and stood beside her chair, and she reached down and patted his head just as Merlin had patted the cat.

The animals imprisoned in the upper limbs of the wicker man began to feel the heat of the flames and struggled frantically to escape. The pigs squealed shrilly and the geese bugled. The doves and chickens in the wicker head cried loudly, and the moans from the trapped men were louder. One of the Romans began to sob loudly as the colour of the smoke changed from pale grey to oily black. In only a few moments, the flames had eaten their way halfway up the wicker body, and the animals in the lower part of the arms were dead.

'Stop it!' Merlin shouted, springing up out of the bushes.

He ran into the clearing.

'Mab! Queen Mab! Stop it!'

He clutched at her skirts, but somehow he could not get her attention. He grabbed the Druid standing beside her and shook him, but the man did not even look at him when Merlin pushed him out of his place. It was as if Merlin weren't here.

Frantically, Merlin looked around for something he could use to quench the flames. He saw a water-bucket standing beside one of the carts and tried to pick it up. But the bucket was as heavy as if it had been bolted to the ground, and the water inside was as thick as honey. When he cupped a handful up to throw on the flames, it trickled through his fingers and sprang back into the bucket, not even leaving ripples in its wake.

This was magic.

'Stop! Stop! I order you to stop!' Merlin cried frantically, gesturing at the flames. 'Stop burning!'

Nothing happened.

The men inside were screaming now, crawling over each other as they desperately sought any way out of the fire.

'*Stop!*' Merlin screamed at the top of his lungs.

Nobody saw or heard him.

He ran toward the wicker man, hoping that at least he could tear it open and thus save the men inside, but it was as impossible as moving the bucket had been. The flames didn't even burn him when he thrust his hands into them, though the stench of smoke was everywhere, making him cough.

At last he could stand his helplessness no longer. He ran from the scene of that horror, unable to watch as men were burned alive, and kept on running until he fell, dizzy and breathless, to the forest floor.

He did not know how long he lay, half-unconscious in the pearly twilight, his fists clutching handfuls of forest loam.

The Cath Palug was gone, back to its treetop home, and Merlin did not miss the creature. All he knew was that something deep inside him had changed today, and that he didn't like the way the change made him feel.

Were these what the Old Ways were? Was this what Frik had brought him here to see?

He might have lain there forever, unwilling to move or go on with his life, but the gnome found him.

'Well,' Frik said brightly, 'how was your outing?'

Merlin stared up at him in disbelief, suspecting a trick. But the gnome looked just as he always had. If Frik suspected what Merlin had seen, he gave no sign of it.

'I saw a cat,' Merlin said slowly.

He sat up and looked around. A few feet away a bright red door with a brass knocker was set into the trunk of an enormous tree. It must be the way back to Mab's palace.

'Ah,' Frik said, in the polite fashion of one who does not know what to say. 'Well, the Forest always has something new and interesting in it – or old and interesting, perhaps I *should* say. You oughtn't to have wandered off that way, but perhaps we'll come back again some time and you can get the full tour. Well, come along now. You'll be late for dinner.'

*   *   *

It was not until he had studied for some time longer that Merlin realized what he had seen that day. The Forest of the Night was the memory of the past, and that was what he had seen. An echo of things past, before the new religion had come to trouble the Old Ways, a memory from the days when Mab was at the height of her power. A ghost, nothing real at all, safely buried in the past.

But forever after, Merlin could not summon fire without flinching.

CHAPTER SIX

THE COURTS OF DECEPTION

*I*t was the day of his most important triumph, and Vortigern wanted to look his best. Today he would marry a new wife, and strengthen his ties to Britain for all time. Let that raddled old hag Lionors bray and posture in Normandy with her puling brat Uther. From now on, Vortigern would be able to ignore them.

You know the old saying: lucky in war, unlucky in love, he thought to himself. He inspected himself in the mirror, turning this way and that, admiring the gleam of the crown on his head. This was not the first time Vortigern had dressed for a wedding.

His first bride had been a beauty, a young nun from a convent his men had sacked. Vortigern had once had high hopes for Brede. In marrying her he could reinforce the bond between the new religion and the Old Ways, and beget a son to inherit the crown when he was gone. Unfortunately, Brede had not fully appreciated the great honour Vortigern was bestowing upon her, and had jumped from the castle's highest tower when the Bishop of Winchester had come to bring her to the ceremony. As Vortigern recalled, he had been very irritated by her behaviour, and even beheading the Bishop had not made him feel better.

Several years later, he'd tried again. Princess Argante

had been the daughter of one of Britain's oldest families. A marriage with her would bolster Vortigern's social position and put an end to a certain amount of rebellious grumbling among his barons.

Unfortunately, Argante's family had not approved the match. Her father had besieged the castle where the wedding was to be held, and Vortigern had been forced to take the girl hostage to compel her father's good behaviour. Unfortunately, Argante's father hadn't been very flexible, so Vortigern had beheaded both him and his daughter. So in a manner of speaking, the marriage hadn't worked out.

This time, however, matters were different. This time, his marriage would last, and secure his northern border from invasion into the bargain. Vortigern's new intended was Ganieda, Queen of the Border Celts. She was a warrior from a sorcerous lineage, and he was holding her entire army hostage for her good behaviour.

Ganieda and her men had surrendered to his army at Badon after weeks of heavy fighting, but Vortigern had no intention of ransoming an enemy army back to their northern kinfolk to cause him more trouble. He'd proposed an alternative to the queen who led them: marry him, or he'd execute every one of her men.

Ganieda had been a good general with proper concern for her troops. She'd agreed to his terms at once. And today they would wed, cementing an alliance that would defeat, once and for all, Uther's hopes of retaking the throne.

Deep under the Hill, Mab watched Vortigern in one of her scrying crystals. She'd kept her eye on him down through the years; he'd been a huge disappointment to her, but she did have to admit that he had certain uses.

For one thing, he would occupy the throne until Merlin was ready to claim it as a ruler of spirit as well as of flesh, a ruler who would lead her people back to the Old Ways. After Vortigern's rule, the people would greet Merlin with tears of joy. So Vortigern had his uses.

But meanwhile, the Saxon despot would require careful handling. She didn't want to get rid of him before she had finished with him, but she had no intention of allowing Vortigern to found a dynasty whose successors would trouble Merlin after his death. Unfortunately, kings took a real interest in having heirs, so Mab had been forced to keep a close watch on matters.

She'd been pleased when Brede had jumped from

the highest tower of Winchester Castle, and it had taken very little manipulation to get the Lady Argante's father to raise his standard against Vortigern at that very opportune moment, but Ganieda was another matter entirely.

Queen Ganieda was no flighty young girl, but a warrior princess used to ruling her Border Celts with pitiless efficiency. She was pragmatic enough to wed Vortigern for power, and the two of them together could pose a serious obstacle to Mab's ambitions for Merlin and Britain.

This time, Mab mused, she would have to intervene more directly . . .

The wedding festivities had gone on all day, and the wedding feast would continue for some hours yet, but the Lady Ganieda, now Queen of England, had already retired to the royal bedchamber to await her eager groom.

He was not what she'd looked for in a husband, but Ganieda doubted very much that she was exactly what Vortigern had looked for in a bride. Past her first youth, as hard and battle-scarred as the men she led, Ganieda was more a warrior than a queen.

But perhaps, she thought, gazing into the mirror as

she brushed out her long red hair, one needed to be both to rule Britain. And for a share in Vortigern's power, she would gladly wed the Devil himself, did that bogeyman of the new religion really exist. And as for the king himself, well, she'd had worse. She was still young enough to bear him strong sons to rule Britain and the Border after he was dead. And so long as Vortigern kept his promises, she would keep hers.

Unseen by any mortal eyes, Mab flickered into existence in a corner of the chamber. This Ganieda was trouble – she could smell it. Best to get rid of her at once, before she could pose too great a threat to Merlin. For the throne must be his, as soon as his training was complete.

Invisibly, Mab appeared at Ganieda's side.

Are you sure you can trust Vortigern to keep his word? Mab whispered soundlessly in Ganieda's ear. *You know how ruthless he is. What if this is all some sort of trap? Perhaps he has already slain your men . . . and will kill you as well, when he's finished with you. There's no escape from his castle. There's no one you can turn to. Everyone within these walls is his ally, and what of the future? When Uther returns you will be branded a traitor to Britain, your children slain before your eyes, and your lands put to the sword. That is your future. There is no hope at all . . .*

On and on Mab whispered into the new queen's ear, as Ganieda gradually grew pale and still, staring into her mirror with wide grey eyes.

Vortigern was accompanied to his bedchamber by several of his more trusted barons, as well as some he simply wanted to keep a particular eye on. There were a large number of steps in the winding staircase that led to his tower bedroom, but Vortigern didn't mind. He would only have to travel them in one direction.

He was not, the king assured himself silently, drunk. He had perhaps had a few more horns of mead than was strictly wise, but if a man couldn't celebrate on his own wedding day, when could he celebrate? And this alliance would put an end to those whispers from across the Channel that his days were numbered. Uther was still only a boy, and if the people of Britain had to choose between the unknown quantity of Uther and their own prince, born and raised in Britain, Vortigern knew which they'd choose – assuming they knew what was good for them.

I shall name him . . . Vortigern. It's a good name for a

king. He shall be Vortigern II, and Uther will not even be a memory . . .

His thoughts made Vortigern smile, and he was smiling when he opened the door to his bedchamber.

The sight that he saw then made him stop dead, but the men behind him had had quite as much to drink as he had, and their momentum jostled him on into the room, before Ardente, the man at his back, saw what Vortigern had seen and stopped short with a strangled cry.

The curtains of the royal bed were pulled back, and Ganieda lay in the middle of it, dressed in her wedding-night finery. The small gold-and-pearl dagger that had been, by Saxon custom, Vortigern's wedding present to her was buried to its hilt in her heart, and her hands were still clasped about it.

There was blood everywhere.

Blindly, Vortigern turned away from the sight, shoving through the press of men at his back until he was past them. He ran down the stairs, shouting for his personal guard. By the time the night was through, no man in Ganieda's army would be left alive.

And in the bedchamber above, Mab surveyed her night's work . . . and smiled.

*   *   *

After his adventure in the Forest of the Night, Merlin felt as though he was seeking the answer to a question without knowing what the question was. That impulse drove him onward, through ever more esoteric books and ancient scrolls. He studied harder than ever before, though at times his studies made him feel as if he were wading through quicksand, working very hard but making little progress.

He enjoyed the pure knowledge, but more and more, the study of magic made him feel as if he were doing something unfair, something that could lead only to trouble. Slowly Merlin was coming to the realization that if he were to become a full wizard and Mab's champion, he might be forced to do things that he despised.

He wished that Blaise or Herne were here for him to talk to; the only people he saw were Mab and Frik. The pixies, trolls, and small fluttering sprites who were Mab's court – elfinkind diminished by time and human disbelief – hardly counted as conversational companions, and Merlin had seen no other creatures here in the Land of Magic. And while he still trusted Mab and Frik to have his best interests at heart, a seed of doubt had been planted in his soul by what he had seen in the Forest of the Night, and slowly, day by day, that seed was growing.

*　　*　　*

'Good morning, Master Merlin,' Frik said, sweeping into the room in his cap and gown.

Over the passing weeks, the library had come to take on the look of an old-fashioned schoolroom. There was now a lectern at one end of the long table before the fire, and a blackboard behind it, its surface covered with detailed drawings of pentagrams, sigils and magic circles. In one corner of the room an athanor bubbled furiously, the result of Merlin's dabbling in alchemy. A worried-looking frog wearing a tiny gold crown sat upon a shelf in a deep glass bowl, slowly blinking its bulging eyes.

Merlin trudged into the room with a book under his arm, his hair still damp from his morning wash. He sat down in his seat, and opened his book with a sigh.

'Is something wrong?' Frik asked archly.

Merlin shrugged. 'It's just that . . .' he stopped.

He wasn't certain *what* was bothering him.

'Well, do go on, Master Merlin. I'm certain that all of us are terribly interested in your deliberations,' Frik said cuttingly.

'All of *whom*?' Merlin demanded with sudden unpent intensity. 'The two of you are the only ones I ever see; is anyone else left? You and Mab talk about the Old

Ways – but I'm not sure what they are or even if any of them are left! I just –'

'Oh, dear,' Frik said quietly. 'A certain person *did* neglect your education, didn't she? You'd suppose that a bit of gratitude would have been in order after all that madam did for her, but I suppose long association counts for nothing. Well. I can see that certain reparations must be made. Master Merlin, what do you know about the true nature of the world?'

After several weeks of study, Merlin knew the answer to this question by rote.

'The world is composed of Earth, Air, Fire and Water. Each of these realms is ruled by its Elemental King: the Sylph for Air, the Undine for Water, the Salamander for Fire, and the Gnome for Earth.' Frik bowed to acknowledge this truth.

Merlin continued: 'The world is composed of three realms for men, three for the dark forces, and three for the bright. The three worlds of men are Anoeth, the Land of the Dead; the mortal world which we know; and the Land of Magic, which lies within the Hollow Hills beyond the Enchanted Lake . . .'

'Yes, yes, yes, very good,' Frik said, unimpressed by his pupil's recitation. 'But don't you wonder why Anoeth and the Land of Magic are counted as part of the world of men when mortals only go to one of them after they die and never go to the other one at all?'

Merlin stared at him blankly. Frik had never spoken to him in this way before.

'*Think,* Master Merlin!' the gnome begged him. 'They're called the Three Realms of *Men.*'

'Is it . . . because mortals used to travel through all three?' Merlin asked hesitantly.

'*Yes!*' Frik said in delight. 'What's the point of having a space–time continuum if you never *use* it? But of course as magic began to leave the world, this sort of travel became less popular. Anoeth is not without its dangers, and it takes great craft and cunning to reach the Land of Magic at the best of times. As they began to forget us, mortals became fearful and unwilling to seize their opportunities, and now, well, I suppose nobody travels much at all. But *you* must know all three realms well, Master Merlin. Only think how awkward it would be if Lord Idath didn't recognize you!'

'Who's Lord Idath?' Merlin asked.

'*That* is precisely what I mean,' Frik said firmly. 'What are they teaching children in the schools these days? I shall have a private word with Her Majesty, dash off a letter of introduction or two . . .'

*   *   *

'Are you sure this is the right direction?' Merlin asked hesitantly.

Frik had roused him early that morning. The gnome had bundled Merlin into his Aunt Ambrosia's warm cloak and urged him to eat a hearty breakfast. Then, with a great air of importance, he had led Merlin out through the doors of Mab's palace, down the grand staircase, and back into the boat which had brought Merlin to the Land of Magic.

They carried lanterns containing captive sprites for light, but Frik had refrained from using the occasion to don one of his peculiar costumes. He scuttled along in his own persona, a dark and faintly twisted figure, whose long pointed ears cast a shadow on the cave walls as if of horns.

They sailed across the dark lagoon, but instead of breaking out into the open air and the Enchanted Lake, as Merlin half-expected, they sailed to a shore still within the vast cavern. The beach upon which Frik grounded the boat was of bright blue sand, blue as the October sky, and Merlin paused for a moment to admire it.

'No time . . . no time,' Frik said quickly. 'We've miles to go before we reach our destination, young Merlin, and it wouldn't do to be late. He's a very timely person, is Lord Idath.'

Obediently Merlin followed Frik through the caverns. He became lost instantly, but Frik always seemed to know where he was going, even when the cavern opened out into that same sunless, moonless landscape that Merlin had seen before in the Forest of the Night.

He looked around apprehensively, but the only trees he saw were small stunted ones, their trunks and branches as black and glistening as if they'd been in a fire.

Though the light was fairly bright, the diffuse, silvery radiance cast no shadows, and gave everything a curious flat appearance. Try as he might, Merlin could not see the sun anywhere in the silvery sky.

Beneath his feet, the ground rang as hard as if it were frozen in the depths of winter, and wisps of mist blurred the ground and the horizon, until it was difficult to see anything at all, but the air was only chilly, not truly cold. A thin cool wind seemed to blow from no particular direction, and sniffing it, Merlin caught the faint, far-off scent of the sea.

Though this was obviously outdoors – at least in comparison to the Land of Magic – Merlin didn't feel as if he was any freer. The earth, for all its flat vistas, seemed cramped, and the sky had no sense of *depth* to it, as if it were merely a piece of painted canvas. Though he knew they were covering a great deal of ground, the landscape did not change, and they didn't seem to have got anywhere.

'Where are we?' Merlin asked finally, after they'd been walking for a long time. Having been used to living an outdoor life, the walk was no trouble to him, but Frik seemed to be labouring a little, and when Merlin spoke, the gnome took it as an excuse for a rest.

'Why . . . we're nowhere in particular,' Frik answered, sounding rather surprised to have been asked. 'This is the World Between the Worlds,' he said, as if that were an answer to Merlin's question. He sat down on a rock, brandishing a fan he suddenly produced out of nowhere. 'It's quite a long and twisted path, but at all costs we must be there by dark.'

'Why are we going this way, then?' Merlin asked. 'You and Mab can appear anywhere you like in the twinkling of an eye. Why don't we just go that way?'

'Well, for one thing, Lord Idath does not appreciate it when people drop in unannounced. For another, *you* must learn all the landmarks to the Land of Winter. Some day you may need to go there by yourself – and get back again, too.'

Herne had told Merlin ghost stories when Merlin had been much younger. They'd given him nightmares until Aunt Ambrosia had told him firmly that they were only stories, and nothing that could hurt him. Discovering now that the shades of the dead were real and present was an experience Merlin didn't care for.

'I suppose so,' Merlin said doubtfully.

He plucked up a weed that had been growing by the roadside. It looked like a yellow flower he saw at home, but here the leaves and petals were both grey, as though the soil in which it grew had leached all the colour out of it.

'Now come along, Master Merlin,' Frik said, as though it were Merlin who had been dawdling.

The path into Anoeth angled sharply uphill after that, becoming so steep that in some places Merlin ended up hauling Frik along after him like a sack of laundry.

As the land rose, Merlin could see for a great distance, but all there was to the grey landscape was mist and rock and the sparse vegetation that was as grey as the earth it sprouted from. He could not even see the cave mouth through which he and Frik had entered this realm.

For some time, Merlin had been conscious of a vast roaring sound. As they came closer to the source, Merlin had recognized it as the sound of a rushing stream, but he was not prepared for what he saw when he and Frik reached its banks.

Alone in all this grey land, the river had colour. Its waters were the bright crimson of flowing blood, ranging from dark ruby to pale vermilion, rushing and foaming along its narrow bed with furious speed. Anyone who fell in would be carried along faster than a horse could run, his body battered against the black rocks that thrust up from the stream-bed like rotted teeth. There was a sharp tang of copper in the air, and the river steamed as it flowed, as if it really were fresh blood.

'Ah,' Frik said. 'We've reached the halfway point. There's a bridge a few yards upriver. We can cross after lunch.'

He seated himself and raised his hands, preparing to gesture their meal into existence.

'Uh,' Merlin said, feeling slightly queasy.

It was not that he was any stranger to death. Life in the forest was an ongoing dance between hunter and prey, in which one died so that the other might live. The wolf killed the deer, and the wolf's body, in death, became the grass that fed the deer. All life was a circle, each creature taking its turn to die so that life could go on. But though Merlin accepted that fact intellectually, the thought of eating lunch on the banks of a river that looked and smelled like fresh blood was a little too much for his stomach.

'I think I'd rather go a little further first,' he said hastily.

After a few minutes' walk along the bank, they reached the place where the path they were following crossed over the river. The river cut deeper into its bed, until they were walking along the edge of a cliff high above it. Spanning the torrent was a bridge the likes of which Merlin had never imagined. The gleaming lace-like structure arched high over the water, and was made of interwoven sword-blades, their steel gleaming in the pearly light of the Otherworld day. Through the roadbed of the bridge, in the open spaces left by the latticework of swords, the red river could be seen racing turbulently below. There were no side-rails. One slip, and the slashed and bleeding body of the luckless traveller would be cast into the torrent.

Merlin stopped and stared. Frik noticed his mystification and assumed a lecturing stance.

'This – as you would know if you'd paid attention to your geography lessons, is the Bridge of Blades, which spans the River of Life, which forms the boundary of Anoeth, *which* is where we are going. It may look rickety, but it's perfectly safe, I assure you.'

'What if I slip?' Merlin asked, looking at the gleaming edges of the swords.

'Don't,' Frik suggested.

Though from experience Merlin knew that his gnomish tutor was both cowardly and lazy, Frik sprang quickly onto the bridge, skipping lightly across the span. Determined not to be outdone, Merlin followed him, trying to match his pace.

The bridge surface gave springily beneath his feet, and the blades creaked and sang as they slid over each other. Merlin tried to keep his eyes on the far shore, where Frik waited impatiently, and to forget the nature of the surface on which he walked. He succeeded far too well, for with only a few steps to go he slipped and fell.

For a moment he hung suspended in space, as if he had taken a giant step sideways. One foot hung over the river, the toes of the other still touched the bridge. He lunged forward, arms windmilling, trying to reverse the direction of his fall, but his momentum was too great. All he managed to do to save himself was to grab one of the sword-hilts as he fell.

The sword slid a few inches out of the weave, but it held, angled slightly downward and vibrating with the stress he placed upon it. Merlin clung to the hilt with both hands, desperately trying to hang on. His shoulders ached with the strain, and his feet dangled above the long drop to the surface of the river, and the misty sky above seemed like a great hand reaching down to crush him into the earth. His heart hammered with the awareness of the danger he was in.

'Use your magic!' Frik shouted from the far shore.

'I can't remember any of it!' Merlin shouted back.

All the spells Frik had taught him were for mundane things like setting fires or summoning storms. None of them seemed to be suitable for saving him from falling into a river that would grind his bones like corn between millstones.

I need to get out of here! his mind shrieked.

To escape.

To *fly* . . .

'Fly!' Merlin shouted, without quite realizing what he was saying. 'I want to fly! I want to *fly!*'

Suddenly he felt the shimmering transformation of magic course through his body, but this time it did not end with the lighting of a candle or the elongating of a branch. This time the magic turned inward, transforming his very self.

His arms lengthened, the bones becoming light and thin and hollow. His fingers spread, becoming the support not of a hand, but of a wing. In the same moment his body, lighter and curiously shortened, sprouted a thick coat of ruddy gold feathers, and he lost his grip upon the sword. He became, in fact as well as name, a *merlin*, creature of the air.

With a cry, the wizard-turned-hawk tumbled down toward the water, as deadly to him in this form as in the other. At the last moment, one awkward flap of his wings carried him to safety, and a second carried him up out of the gorge and into the pearly sky.

He was flying.

He felt a rush of pure joy sing through him as the cool air slid through his feathers. The sky was not flat as he had thought it before – it was an infinite land, a palace to which he had been given the keys. It seemed as if all his life until this moment had been spent crawling painfully and slowly across the surface of the earth, and now the freedom of the heavens had been opened to him. Acting on instinct, Merlin reached for the winds. An updraught carried him far above the earth; he spread his wings and angled the feathers to catch every breath of air. He opened his beak and shrieked – a harsh avian cry of triumph for the sheer joy of flight – and tumbled down through the temple of the winds.

He forgot his other self, circling higher and higher, flying in great circles for the sheer animal joy of it. But no matter how high he flew, the nacreous sky did not turn to blue. The sun that shone on the living world did not shine here. Baffled in his hunt for clear air, the hawk turned his attention elsewhere.

With strangely altered sight he considered his new domain. The world was oddly distorted, flat yet amazingly sharp and vivid at the same time. The earth below seemed to rise up at the edges like a great shallow bowl filled with sky, and in all directions the vista was the same. The mists that had baffled his human eyes were no barrier to his hawk's vision. Merlin could see every stone, every tuft of withered grass on the ground below. He could even see the gnome, his figure made tiny by distance, leaping and yelling on the bank of the red river as he tried to attract Merlin's attention, but Merlin was too beguiled by the sensation of flight to pay any attention to Frik. The whole world was now open to him, and he could see for miles in every direction.

Save one.

Beyond the gorge through which the red river fell, the land rose sharply, into peaks as sharp and craggy as the mountains of the moon. At the very top of the highest crag there was a palace, gleaming bone white against the stone. It shone as brightly as the blades of the bridge. What was it, and who lived there?

To think was to act. Merlin caught a soaring updraught and swooped up into the heavens, climbing until the river was only an insignificant red thread meandering through the grey land below, and even the white palace was a tiny speck against the silvery mountain crags.

But reaching the castle was harder than he had thought. Gusts of wind buffeted him back, causing him to tumble hundreds of feet in seconds. Each time he saved himself at the last moment, slicing upwards through the sky as if his body were a blade.

His human form, the waiting gnome – these things were forgotten. All that mattered to Merlin now was his flight and his goal.

At last he won through to a lake of calmer air directly

over the castle, where he could soar in a wide circle and inspect his target at leisure.

The castle was a ring-shaped structure, with eight tall towers surrounding an octagonal centre court-yard. Each tower flew a long forked banner: two were black, two were white, two were red, and two were silvery grey. Men in elaborate armour and horned helms patrolled the castle walls, their spears and shields clashing as they paraded. Despite the barrenness of the surrounding landscape, the foliage within the castle wall itself was lush and even gardenlike.

Looking down into the courtyard, Merlin could see the thatched roofs of extensive stables. Flowering vines climbed the walls, and fruit trees in tubs adorned the compound. Set into the castle walls, facing each other, were two massive sets of gates. One set was the trans-lucent golden colour of horn, the other the glistening cream of ivory. They were carved in elaborate knots and spirals and whorls, until even his hawk-sight was dizzy with following all the convolutions of the tangle.

As Merlin circled lazily above the castle, pleased to have reached his goal but no longer knowing why it was so important, a tall man walked out into the courtyard. The nacreous light that illuminated the land was growing dimmer now, but it still gleamed off his red hair and struck sparks like buried embers from the flowing locks.

He was dressed for the hunt, all in dark green leather. Silver-stamped grey leather boots adorned with jewelled golden spurs reached to mid-thigh. His leather tunic was trimmed in grey fox-fur and studded all across the shoulders and front, and each stud was in the shape of a small silver skull. His gauntlets were jewelled along the turned-back cuff to match his spurs, and sewn with small crescents of lacquered metal, so that they glittered like a dragon's scales. The black cloak that flowed from his shoulders rippled like smoke, or like the night itself, and the hawk thought it spied the twinkle of stars deep in the fabric's folds.

When he reached the centre of the courtyard, the castle's master looked up into the sky. He whistled shrilly between his teeth, and held up his fist.

Merlin felt the hunter's grey gaze transfix him like winter ice.

The circling hawk was seized by an irresistible impulse. Without conscious deliberation, Merlin folded back his golden wings and dived towards the man below. At the last moment, he spread his wings wide and yanked himself to a halt, his talons spreading to grasp the upraised fist as he settled to a stop.

'Here's a pretty hawk for my mews,' the hunter said in a deep rumbling voice, stroking the bird's feathers with an outstretched finger. 'But I do not think you will become a subject of my kingdom for many years yet, Master Merlin.'

As if the mention of his name had reminded him of who he was, Merlin felt another great wave of magic kindle within him.

The transformation rushed over him in reverse, and he fell sprawling on the cobblestones of the courtyard, in human form once more.

Merlin lay there for a moment, blinking up at the grey-clad hunter, his heart beating as fast as that of the bird he had been only moments before. He felt as if the track of his life had been wrenched out of its bed, as if something enormously significant that he could somehow not quite remember had happened to him.

He'd become a hawk.

He knew that much, but the details were oddly vague, like the dream that vanishes upon waking.

The cobblestones of the courtyard were hard and cold against his back. He drew a deep breath.

'Master Merlin!' Frik flickered into evidence at his elbow, glanced up long enough to get a good look at the hunter, and fell to his knees in obeisance. 'That is to say – Lord Idath – terribly sorry, and –'

'How did you know it was me?' Merlin asked the hunter, getting to his feet.

If this was Lord Idath, he didn't look particularly terrifying. In fact, he reminded Merlin just a bit of his friend Herne.

'In the Land of Winter, we tell nothing but the truth, young Merlin,' Idath said in his deep voice. 'There are no lies, and no illusions: no matter your seeming, I knew it was you.'

'That was no illusion,' Frik said fervently. 'Master Merlin, I thought you were lost for certain. I don't know what madam would have done if I'd come back without you.'

'She would have turned you into a rock for a thousand years,' Idath told him genially, and the goblin shuddered.

'Then I really turned into a bird?' Merlin asked, fascinated.

He glanced toward the sky. Had he really flown through that as easily as he could swim through water? He felt a sharp longing to leap into the sky once more, and sail along the wind on a merlin's feathered wings.

'You did – but don't try that again soon, young wizard,' Idath said. 'It's easy to lose your way when you change your form, and to forget who you are. And when image becomes truth, then illusion becomes real. Remember that.'

'I won't forget,' Merlin promised.

'Well, now, here we are, all matey,' Frik chirped fulsomely. He glanced toward the sky a little warily, rubbing his hands together briskly. 'A lovely evening for a good gallop, wouldn't you say?'

'Begone with you, foolish one,' Idath said impatiently. 'Tell Mab I'll return her apprentice to her safe and sound once he's done what he's come here to do.'

'What have I come here to do?' Merlin asked.

Now that he'd got over his disorientation, he found he rather liked Lord Idath.

'You've come to ride with my Hunt, Master Merlin,' Idath said, putting an arm around Merlin's shoulders and leading him toward the stables. 'To pass through the gate of dreams, to gain visions, to learn the boundaries of life and death.'

As Merlin and Idath reached the stables, the door slid open, and the grooms began to lead out the horses. Through the doorway, Merlin could see the grooms rushing back and forth, saddling and bridling the animals and leading them out into the courtyard.

He could smell the scents of horses and fresh hay, and the rich aroma of well-cared-for leather.

Idath's mount was led out first. He was a splendid grey stallion whose eyes gleamed as red as a wolf's. His coat was polished until it gleamed like the river stones, and he set his feet on the stableyard cobbles as though his hooves were made of fine glass.

'He's beautiful,' Merlin said reverently.

Idath stroked the stallion's velvety nose. 'His name is Tempus – he is that which no man can elude; that which no one can halt. But he is not for mortal man to ride, nor even a wizard. Here is your mount. Sir Rupert, meet Merlin. He's a wizard.'

Pleased to meet you, Master Merlin, Sir Rupert said, tossing his head. He was a placid grey horse with a dark mane and tail and he regarded Merlin with wise brown eyes, his ears flicking back and forth.

'I am pleased to meet you as well, Sir Rupert,' Merlin answered.

He was a little disappointed not to have been given a fiery charger like Idath's to ride, but he didn't wish to seem rude.

'Oh, Sir Rupert will be a better companion to you

than someone like Tempus,' Idath said, as if he had guessed Merlin's thoughts. 'He may look like a common palfrey, but he has more than a touch of the Old Magic running through his veins. He will serve you well, and will always be there when you need him. Now mount up, for we have far to go.'

A groom ran forward and boosted Merlin into Sir Rupert's saddle.

Easy, lad, the horse said, stepping sideways to shift Merlin's weight into balance.

Merlin, who was not used to horses, clutched at the saddle.

The light had dwindled as they stood talking, and servants came out of the castle with torches to light the courtyard. All around them now were mounted riders, both men and women. The noise level had increased as more and more members of the Hunt arrived and were mounted, laughing and calling to one another, greeting old friends. Some wore armour, and some wore masks, and some needed no masks, for they had the heads of beasts.

Here we go. Oh, this will be fun. I do so love a good run.

'I hope you're right,' Merlin said uneasily. He gathered up the reins and tightened his legs around Sir Rupert's middle.

'Release the hounds!' Idath shouted, and from somewhere an enormous pack of hounds boiled into the
stableyard. They had white bodies and red ears, and
their eyes gleamed with a fierce red light. They yelped
and babbled around the horses' legs, adding their
baying to the din.

Idath reached down and took his helmet from a
waiting groom. It seemed ordinary enough, but as
soon as he set it upon his head, great ivory antlers
sprouted from its brow-band, growing and branching
until Idath wore the glorious crown of the king stag.

As Merlin gaped at the transformation, the Hunt
Lord reached into the air and plucked down a jewelled
hunting horn. Placing it to his lips, he blew a single
mournful note, that drowned out the baying of the
hounds and the shouting of the riders. As if it were
a signal, two servants flung open the ivory gates.

With a laugh, Idath spurred Tempus forward, reaching down to snatch a burning torch from one of the
servants as he passed.

Sir Rupert bounded forward in pursuit; Merlin,
caught by surprise, lurched sideways in the saddle,
then clung frantically.

Duck! Sir Rupert commanded, and Merlin crouched
low in the saddle as Sir Rupert sprang into the air,

vaulting a brace of hounds in his path and clearing the archway.

The rest of the Hunt followed, shouting and clashing as all of them tried to pass through the ivory gates at once. The hounds boiled between the horses' legs like water through a mill-race, fanning out into a ghostly living carpet at both sides of Idath's steed. They gave tongue as they ran, their yelping sounding eerily like the calling of the geese flying south through the winter sky.

The sensation of sheer speed was as intoxicating to Merlin as flight had been. The air whipped past his face so fast that there was no scent to it, only a bright coldness like starlight and fresh snow. Merlin found himself shouting along with the others, a wild yell of unfettered delight.

Careful. Here comes the first jump.

Sir Rupert's warning came only a moment before he checked, then launched himself into space.

Merlin glanced down, but saw nothing more than a faint glittering below before Sir Rupert jolted to earth once more.

By now the rest of the Hunt had caught up with them, and the night was filled with the drumming of many hooves, and the wild battle-cries of riders further back in the pack. The horses slowed the pace a bit after their first wild rush, and now the hounds surged ahead in a body, red eyes flashing as they tasted the wind.

'Where are we going?' Merlin shouted to his mount. 'What are we hunting?'

He could recognize no landmarks in the grey land: though it was night, it wasn't fully dark. The same radiance that had lit the day persisted, though dimmer, and the mist that rose from the ground gleamed like pearl.

'We hunt souls, young wizard,' a rider next to him shouted. He rode a piebald horse, and all he wore was a spotted catskin kilted about his waist, and on his head an untidy crown of wild grapes and ivy twisted together. He carried a harp in his free hand. 'We are the Wild Hunt, and all mortal kind's forgotten gods and terrors ride with us.' He laughed wildly, and a few moments later his horse had pulled ahead and he was gone.

'What did he mean?' Merlin demanded of Sir Rupert, but he thought somehow that he already knew. Idath was the Hunt Lord, and the Lord of Winter, but he was also the Lord of the Dead, Hunter of Souls.

Merlin saw his fellow horsemen in glimpses: the hollow eyeholes of a gilded mask, a crimson cowl that seemed to have no tenant. Long white fangs gleamed in beastly muzzles, branching horns curled from broad foreheads, and glowing eyes gleamed from beneath jutting brows. One rider had no head at all, and under his arm in place of it he carried a candle-lit orange gourd that had been carved with a demon face. Merlin closed his eyes very tightly. Those he rode with now were far more inhuman than the members of Mab's court in the Hollow Hills.

Jump! Sir Rupert said laconically.

This time Merlin managed to take the jump *with* his mount, rather than being dragged along behind.

As soon as they landed again, he realized that something was different. The air was warmer. He could smell growing things. The sky was truly dark, and far above, a fat silvery moon sailed through the midnight heavens, bright as a coin.

'We're home!' Merlin said in astonishment.

'Of course, young Merlin. My business is with the race of men,' Idath said. He'd reined in so that Tempus and Sir Rupert ran side by side for a few moments.

'Was he right?' Merlin asked him. 'The man in the leopardskin? About the souls, and being forgotten, and all?'

'No,' Idath answered. His red eyes gleamed below the rim of the helmet, and his white teeth were very sharp. 'Let others despair, let Mab plot and scheme to regain her sovereignty: it is of no concern to me. I will never be forgotten so long as mortals fear the shadow that comes at midnight, the howl in the dark. I am the Lord of the Wild Hunt, and as long as mortals cower by the fireside there will be a place there for me also.' He laughed, and spurred his horse ahead, leaving Merlin and Sir Rupert behind.

Merlin shuddered. He had liked Lord Idath, and a part of him still did, but he recognized that the huntsman he had met in the castleyard was only one of Idath's aspects. As Lord of the Dead he was a terrifying figure.

But he did not have time to reflect on such things. The horses were running flat-out, and he had to work to keep his seat. Mortal hunters would have tired, or slowed, or stood around waiting for the hounds to pick up a scent. The Wild Hunt did none of these things – its riders rode as if the gates of Hell gaped open behind them.

They reached a road, and ahead Merlin could see the lanterns hung at the entrance of a village. Though the village gates were chained shut for the evening, the Hunt poured through the gates as if they were not there at all. The sound of the horses' feet changed as they ran over cobbled lanes, and the baying of the hounds echoed through the narrow village paths.

Sir Rupert slowed on the twisting streets, jostled by the riders who surged past him, vying for pre-eminence. As they raced onwards one of the horses fell, pitching his rider over his head. The riders following did not have enough room to stop or turn aside, and crashed into him, collapsing in a desperate tangle of hooves. There were screams from behind as others saw the obstacle – Merlin could see it, too, but to stop was to be trampled.

'Sir Rupert!'

Hush. Let me concentrate.

Merlin felt his mount gather himself once more, then Sir Rupert sprang into the air, clearing the jumble of fallen horses by no more than inches. He seemed to hang in the air forever, and landed with a jar that knocked the breath from Merlin's lungs. Sir Rupert scrabbled for balance, his hooves skating over the slippery cobbles, then he regained his footing and bounded out of the way as the next members of the field leaped over the fallen horses.

In moments the town was a dim blur behind them. Merlin realized he was breathless and aching, chilled to the bone by the whipping wind and thoroughly unsettled, but there didn't seem to be any way to retire from the Hunt, even if he had known somewhere else to go.

He was in a gap now between two packs of riders – the entire Hunt was strung out for half a mile, whooping and howling and brandishing torches and captured plunder – and he could see a little of the land around him.

The terrain through which they ran seemed strangely altered from the Britain that Merlin knew. The countryside was dotted with lights – not many, but they burned with a fixed white intensity strange to him. The very air smelled different; it held the taint of metal and distant smoke.

Close behind him he heard the hoofbeats of an approaching rider; and, turning to see who it was, he caught a blurred glimpse of a small dark bearded man with the horns of a goat. He rode without saddle or bridle, and his mount ran in blind terror, its coat foamy with sweat. As he passed, he turned suddenly and shouted into Merlin's face.

Go and tell them in Arcadia that great Pan is dead!

Merlin recoiled in surprise, dragging back involuntarily on Sir Rupert's reins. The horse slowed, shaking his head and dancing sideways in displeasure.

'I'm sorry,' Merlin said apologetically. 'I was just startled.'

You have to expect a few shocks if you're going to ride with this crowd, Sir Rupert answered a little crossly.

He stretched out his neck and set himself to regaining his lost speed.

The thunder of the hooves ahead rang hollowly as the animals passed from turf onto stone once more. They were onto the causeway before Merlin quite realized where he was. They had reached the coast and were still riding west; on both sides of him there was the hissing of the sea as it foamed against the sea-wall. At the end of the causeway the little strip of land broadened, and a mighty castle was built on the outcropping, but when they reached it, Merlin saw that the castle was long deserted. The full moon shone down on brave stone walls that were now no more than ruins: the castle's ancient defences now a hollow shell.

The riders clattered through the forecourt and the inner court – surrounded by the red-eared hounds of Anoeth – then up a stairway to the battlements, their iron hooves striking sparks from the flints in the stone.

When Idath and Tempus reached the top they jumped,

followed by a wave of hounds. The other riders followed, wild as otters.

Merlin clung desperately to his seat as Sir Rupert lunged up the stairs. When he gained the top it seemed for a moment that the blast of salt wind that blew landwards with gale force would be enough to hold them there. In a lightning glance, Merlin could see that the moon cast a wide silver track upon the glittering water. Then Sir Rupert, too, jumped.

Merlin yelled as his mount fell through the blackness but moments later he landed upon a shifting, springy surface. Sir Rupert began to trot, slowly building up speed, and as he did, Merlin realized that he could see the other members of the Hunt riding up ahead. Their mounts ran tirelessly along the moon-track far in the distance, but none of them was galloping over the ground any longer. Now there was no more beneath their running feet than the storm-driven ocean waves, and still they ran, into the west.

Merlin never knew afterwards how long or how far the Hunt had ridden, or who had joined them, or even if they had coursed any prey. He rode over sea and land, village and town, and the strange sights he saw blurred into dreams almost at the moment he saw them. Slowly the world seemed to grow unclear, the sound of the Hunt more distant, as if, no matter how hard Sir Rupert ran, he were dropping slowly behind.

In the end the wonders he saw lost all their power to move him, and he was conscious only of a vast dragging weariness – for though he was fairy-born, Merlin was still mortal, and those who ride with the Wild Hunt must be more than mortal, either at first or at last.

Finally all was silence and darkness. Merlin drifted through the void for a long time, slowly becoming aware of the stillness. As memory seeped back the peace unaccountably began to trouble him. Wasn't there something he ought to be doing?

He opened his eyes with a jerk and found himself staring into a pair of great goggling, protruding, unblinking eyes.

'Yah!'

The gnome had been bending over him to see if he was awake.

Merlin and Frik recoiled in opposite directions: Merlin back into his pillows, Frik to the foot of the bed.

All around Merlin the world as he knew it seemed to clatter back into orderly place with almost tangible force. He was lying in his own bed back in his own room in Mab's palace. Sprites flitted in and out of the windows, their glow glinting off the crystals that covered the walls.

Had any of it really happened – the journey to Anoeth and all the rest? He tried to sit up and found that all his muscles were bruised and aching.

'Ow,' Merlin complained.

He swung his feet over the edge of the bed, and discovered that he seemed to have slept in his shoes. One of them, anyway. He wasn't sure he wanted to know where the other one was.

'Well,' said Frik bracingly. 'And what did we learn from our little adventure?'

'I'm not sure,' Merlin said. He rubbed the back of his neck. 'Everything seemed so . . . peculiar. Even for here. I'm not sure what happened. Was it all a dream?'

'Ah,' Frik answered. He tried to look wise and mysterious and didn't quite succeed. 'Everything is, in the end.'

He is more powerful than he knows. Too powerful for us.

He wasn't entirely comfortable with the inner colloquy, but one might as well talk to one's self as to the walls, Frik supposed, since while the walls talked back, they also tended to tattle. And it wasn't, after all, as if he could have a chatty heart-to-heart talk with Queen Mab.

He paced restlessly beside the mermaid's lagoon, gazing morosely into the depths of the black water and trying to ignore the still small voice that wasn't conscience, because gnomes didn't have consciences. And certainly no one who served the Queen of the Old Ways had any right to a conscience.

Served. Now there was a bitter word. He was a gnome, an ancient member of a terribly-well-thought-of and magical race. Once he and Mab had plotted together as equals. Occasionally she had even listened to his advice. But paradoxically, she had become more arrogant and more demanding as her influence waned, until she tyrannized him just as Vortigern did mortal kind.

Vortigern. A name it wasn't prudent to utter in Her Majesty's hearing these days. While it was true that Vortigern persecuted the Christians, there was no distinction in it: Vortigern persecuted *everybody*. For every Christian who renounced the new religion, there were two pagans who renounced all gods entirely since none of them seemed to be of any help against the tyrant king of Britain. Worse than that, in the years since the Holy Grail had disappeared from Avalon many of the monks and nuns of that holy isle had wandered the land in search of it, and in their travels they preached Avalon's gospel of love and acceptance. The harsh Christianity which Constant had imposed upon the people was being replaced by a doctrine which was . . . quite tolerable, really, when you came right down to it.

Frik shuddered at the direction of his thoughts. Let Her Majesty catch him even *thinking* something like that and he'd have no worries about either the future or his relationship with his employer. He'd spend the rest of eternity as a plaster lawn decoration, clutching a fake fishing rod, somewhere in Surbiton.

But the fact remained: like it or not, Vortigern was driving the people into the arms of the new religion. And the magic of the Old Ways was growing steadily weaker.

Except for Merlin's.

He ought not to have been able to do what he did, Frik worried. The moment yesterday when Merlin had turned himself into a hawk through sheer will and an improperly-phrased spell was still vivid in Frik's memory. Fortunatcly he'd been able to avoid reporting the incident to Her Majesty. It would have led to quite an ugly scene, and questions that Frik had no way of answering.

Their magic – Mab's and his and all that of the Old Ways – was a magic of illusion. Nothing they did had any true objective reality. Their spells drew their power from belief and their effect from trickery. They were a thing of the fairy realm, as ephemeral as summer snow, though often far more dangerous.

But Merlin's magic was different. Frik could make himself appear to be a bird. He could use his magic power to fly. But Merlin's transformation had been no illusion. It had been as real as wood and stone.

When he forgets his lessons, he's far more dangerous than when he remembers them.

Somehow Merlin had the ability to dream true – and to make his dreams real.

It's his mortal part. Mortal dreams have power, everyone knows that. Haven't they almost dreamed us out of existence? Merlin is only half-mortal, but somehow he seems to have combined his powers. He's unique, and that makes him all the more dangerous.

Frik stooped and picked up an expended crystal from the ground at his feet. He rolled it back and forth between his fingers. You were seeing more and more of these lately around the Land of Magic, as the magic in the Hollow Hills seeped away like water from a cracked jug. He shrugged, tossing it out across the surface of the water.

'Hey!'

A mermaid surfaced with an angry splash of her tail, the crystal in her fist. She flung it back at Frik with a great deal more accuracy than he had shown. Frik ducked out of the way, cowering behind a rock, then straightened up slowly.

He'd reached a decision.

If the magic of Merlin's mortal part held such power, it was up to Frik to make certain that the boy never discovered his own strength. He'd bury Merlin's native abilities in fairy spellcraft until the boy was too dizzy with bookish knowledge even to realize what he had. With luck, Frik could extinguish the young wizard's dangerous mortal magic forever.

CHAPTER SEVEN

THE COURTS OF MAGIC

*U*naware of Frik's plans for him, Merlin continued with his studies. He met many strange and wonderful creatures in Mab's realm and its neighbouring lands. He learned of the unseen forces that held the world together, of the secret ways of other worlds that existed beneath the surface and behind the mirrors in the world he had always thought of as real. But most of all, his days were filled with the endless practice of magic.

He mastered the countless spells that made him a Wizard by Incantation, only to discover that he needed to forget them all again as he became a Wizard by Gesture, for each higher level of spell automatically erased its lower-level counterpart. Each time he learned a Hand spell, its equivalent Incantatory spell vanished from his mind, as – some time in the future, if all went well – each Thought spell would erase the Gesture it duplicated.

There were only a few Incantatory spells that were not duplicated by gestures, but those he would remember until the end of his days. As a Hand Wizard in training, Merlin's days were now spent in the practice of endless repeated gesticulations – right hand to create, left hand to banish.

As the days turned to weeks, slowly a vast and

profound boredom began to take hold of Merlin. He thought the matter over carefully, for Frik had seen to it that he learned philosophy in addition to metaphysics and etiquette, and eventually he came to realize what was bothering him. His future was a lie.

When he learned something – when he went on adventures in Mab's realm or outside it – that was *real*, because it affected him and changed him deep inside, in his heart. But the wizardry he was being taught . . . that wasn't real. The fairy magic was all based on illusion, cold and heartless and as misleading as moonlight. It didn't affect anything real.

In the most profound sense, it didn't matter.

'Now you try.'

The long table in the schoolroom had been cleared of the clutter of books and scrolls. The familiar – though now rather battered – silver candlestick sat in the middle of the table, and Merlin and Frik sat in chairs on either side.

Frik had been working with him all week on Summoning Fire by Gesture. Since his sojourn in the Forest of the Night, Merlin had disliked fire intensely. Frik said that fire elementals were the easiest to call, and so the mastery of Hand Wizardry must begin with them, but every time the bright flame flashed into being before his eyes, Merlin could hear the screams of the trapped soldiers in his mind.

Was that what he was being trained for?

'Master Merlin!'

Merlin blinked owlishly, focusing on Frik.

'If you please,' the gnome said, pointing to the candle.

Right hand. The flame blossomed at the tip of the wick.

Left hand. The light vanished as if it had never been.

'Now you,' Frik said.

'Must I?' Merlin muttered.

Sighing, he pointed his finger at the candle. Light. He suppressed a pang of queasiness. Why couldn't they do something else? Something important. Something worthwhile. The more he learned about Mab's realm, the unhappier he became. Mab had told him that he was supposed to be the one who would lead the people back to the Old Ways, but Merlin had grown up helping Ambrosia in the forest with the needs of the local farmers and villagers, and he knew that the Old Ways of sacrifice and service to the Fairy Court were things that the people could not bring themselves to return to in these days of war and chaos. The future Mab wanted for him was already a part of the dead past.

'Now put it out. Left hand, left hand. You must concentrate,' Frik said fussily.

Merlin reached out his hand, but his mind was elsewhere. He disliked the Land of Magic, but if he condemned Mab, he had to condemn himself, because she had created him and part of her would be in him always . . .

The candle exploded, spraying hot wax all over Merlin, Frik, and the table. Merlin recoiled with a cry.

'That happened because you weren't concentrating!' Frik sputtered. 'Try it again.'

'I don't want to try it again,' Merlin snapped, pushing himself to his feet and brushing uselessly at the hardening spatters of candle wax on his tunic and in his hair. 'There isn't any point. There isn't any point in any of this. None of it's real.'

He turned and stalked out of the classroom.

Deep in the dark heart of the earth, Mab brooded. The only sound within her sanctum was the muffled creaking and groaning of the rock itself, echoing through the chamber like the far-off music of whales, and the only motion, the faint breeze generated by the beating wings of the sprites who flitted through the air of her underground realm carrying out Mab's silent commands.

Here she was supreme, unchallenged, and soon her power would extend over the mortal realm as well. And afterwards, who knew? In the end, perhaps even the haughty Lord of Winter would bow the knee in acknowledgement of Mab's supremacy in the Three Worlds of Men. When Merlin ruled . . .

Mab smiled at the thought of her protégé, her child. He would rule the people of Britain, and she would rule him. She would cast down every Christian church and chapel in the land and raise up vast temples to the Old Ways. She and her people would reign supreme again.

When Merlin ruled . . .

Mab gestured, and an image appeared in the vast crystal ball before her. The globe was so perfectly transparent that it seemed almost invisible; only the reflection of light across its surface betrayed its presence. In its heart, the whole cavern of glittering rainbow crystals and Queen Mab herself were reflected, inverted and in miniature. Now a glowing image of Merlin appeared – not as he was now, but as he would be: a man grown, clad in green and silver armour and carrying a banner with her image upon it. Around him were throngs of cheering peasants, flinging flowers into his path as he rode his gleaming white destrier slowly along at the head of a cheering army toward the steps of a vast gold-roofed temple hewn from white marble. Each of its pillars was carved in the shape of a coiled dragon, and great stone serpents roared their defiance from each corner of the eaves. From the roofpeak a lofty spire reached high into the sky, and at its apex the symbol of the Old Ways gleamed in beaten gold. On its steps stood nine white-robed maidens. Each maiden had nine acolytes dressed in red, and each acolyte had nine black-cowled servants, and all the people in all the land would worship Mab.

This was how it would be, once the people welcomed Merlin as a saviour. But Mab had to plan carefully in anticipation of that great day, so that everything would go as she wished.

She'd been spying on Vortigern.

After Queen Ganieda's death, he seemed to have given up on matrimony to concentrate on architecture instead. He was building an enormous castle in the west, named Pendragon in honour both of his own totem, and of the Great Dragon which was rumoured to make its lair in that realm.

The Great Dragon . . .

The Great Dragon – Draco Magnus Maleficarum – was the last of its kind. Before man, the creatures had ruled over the entire world, filling the sea, the air and the land with their endless fiery combats. But as the aeons passed, their numbers had dwindled until only this one was left, the last dragon, its existence little more than a myth. For centuries it had slept undisturbed in a deep cave beneath the soil of Britain.

She would change that.

Vortigern needed something to worry about to take his mind off Uther. Left to himself, the royal barbarian would probably send assassins to Normandy to strangle the king-in-exile at his schoolbooks. Mab didn't want that. Once Vortigern no longer had to guard against threats from outside, who knew what might happen to Britain? Vortigern might stop persecuting his people and become a moderately sensible ruler. He might even make his peace with Avalon, allowing the new religion to spread its roots deeper into society than it was now.

No, she couldn't permit that.

Reaching out, Mab sorted through a pile of the cracked, drained crystals whose proliferation had so puzzled Frik until she found one that still had some power in it. She raised it in her hand and concentrated on her crystal ball once more.

The image of the Great Dragon appeared, curled in its cavern nest. Its hide was green and gold and brown, the colour of the earth above, and its great wings were furled in sleep.

Mab held the crystal out over the dragon's image. Magic drained from the crystal, leaving it dull and inert, and sifted down into the dragon's body, energizing it.

Soon it would wake.

And Vortigern would have more to worry about than a boy king plotting in France.

Frik hesitated outside Mab's sanctum. He'd hoped to leave Merlin practising Hand Wizardry on his own, but there was no point in attempting to get the boy to study when he was in this mood. It would probably be just as well to let Merlin have some time to himself; Frik was already late for his report to Mab on her protégé's progress. She insisted on these meetings, even though Frik provided her with daily written reports, and there was nothing to do but go along with her.

So far Frik had accomplished one of his goals: to keep Merlin from discovering his own uniquely human magical potential. Merlin had comparatively little taste for the disciplines of fairy magic, but Frik had Mab to satisfy, and Mab wanted Merlin to become her champion, a Wizard of Pure Thought who would supplant Vortigern and rule Britain as her instrument. Unfortunately, it didn't seem possible to have things both ways.

The magic lessons had been going badly ever since Merlin had come back from Anoeth and begun to study the second stage of wizardry. His progress had become slower with each day, and Frik knew why. It was nothing he hadn't seen before.

Merlin's heart had already made the choice his mind refused to consider. The changeling had chosen to side with his human half.

The boy was homesick.

'Well, how's he doing?'

Mab pounced upon Frik the moment he entered the room. She looked like some exquisite and dangerous predator. Her jewel-coloured eyes shone against the dark painted shadow that surrounded them. Her skin shimmered pallidly. Frik realized with a pang of discovery that Mab was as hard and glittering as anything in her crystal kingdom.

'You've read my report?' Frik asked, hedging.

He had not dared to don any of his many disguises for this meeting, comforting though they would have been. Mab's temper was too volatile these days, fluctuating between impatience with Merlin's slow progress toward wizardly perfection and delight at his simple presence in her realm. And what Frik had to tell her would not improve matters.

'Yes, yes,' Mab said peevishly, 'but I want your personal impressions.'

This is it, then. Mentally Frik crossed his fingers and hoped for the best.

'He's certainly got the ability,' Frik began, hoping to start on a high note. 'He could be the greatest . . .'

'I knew it!' Mab broke in eagerly. She didn't seem to – or didn't wish to – hear the equivocation in Frik's words.

'But he never will be,' Frik added quickly, wanting to have the worst out of the way immediately, before she could say he'd misled her. Mab froze, staring at him intently. Even the gems she wore didn't glitter, she was standing so still.

'He won't get past being a Hand Wizard. He doesn't want to do it. In his heart, he doesn't like magic,' Frik said in a rush, realizing the truth of the words as he spoke them.

For a moment he thought she was going to take it well. Then she flung down the crystal she'd been holding. It crashed into the pile of expended crystals heaped in one corner of the chamber, and caused them to cascade noisily across the floor.

'Doesn't like it?' Mab hissed in a bloodcurdling whisper.

She rounded on Frik, her face very close to his, inspecting him minutely as if by the force of her will she could change the truth behind his words. He'd known she wouldn't like the news, but somehow he'd also assumed that she would be as resigned to the facts as he was.

'I–I–I know it's shocking, but that's the way it is,' Frik stammered uncomfortably.

It was hard for him to imagine not 'liking' magic – to Frik, magic was as universal, as inevitable as the air itself. Yet the fact remained and Frik, at least, was willing to face it: Merlin disliked magic.

Mab spread her arms threateningly, seeming to tower over her servant in that moment. The gnome half-closed his eyes and did his best to efface himself.

'We've got to make him like it! I have work for him to do,' she proclaimed.

Even though he'd exerted himself to deliberately mislead and manipulate the boy, Frik had developed a sneaking admiration for Merlin – his resourcefulness, his stubborn human integrity. Merlin's dual heritage was tearing him apart, anyone could see that. The boy was suffering, yet all Mab thought about was *her* plans, *her* desires.

'The truth is, he wants to go home!' Frik said, goaded into honesty.

'Home?'

In an eyeblink, Mab was on the other side of the chamber, her image shimmering with fury.

'Home?' she repeated, as if demanding an answer from the hoarded crystals.

'Home?' she said again, at Frik's side and more furious than before.

'Bring him to me.'

But Merlin had unwittingly placed himself beyond the reach of Mab's wrath. When he'd left the schoolroom, he'd gone looking for some place that didn't remind him of his failures. But no matter where he turned, all he found was vast underground caverns, deep subterranean lakes, forests of crystal that he'd seen a thousand times before. The immense oppressive weight of the rock seemed to press down on him, crushing him into immobility, and Merlin yearned desperately for the vast open spaces of the forest in which he'd spent his childhood. He wanted to go home.

Home. He slid down the wall and sat down on the floor, leaning his head and back against the wall. The cold of the stone sank into his flesh like some malign opposite of sunlight, its chill making his muscles ache. He held out a hand and stared at his fingertips. Right hand . . . left hand . . . it didn't matter: in his heart, Merlin knew that he wasn't living up to his full potential. He'd been summoned here into the Land of Magic to learn, but all he'd learned was that he'd never match Mab's skill with magic – or even Frik's. He was not willing to do the things that they did.

But what could he do – what was he *supposed to be* if not her champion? He'd wanted to do right, to be good, and he was further away from understanding what that was than he'd ever been.

Merlin closed his eyes and inhaled deeply, wishing he could breathe in the familiar scents of home. But all he could smell was dampness and stone and water, the sterile dead odours of the crystal caves. The sense of being trapped, imprisoned in a desolate vault, was frighteningly strong.

He shook his head, almost overwhelmed by the sudden bleakness of his contemplations. *I don't belong here. I don't know what to do. I need someone to show me the way!* he thought desperately.

In the rock above his head a spark of light blossomed. As it grew in intensity, the rock seemed to become transparent, until for all its massiveness it seemed as insubstantial as water. And through that water a glowing figure moved, swathed in a long flowing silver gown. A necklet of live fish swam like brilliant captive stars around her neck.

'Why did you call me, Merlin?' the Lady of the Lake asked.

Merlin turned toward the voice, startled, and saw a woman he had never seen before. Her eyes were the pale blue of wintery skies, and her hair and eyebrows shimmered with the whiteness of fresh snow. She moved languidly, her hands fanning to hold her place, as though the stone in which she had manifested herself to him was in truth the liquid it appeared to be. He could tell she was a powerful creature of magic – yet he did not know who she was. Mab had introduced him personally to most of the denizens of her realm and told him about the rest . . . but who was this pale shining creature?

'I didn't . . .' Merlin began.

'You did,' the bright lady corrected him, smiling.

She seemed to radiate a wonderful unfettered aura of freedom; she emanated a stillness that was not passivity, but instead held such mystic insight and enlightenment that he sensed she had no need to rush fruitlessly about constantly doing things. It was in some strange way the opposite to all the magic that Merlin had learned in his sojourn in the Hollow Hills: a wisdom that lay not in *doing*, but in *knowing*, and Merlin's heart opened to it as if *this* were his true nature.

'Who are you?' he asked.

He sat up, leaning toward her and pushing the hair out of his eyes.

'I am the Lady of the Lake,' she told him.

Her voice was soft, humming with power, a chorus of possibilities.

'How are you getting on with my sister Mab? We two do not get on.'

The Lady of the Lake was Mab's sister? That made matters even more puzzling. Merlin trusted his instincts, and his instincts told him that the Lady of the Lake was good and wise. It seemed as if Mab's decision not to speak of her sister must be deliberate, but what possible reason could there be for it? Were they enemies? As far as Merlin knew, all the fairy kind agreed with Mab's plan to bring back the Old Ways – how could someone whose own existence was at stake not wish to see the Old Ways brought back?

'Why?' he asked, with a directness verging upon bluntness.

The Lady blinked slowly, her hands moving with hypnotic deliberation at her sides.

'I don't approve of what she's been doing,' she answered. Her voice was remote. 'Creating you and letting your mother die like that.'

The words seemed to press down on him as if they were the stone that hung over his head. His mother! He'd visited Elissa's simple grave deep in the forest many times, wondering about the woman who had given him life. Aunt Ambrosia had never spoken of his mother to him, and now, with an awful certainty, Merlin knew why. It was because his Aunt Ambrosia had been careful never to speak against Queen Mab.

'She let my mother die?' he said slowly.

A sensation for which he had no name was growing in Merlin's chest. It was as destructive as fire, as cold as the water of the Enchanted Lake, as hard and unyielding as the crystals that Mab so loved.

'Oh, dear,' the Lady said mournfully. Her pale beautiful face remained expressionless, though her voice held regret. 'I shouldn't have told you, but it just slipped out.'

She let my mother die. Mab let my mother die.

Merlin was stunned, as if he were trying to understand a lesson beyond his comprehension. He got to his knees and then to his feet, hugging himself against the cold of the cave and gazing into the Lady's moon-pale eyes.

Somehow he'd always assumed that Mab cared for him as a mother should. Aunt Ambrosia had loved him, and he'd presumed that Mab, who'd created him, loved him just as his foster-mother did. He'd been able to do all the strange and sometimes frightening things she asked of him because he'd thought she had his ultimate good at heart.

But Mab had killed his mother, and the illusion of her compassion was stripped away, leaving Merlin enveloped in confusion and bewilderment. Why did Mab want him if she did not love him? If she was not being honest about that, what else had she been dishonest about? Did she truly want him to be her champion? Did she mean him to kill for her?

Ambrosia would know. His foster-mother would

understand his bafflement and distress. She would know how to straighten things out. She would tell him the truth.

'I want to go home,' Merlin said in a low voice.

'You should,' the Lady of the Lake said. 'Ambrosia is very ill.'

'No!' Merlin said in horror.

He understood in that moment how Nimue had felt as she sank into the quicksand: safety was visible, but it was slipping away and there was nothing she could do to stop it.

'I have to go to her.' He straightened, and gazed into the Lady's face. 'Tell me how to reach her.'

When he left Mab, Frik went to the classroom, to Merlin's bedroom, to all the places in Mab's palace where he usually found the boy. There was no sign of him.

'Where is he?' Frik demanded in frustration, giving up and returning to the classroom. If gnomes had possessed imaginations, Frik would have said that the room looked more than empty; it looked abandoned, as though Merlin was never going to return here.

But that was ridiculous.

'He's gone,' Mab growled, appearing behind him.

245

Frik tried on several different expressions, none of which really fitted the occasion. 'Gone?' he bleated.

'He's on his way home to that viper-tongued witch, Ambrosia.' Mab's eyes gleamed with fury, and at that moment Frik was very glad not to be her enemy.

'But–but–but–but how can he get across the lake?' Frik demanded indignantly.

The Enchanted Lake was the border between human realms and the Land of Magic. Merlin had not been back in human lands since the day he'd come to the Hollow Hills – even the Wild Hunt, which crossed through all lands and all times, brought the magic of its own domain with it, and no one left the Hunt without Lord Idath's consent. Frik had been certain Merlin could not escape.

Besides which, the boy should not even have known he wanted to escape, much less have been able to. Not until time had done its work in the mortal realms, and all who had a claim on Merlin's human heart were safely dead.

'My dear sister . . .' Mab whispered, venom in her voice.

There had never been war between the Mistress of Magic and the Lady of the Lake, for their interests had always been too different, but now – or so it seemed to Frik – things were about to change. If the Lady of the Lake had helped Merlin to cross her territory and return to human lands . . .

'No!' Mab cried. 'Vortigern betrayed me – and now Merlin? Why must everything I love turn to ash? I won't allow it – I won't lose him!' she vowed.

'But madam –' Frik began.

Soft words and fair dealing were the only way to get Merlin's co-operation, and Mab wasn't inclined toward either at the moment.

Mab turned on Frik, her breath coming in a hiss. She gestured, and with the merest thought sent him flying across the chamber into the pile of used-up crystals. He landed with a great crash, and at the moment of his impact, Mab clenched her fists against her chest and vanished.

Merlin did not need the Lady of the Lake to tell him that he was in danger. It seemed to him that he'd been blind and foolish all the time he'd been here in the Land of Magic. Mab did not hate him – but she did not love him, either. All she loved was her plan to make the Old Ways supreme once more with Merlin as their defender, and she would destroy anyone who got in her way.

Even the one she had appointed as her champion.

As he inched along the cavern paths, the Lady of the Lake swam through the rock above as if it were the water of her lake. Merlin followed her glow through chambers in the crystal caves that he had never seen before, along a twisting route that made him edge carefully between boulders or walk along hunched over to pass beneath the tilting roof. He knew that Mab's underground kingdom was dangerous to any but his mistress, but at this precise moment he didn't care. Nothing was more important than getting home.

Home to those who *did* love him. How could he simply have *forgotten* about Ambrosia, about Nimue, about all of his friends? He'd never even tried to send Ambrosia word of how he was!

That was Mab's doing. Mab's was the fairy glamour that clouded minds and led wills astray. Frik had taught him what they were – creatures of magic whose magic was based on illusion and misdirection – but Merlin had thought it was only part of his lessons and never applied it to himself. He knew better now. He'd been so arrogant – he'd thought that just because she wanted him as her champion she wouldn't do the same things to him that she did to everyone else.

I've been such a fool!

'Merlin . . .'

The Lady's echoing voice broke into his thoughts, and Merlin realized that for the last several minutes he'd been able to hear and smell water. They must be getting near to the cave mouth that opened onto the Enchanted Lake – but without Frik to guide the boat through the lagoons and canals that led to the entrance, Merlin knew he had no chance of reaching the outside.

'. . . here . . .' said the Lady. 'You can ride him to the vessel . . .'

Merlin looked around the edge of a boulder at the still black water. Then suddenly there was a gleam in its depths, and an instant later a horse's head broke the surface.

It snorted and shook its head, spraying Merlin with a shower of droplets from its long white mane. Merlin mopped water from his face with the sleeve of his jacket and stared at the animal. It was a deep dappled grey, its mane as white as the tips of the waves on a stormy day, and its forelegs churned the water as it swam. The rest of its body could not be seen beneath the surface of the water, but as Merlin stared it became impatient with him, thrashing its tail against the water and rising up higher out of the pool.

'Hey!' Merlin cried, with mingled irritation and astonishment.

Now he could see its body clearly for the first time. The animal's torso was covered in gleaming scales, and it did not look like any horse Merlin had ever seen. Where its hind legs should have been it had a long muscled tail with broad fins, the colour of the scales gradually darkening from a silvery ivory to a deep sea-green.

'It's a sea-horse,' the Lady said, sounding amused for a moment. 'Mab does not control as much of the elements as she hopes – the creatures of water are still my allies. You must hurry, Merlin. Mab can be so thoughtless and cold.'

The thought of having to remain in Mab's realm while Ambrosia was ill galvanized Merlin into action. He sat down on the rock ledge, then slipped into the water.

It was bitterly cold, and he floundered for a moment before reaching out and grabbing the creature's mane. It felt like any other horse's mane – though wet – and as the animal bobbed in the water like a chunk of wood, Merlin managed to get his leg across its back and pull himself onto it. His weight did not push it under water as he had feared, though its powerful tail now thrashed constantly to keep its body above the surface.

'Go safely, Merlin. You will need all your cunning to prevail,' said the Lady.

He had no chance to answer her, for the sea-horse lunged forward at that moment, its powerful legs and tail churning the black water into foam, and it was all Merlin could do just to stay on its slippery scaly back. It was like riding a trotting horse – but this horse 'trotted' not over turf, but through icy water that tugged at its rider, trying to pull him from its back.

At times only his grip on its mane kept Merlin with the animal, and the faster it went, the more he choked and gasped for breath as the waves of its motion flung icy clear water into his face. He shivered both with cold and with dread as the sea-horse swam, for he was soaked to the skin and Mab's caves were as cold as the Mistress of Magic herself.

It was so easy to think badly of Mab that Merlin was ashamed of himself, but it made a kind of terrible sense. The Lady of the Lake had called her sister thoughtless and cold, and when Merlin came to think about it those words summed up Mab's character perfectly – she was as cold as the caves in which she dwelt, and once she had chosen her goal, no other consideration could be allowed to matter.

Even love.

The strange reluctance Merlin had always felt acquiescing with the plans of the fairy queen who had created him was no longer a mystery.

All along, his heart had suspected what it had taken the Lady of the Lake to tell him: that Mab was as merciless and amoral as the forces of Nature herself. But Merlin could never be like the Queen of the Old Magic, by the power of his human mother. And just as humankind did what it could to relieve Nature's ruthlessness, so Merlin must fight Mab.

As he'd been brooding, the sea-horse had swum from the smaller cave into one of the lagoons which linked Mab's palace to the canal leading into the Enchanted Lake. He heard the mermaids cry out as they spied him, and heard the faint droning as a cloud of sprites flew toward him, their high shrill voices echoing off the cavern walls.

Though the mer-creatures might aid the Lady of the Lake, the sprites were wholly Mab's creatures.

As the first sprite reached him, Merlin felt a stinging burn on his arm as it shot him with a tiny arrow. He gasped with shock, and just at that moment the sea-horse flung back its head and dived deep beneath the surface of the lagoon.

Merlin clung tightly to the sea-horse's mane as it plummeted downward. Then, to his silent horror, it levelled off far beneath the surface and began to swim onwards.

Merlin's lungs burned desperately for air. It seemed a very long time before the sea-horse headed for the surface once more, flinging its body up into the air while Merlin gasped and sputtered for breath. It hardly seemed that he managed to take a full breath before it dived again.

Choked and blinded by water, Merlin could not tell if they were still pursued. He lost count of the number of times the sea-horse surfaced and then submerged itself again, dragging him with it as if it were a seal and he just a tangled scrap in a fisherman's nets.

At last they did not dive again. For several seconds all he could do was lie against the horse's neck and pant while the water dripped from his hair and ran down his numbed face.

Warily, Merlin opened his eyes. He could see light up ahead – the mouth of the cave – and, just outside the entrance, the boat that had brought him here, bobbing lightly on the surface of the lake.

Painfully Merlin prised his cold-stiffened fingers from the sea-horse's mane. There was a narrow walkway here – Frik had run along it to reach the boat on the day Merlin had arrived – and Merlin dragged his shivering, cold-cramped body up onto that slippery refuge.

'I thank you for the ride, Master Salmon – I think!' he said.

The sea-horse shook its mane, laughing at him silently.

'Well, go on. What are you waiting for? Scat!' Merlin said.

Nothing anyone could do would be enough to induce him to mount that creature's back again, even if it meant returning to the Land Under Hill as a helpless prisoner.

As if it had read his mind, the sea-horse snorted and turned away. There was a thrashing in the water, a flash of green-webbed tail, and then it was gone.

Merlin turned all his attention toward getting into the boat. It floated just out of reach, on the far side of the boundary that separated the Lady of the Lake's domain from Queen Mab's. All he had to do was get to it before someone stopped him.

With painful slowness Merlin dragged himself along the narrow ledge. The wind that blew from the Land of Magic to the mortal world cut through his sodden clothes like a knife of elemental cruelty.

The winter wind gets crueller every year, she thought, pulling her grey shawl tighter around her thin shoulders.

It had been eighteen years now since Elissa died, and the first snow always made Ambrosia think of her and of the first winter the two of them had spent wandering, at the mercy of the elements, while Elissa's fragile body grew great with child.

Funny how every thought comes back around to the boy these days, Ambrosia thought without humour. She missed him more with each day he was gone – not for herself, she told herself fiercely, but for what Mab might be doing to him.

'Ah, girl, you're getting old – and maudlin with age,' Ambrosia said aloud.

She levered herself painfully up from her seat by the fire, trying not to see how small and empty the forest hut was now that Merlin was gone.

There wasn't much employment for a wise-woman in winter, other than the odd birthing, but there was still plenty of work to do: wood to chop and water to draw. Herne was always ready to turn his hand to that, bless him for his help. She wasn't any too spry these days. The pains in her chest came more and more often, along with the weakness in her arms and the dizzy spells, and she yearned for the warmth of the summers she'd known as a young girl. The winters had been warmer, too, as Ambrosia recalled – not this icy north wind spitting snow that found every chink in the walls of the hut.

Once she would have swept it up before it could melt, but nowadays the effort was too much for her. Let it melt. Who would there be to care in a year or two?

Or even a month or two. You're fooling yourself if you think you're going to be around to see in the spring.

She wished she could see Merlin for one last time. Only to see how he fared.

Only that.

Her chest ached, and with more than the cold. Perhaps a cup of herbal tea would ease it, and making herself the tea would do something to take her mind off the boy. With painful care Ambrosia measured dried herbs – comfrey, foxglove, horehound – into a thick brown drinking horn. She always kept a kettle on the hob in the winter, and the water should be hot enough to make an infusion.

But again her mind wandered away from the task at hand, back to her worries – and Merlin.

What was Mab teaching him, there in her palace in the Hollow Hills? Was he happy learning to master his magic, or did he miss the simple pleasures of home? Was Mab being kind to him – or was she turning him into the same sort of heartless monster that she was?

Roughly, Ambrosia rubbed away a teardrop. She knew the answer from long experience – Mab had no kindness in her. But Ambrosia could hope that the Queen of the Old Magic had enough self-interest left to see how special Merlin was. For all his impetuous nature, he was kindness itself, and he would be kind to Mab as well, if she would only let him. If she broke his spirit with her cruelty and indifference, it would be more than Ambrosia could bear. And she would know if that happened – she had no doubt of that. You couldn't raise a child from the moment it first drew breath and not be linked to it, certainly not if you had once been a priestess of the Old Ways, as she had.

Only let him be happy, and I won't even ask that he be safe! She did not know to whom she made this promise, for in her lifetime Ambrosia had broken with the old gods and never accepted the new, but she made it sincerely. Only let Merlin be happy.

She sighed and reached for the kettle, when suddenly the air in the little forest hut turned bitterly cold – a chill not of the body alone, but of the soul. Ambrosia hunched her shoulders against it involuntarily, the ache in her chest spreading with her dismay.

'Where is he?' Mab hissed.

Ambrosia did not even bother to turn around.

'Ah, here you are again, still a chip off the old glacier,' she mocked, pouring her tea as if a visit from the Mistress of Magic were an everyday occurrence.

'Where's Merlin?' Mab repeated, and this time Ambrosia did turn around, steeling herself to show no surprise.

The Queen of the Old Ways looked less like a human mortal than Ambrosia could ever remember seeing her. Her dark and glittering robes were encrusted with elaborate decoration, hanging stiffly from her body like folds of carved stone. Her face looked less like a living face than an image of a face – a beautiful jewelled mask, made inhuman by fury.

'So you've lost him, have you?' Ambrosia asked coolly.

She did not want Mab to see what joy she took in the knowledge that Merlin had run from her, but if he had, then surely it meant the she-spider's sorcery had failed her, didn't it? It meant that Merlin had seen through Mab and rejected what she had to teach him. His human mother's heritage had won out after all.

'Don't provoke me, Ambrosia!' Mab snarled. 'I'm in no mood for your gibes!'

The Queen of the Old Ways was more than simply angry – she was as furious as Ambrosia had ever seen her, and inwardly Ambrosia rejoiced at her adversary's discomfiture.

With so much passion between the two of them, Ambrosia and Mab could never have simply remained indifferent to each other once their paths had crossed. The coin would have had to fall on the side of either love or hate. The battle between what Mab represented and what Ambrosia did was never over and never would be; it would continue forever, the adversaries changing but the conflict going on.

'I'm worried about the boy, too,' Ambrosia said levelly.

You should have looked after him better! her heart cried.

'He'll be here. He's heard you're ill,' Mab cooed.

Any sympathy Ambrosia felt vanished in the face of Mab's feline self-interest.

'I'm not ill. I'm dying,' Ambrosia said, and remembered words of long ago. *'She's not dying. She's dead,'* Mab had said of Elissa on that long-past autumn day. Elissa had given the child into Ambrosia's arms, and Mab had given him a name. And now it had come full circle and Merlin was caught between the two of them – and what they represented – once more.

Ambrosia was abruptly filled with bone-weariness at the thought. Groping her way to a chair, she eased herself into it.

Mab watched her with birdlike interest but no scrap of compassion. The Queen of the Old Ways understood human frailty as little as she understood human love.

'When he comes, send him back,' Mab demanded. She began to pace the hut like a leopard in a cage, her fury making it impossible for her to remain still.

'Can't you make him come back?' Ambrosia asked, unable to resist a last taunt.

Have you found something that you can neither bend to your will nor pretend out of existence? He'll be stronger than you in the end because of his humanity – you mark my words, Queen Mab!

'It's better if you tell him his place is with me,' Mab said, a vindictive smile on her face.

Love might be beyond her capacity, but Mab under-stood spite and vengeance very well. Humans had taught her that, over the generations.

'No,' Ambrosia said, suddenly tired of the verbal fencing. 'No, I won't do that.'

'You defy me?' Mab demanded incredulously, as if she'd only just discovered the fact.

What dreams of victory Merlin must have raised in her heart to have made her so arrogant, so confi-dent!

'Of course I defy you – I've always defied you,' Ambrosia answered irritably.

'Why? *Why?*' Mab cried, and in that moment Ambrosia had the answer to their long conflict.

'It's my nature,' she said simply.

New religion or Old Ways, she realized at last that she would have fought with all her strength against anyone who had tried to compel her belief and loy-alty with nothing more than a demand. And Merlin would do the same – she'd given the boy that much of herself.

She wished Mab would leave so she could lie down to wait for Merlin. She was weary, so weary . . .

'When my boy comes here, I won't say a word. He'll do what's in his heart,' Ambrosia said.

He has *a heart, unlike you.*

As if that final word – heart – were the ultimate act of insolence, Mab opened her mouth in a sound-less wail of cheated rage. Chaos rose around her in a thunderclap, shaking the hut and its contents as a weasel would shake a rabbit. The fire blew out, furniture tumbled about as if it were made of straw. Cooking pots and jars of herbs flew everywhere. The kettle, still half-full of steaming water, flew across the room and struck Ambrosia on the shoulder, knocking her from her seat.

Her anger, the sudden shock of the storm, was too much for Ambrosia's weakened condition. She lay where she had fallen, clutching at her chest as if her fingers could ease away this pain as they had eased so many others.

'Now look what you made me do!'

The cheated selfishness in Mab's voice made Ambrosia laugh weakly, even as she winced at the pain.

Oh, dear, mustn't do that . . .

'Ambrosia!' Mab cried. 'Ambrosia, what is it?'

'You tell me,' the once-priestess whispered painfully. 'You're the great Mistress of Magic . . .'

The air seemed strangely flat once the boat began

moving across the surface of the lake, and Merlin realized after a moment that what it lacked was the scent of magic that he had breathed all during his stay in Mab's domain.

Well, I don't miss it, he told himself stubbornly.

There was an unlighted brazier in the bottom of the open boat – a common enough accessory when the sailing was likely to be hard and cold – and Merlin quickly summoned fire to warm himself and dry his clothes. It was harder to do here than it had been in the crystal caves, and the effort left him weak and gasping. But it was still more – far more – than any mere mortal could do.

I'm not a mortal. I'm Mab's child. I'm a wizard. No matter what else happens, I have Mab to thank for that.

If he could really be certain whether he wanted to thank her for the gift of magic – or curse her for it.

The return trip, sped by the magic of the Lady of the Lake, seemed to go more swiftly than the outward voyage had, and soon the boat's keel was grinding along the stones of the shore. The whole landscape was dusted in white, and the trees were bare of leaves.

It's winter.

It had been summer when he left, but Merlin had literally no idea of how long he'd been in Mab's domain. Had it really only been a few months? Or had it been years?

He had to go home.

Longing for the forest drew him nearly as strongly as his love for Ambrosia, but now Merlin faced another obstacle. The forest was miles from here, and he did not have Mab's magic horse to ride home upon.

Then he realized he did not need Mab's magic when he could summon his own.

He searched until he found what he needed: a fallen branch, polished smooth by the elements, that was long enough to serve as a walking stick – but Merlin did not intend to walk. There were still a few spells that he remembered from his days as a Wizard by Incantation that would serve him now.

He flung the stave into the air.

It did not fall, but hung there against the winter sky as if someone were holding it up.

'Horse and hattock – horse and home – horse and pelatis: go – go!'

The stave shuddered as his wizard-magic filled it, its colour changing from winter brown to gleaming silver, though each whorl of the grain could still be seen against the enchanted wood.

Merlin quickly straddled it, his hands gripping it tightly. The enchanted stave rose into the sky and began to move forward with the speed of a running horse. Merlin soared over the treetops, borne aloft by magic.

He was going home.

CHAPTER EIGHT

THE COURTS OF HONOUR

S *omeone was dying.*

He'd learned to shut out the warnings over the years – you could do anything with practice – and there weren't that many people in Barnstable Forest anyway. All the more reason that this summons to a duty long abandoned took Herne the Hunter completely by surprise.

Once, long ago, he'd ridden with the Wild Hunt, and when he'd received the knowledge of a soul about to pass into Anoeth that consciousness had meant he must turn and go in search of it to bring it to his master, Lord Idath.

But those days were gone – he had relinquished his horned crown and the power of his heritage in the fairy realm to become a simple forester. All who served the Lord of Winter knew that all things must pass, and if the memory of the Old Ways were fated to pass out of Britain, then Herne vowed he, too, would depart gracefully. Why was he being summoned back to his old commitments now?

Herne straightened up, gazing around himself for danger as warily as any other forest dweller. He'd been gathering fell-timber for Ambrosia, and had been just about to shoulder his bundle when the warning came.

Ambrosia.

He knew she was ill – was this her time? There were things he could do to ease her passing and guarantee her safe voyage into the Summerland, that paradise that the Christians now claimed as their own Heaven. But Christian or pagan, all were welcome in the Summerland, and somehow this did not feel like an ordinary summons to guide a wandering soul upon its journey.

Grabbing up his quarterstaff, Herne began to run toward Ambrosia's hut.

'Ambrosia!' Mab cried again, as the once-priestess tried weakly to get to her feet.

This was all part of some trick, Mab was certain of that. And she was running out of time – Merlin would be here at any moment to misinterpret all he saw.

Suddenly she thought of a plan. Merlin would come here looking for his foster-mother – but what if Ambrosia were gone? Mab could whisk Ambrosia, her hut, everything the woman owned, out of this clearing in the twinkling of an eye, and deposit them where Merlin would never find them. Soon he would give up looking and return to the Land of Magic.

And to Mab.

She raised her hands to weave the spell.

'You never could leave well enough alone, could you, Queen Mab?' a man's voice asked from behind her.

Mab spun around, her teeth bared in a feral hiss.

A man in green huntsman's leathers stood in the doorway, gazing at her steadily with cold grey eyes.

She knew him from long ago, when he had not been mortal, but a huntsman still.

'So, Herne the Hunter – you come slinking back to regain my favour,' Mab said.

Herne did not answer. He looked past Mab to where Ambrosia lay on the floor of the hut, and his expression hardened into anger.

'You always did have a high opinion of yourself, oh Queen of the Old Ways. You were never my liege – and I would defy you now if you were.'

Long ago, Herne had set aside his power in order to become the mortal champion of a people beset by the unjust policies of a tyrant king – Britain would remember that about him, he knew, when even his name was gone.

Mab snarled wordlessly. 'This is nothing to do with you, Hunter,' she said. 'Leave us!'

'If it concerns Ambrosia – or Merlin – then it is to do

with me,' Herne answered. 'The boy must have escaped your clutches if you've come back here looking for him. I won't let you trick him into going back with you again.'

Enraged beyond speech, Mab flung out her hand to launch a killing bolt of fairy-fire at her tormentor. But Herne was fast enough to evade it – he ran for the edge of the clearing, and the cover of the trees.

Mab was there before him, materializing in an eye-blink.

'You cannot stand against me. You have given up much, Forest Lord, to be the champion of mortals who have betrayed the Old Ways. You are not my equal in power or in cunning.' She smiled coldly at him. Believing him now to be at her mercy, she raised her hands to dispatch him.

'Perhaps not,' Herne answered. 'But I can call on one who is.'

He raised his hand, and plucked the Horn of Idath out of the wintry air.

The Horn of Idath was one of the thirteen sacred treasures of Britain, each as magical in its own way as the Grail of the Christians, which many said was only the Cauldron of Idath in a new form. So long as all thirteen of the treasures existed, the realm of Britain would endure no matter what evils beset it. Aeons ago the treasures had been lost by their ancient guardians, scattered across the land and hidden from the sight of men and fairyfolk. Only the whereabouts of a few were known today, even by Mab's kind, which had once had the keeping of all of them.

The Horn of Idath was one of those few treasures which remained visible in the mortal world. It had the power to strike terror into those who heard it, to suspend time . . . or to call its maker to aid the wielder.

'You would not dare to summon Lord Idath and his Wild Hunt to your aid!' Mab cried in disbelief.

Herne smiled grimly. 'There's quite a lot I'll dare and you know it, Queen Mab. Do you think I won't tell young Merlin what you've done to Ambrosia? She's ill and weak – is this how you repay her for raising your boy?'

'She didn't do that for me – she did it for herself!' Mab cried furiously. She lashed out at Herne before he could blow the jewelled horn – it spun from his grasp, burying itself in a drift of fallen leaves.

Herne glanced from Mab to the horn. 'So it's still true,' he said, backing away from her. 'Your magic cannot kill, though it can trick others into doing your

killing for you. Is that what you want to make of Merlin
– something that will kill for you?'

'Silence!' Mab cried.

She might not be able to kill Herne directly, but
there were many things she could do to hurt him,
Herne knew. And if she thought to summon a pack
of griffins . . .

He must reach the horn. Desperately, Herne summoned the magic that was left to him, shaping it into
a bolt with which to strike her. She was weaker now
than she had been at the height of her power, and
if he could force her to change to any of her animal
forms – raven, owl, wolf – she would be vulnerable.
Summoning all his strength, he cast his spell.

But his magic had no effect – his power fell away
from Mab's defences like a glittering fall of ice-crystals.
And at that moment, Mab struck.

Herne struggled powerlessly as her magic enfolded
him, realizing in a last despairing moment of consciousness that Mab was more subtle than he'd dreamed. He
did not need to die for her to win.

His whole body stiffened helplessly. In an instant his
toes became roots, tearing through the soles of his boots
and seeking the earth below. His arms were forced
toward the pale snowy sky, his fingers lengthening and

shooting heavenward to become a myriad of winter-bare branches. He threw his head back in a silent cry as flesh became wood. His body, his consciousness, slowed to the vegetable rhythms of the earth as he became one with the green growing things of the forest.

In a moment, Mab's spell had worked its transformation, and where Herne had stood a moment before, a mighty oak now raised its branches to heaven.

Mab stepped back, regarding her work with satisfaction. With a flick of her fingers she summoned a swarm of sprites to seek out and bring the Horn of Idath to her. They found it easily, but it took a dozen of them to lift it, and the sound of their wings buzzed with the strain as they carried the horn carefully to their mistress. Its pale jewelled curve gleamed in the winter twilight.

Only a Lord of Fairy, such as Herne had been – or a great wizard – could sound this horn to summon her consort, Idath, Lord of Time and Death. Merlin would be the last of those, and she would see to it that he never suspected the horn's existence.

Mab took the horn from her sprites and placed it carefully in a fork of the branches of the great oak. When spring came the leaves would hide the Horn of Idath from sight, and in time the branches would grow over it, trapping it and its magic within the trunk of the tree for all time.

'Now you may guard this forest forever,' Mab crooned, running her gleaming hand over the tree's bark.

Now she could deal with Merlin.

The wizard magic in his staff carried Merlin homewards, whisking him through the chill winter air from the shore of the Enchanted Lake through the clouds that lay over the hills and valleys of Britain. Slowly the landscape below began to seem familiar once more, and then he was flying low above the road that led from Nottingham Town to Lord Lambert's castle.

'*Hattock and horse – hattock and home!*' Merlin cried.

The reversal of the spell should have caused the flying stave to descend gently to the ground once more, but Merlin was cold, tired, and worried. The command of the flying spell slipped through the intangible grasp of his wizard's will in exactly the way his control over the candle-lighting spell had earlier.

The stave spun wildly in the air for a moment; Merlin lost both his grip and his balance almost instantly. He was flung through the air to land with a bruising crash in a pile of fallen leaves. Twirling out of control in the air above, the stave burst like a dropped jug, spraying splinters through the air before the largest remaining chunks of wood fell to the ground.

Merlin sat up with a groan.

'It serves me right, I suppose,' he said ruefully.

He got to his feet, rubbing the sorest spots. He was close enough to home now to be able to travel the rest of the way on foot. Quickly Merlin began to walk – and then to run – in the direction of Ambrosia's cottage.

The knowledge that she was dying brought Ambrosia a great peace. At last she could lay down the tangled threads of the responsibilities she'd taken up with her life. She'd done as well as she could for all her loved ones. Most of them had preceded her into the land of Anoeth, where they waited for her in the golden fields of the Summerland. There was only one love that she was leaving behind.

'Aunt A! Aunt A!'

As if her dying thoughts had summoned him, Merlin burst into the hut. His face was pale with fright at the destruction he saw all around him – the after-effects of the rage of a fairy queen. He skidded to a halt and knelt beside Ambrosia where she lay on the floor in a jumble of household goods, reaching for her hand.

Ambrosia smiled painfully up at him, searching his

face with her eyes. He wasn't much older, but he'd changed in the Land of Magic; she could see it in his gaze. He was no longer a boy – there was both sorrow and knowledge in his eyes, the glimmerings of the man he would become. Now Merlin knew all the secrets of his true nature, and till the end of his days he would be forever trapped between the two worlds of mortal and magic, never to belong fully to either.

But Ambrosia was content. *You'll never have him for your accomplice, Mab. He's mine. You gave him to me – to the mortal world – with my death.*

'Dear boy, dear boy,' Ambrosia whispered.

The easy tears of illness filled her eyes.

'What's wrong?' Merlin asked. His voice trembled as he took in the enormity of the destruction and the pallor of his foster-mother's face. He touched a fold of her shawl with trembling fingers, feeling fearful and lost in a way he had never been before. Deep inside he'd expected to find the forest cottage exactly as he'd left it, but all of Ambrosia's careful house-keeping had been destroyed by the fury of a force impossible for Merlin to imagine. His childhood home looked worse than if a bear had blundered into it and smashed everything in a blind rage, and in the middle of this terrible destruction, his Aunt Ambrosia lay dying.

'Nothing's wrong,' Ambrosia whispered with effort. 'Everything's as it should be now.'

Merlin whimpered deep in his throat, trying to deny the evidence of his senses. His Aunt Ambrosia *couldn't* die. He needed her. He would always need her.

He fought back his tears. Ambrosia seemed to be roused by his bewilderment and desperation to give him one last comfort. 'Merlin – Merlin, remember. Only listen to your heart.'

His heart. As though it had ever done anything but confuse him with contradictory warnings he had not understood until it was too late.

And then, as he watched, Ambrosia closed her eyes and was gone, as if a bright candle flame had been quenched, leaving only the wick behind. Ambrosia's body remained, lying on the floor of the hut, but the spirit that had been *Ambrosia* was gone, never to be met with again in this lifetime.

Merlin was alone. He would have to make his own choices, discover his own truths without Ambrosia's help, for all the days left of his life. The last person who had truly loved him was dead.

He did not, in that moment, consider Nimue. For

all her youth and beauty, he had known her only briefly; Ambrosia had raised him. She had been a part of him, understanding him better than he understood himself.

Slowly Merlin rose to his feet. He turned toward the door of the hut, and was unsurprised to find Mab standing there, waiting for him.

Always before he had been dazzled by her, a little overwhelmed. But it was as if now his anger had stripped away her fairy glamour, and she was no longer impressive, even in her elaborate whimsical garb. Despite her high-piled raven hair, Mab was even shorter than he was, and somehow unreal – a strange, dangerous vestige of an ancient time that was justifiably over, never to come again.

'You killed her!' Merlin said.

He saw clearly now, and at last he realized what the cold hard pain in his chest was: rage. Rage at Mab, who had lied to him, misled him, deceived him, taken Ambrosia from him.

Taken everything from him.

'No, I didn't,' Mab said. Her face was as cool and remote as always.

'You killed her like you killed my real mother!' Merlin cried.

Some part of him hungered for Mab's understanding, her grief. He wanted her to weep for what she had done.

'No,' Mab said, shaking her head. She enunciated slowly, carefully, as though she were speaking to a dull-witted child. 'I only *let* her die.' She smiled at Merlin as if she were pleased to have explained it so neatly.

There is no difference! His rage boiled over, mastering him swifter than thought. Merlin raised his hand to strike her, his fist plunging toward her chest as though his hand held a dagger. If he could have killed her in that instant, he would have done so.

But for all Merlin's training and untapped power, Mab was still the stronger. His hand stopped inches from her body, held back by an invisible shield.

'You haven't the power to strike me,' Mab told him, her voice faintly chiding.

'Watch my power grow!' Merlin cried.

He stared into Mab's eyes, feeding his fury with the lack of remorse he saw there. Mab had used him, just as she used everyone. When her tools broke she did not mourn them – she merely cast them aside. Nobody mattered to her.

Merlin called upon everything he knew, everything

he was, trying to force his attack home. His hand moved closer, but he still could not strike. It seemed as though there were some great reservoir of power just tantalizingly out of his reach – something that he could attain if he could only figure out *how*.

But before he could touch it, Mab thrust him aside, as if she'd only been toying with him as she assessed his strength. Merlin fell sprawling to the floor of the hut beside Ambrosia's body.

'That was very good, Merlin. I'm impressed,' Mab said approvingly. She spoke as if she hadn't even noticed his fury and hatred.

'I'll never forgive you – never!' Merlin shouted.

He struggled to his feet, weak and out of breath. He had no magic left, only the power of his human emotions – and he burned like a bright torch with his revulsion against all that Mab stood for. For the first time he understood in his heart why the new religion despised the fairyfolk so: their callous indifference to suffering was as damaging to the human spirit as any hatred could be. The two races could never peacefully co-exist: if the fairyfolk did not rule mankind as its slaves, then mankind must destroy them.

'I'm sorry about your mother and Ambrosia, but they were casualties of war,' Mab said at last. It was as if she had just now remembered that some explanation of her actions might be called for, not as if she meant it. 'I'm fighting to save my people from extinction.'

'I don't care if you die and disappear,' Merlin said furiously.

In that moment he meant it with all of his heart. *Die, disappear, vanish – we have no use for your kind, or for your lying magic!*

'I will, unless I fight and win!' Mab assured him seriously. 'That was why you were created.'

To help Mab, against people like Ambrosia? He could not bear the thought. To be her servant would be to help her do far worse than anything Vortigern had ever done. Merlin shook his head, appalled by the knowledge of how close he'd come to becoming what Mab wanted. In his mind, Mab had become a black serpent, coiling around the things he loved and crushing the life out of them.

'I will never help you,' he vowed.

'You will,' Mab purred, her green eyes gleaming with wolf-light. 'I'll *make* you help me.'

Merlin shook his head mutely. The day had held too many tragic shocks for him to be able to articulate his new wisdom, but it burned within him, transfixing his soul like a burning sword. This day would always live in his memory as the one upon which he'd been given absolute understanding of goodness and evil.

And Mab was evil.

The Queen of the Old Ways smiled, confident of her eventual victory. She turned away from Merlin and moved toward the door of the hut, vanishing as she approached it, going back to her hidden kingdom.

Merlin waited, but nothing more happened. Neither Frik nor any of Mab's other servants came to torment him. He was alone. And for the first time he was on his own. There was no one he could turn to for help.

Blaise? Herne? Perhaps they could help him, but later. For now, his grief was too raw to admit the existence of anyone else's feelings. He picked up Ambrosia's frail body and laid it tenderly down upon her bed, covering her gently with a blanket. Then he turned to undoing the destruction Mab had brought to his home, as if by erasing her works he could erase her very existence.

Frik had known the instant Mab returned to the Land of Magic that the news was bad, and he did not feel the need to learn anything more. If she had returned without Merlin, it could only mean that the boy had successfully defied her, and Frik could not remember the last time something like that had happened.

It was true that her allies had betrayed her – like Vortigern – or disappointed her – like the priestess Ambrosia – but Merlin was different. Or at least he had been, assuming he was still the boy who had left here, and not a stag or a tree or an owl or something even worse. Mab's magic couldn't kill, but it could make you wish it had, and when she lost her temper she could be quite, quite unreasonable. Bearing that in mind, Frik did his very best to become invisible and immaterial.

'*Frik!*'

It didn't work, of course.

Mab appeared abruptly in the cavern where Frik had done his best to transform himself into a limestone pillar. With a sweep of her fingers she dispelled the illusion, leaving Frik standing there in a crouch, feeling faintly ridiculous and very apprehensive.

He'd been wearing a horned headdress and a lot of animal skins, hoping to be mistaken for a cave painting if all else failed. With a sigh, he banished the clothing, lest it provoke her further, and returned to his plain black garb.

'You let him defy me!' Mab raged.

Not only furious, but petty-minded. Always blaming

others even when – *if* – there was no one really to blame.

'Well to be perfectly accurate, he couldn't have got anywhere without the help of your dear sister,' Frik said recklessly. 'If I may say so, madam, it really would help matters if you two could agree to –'

'When I want your advice, Frik, I'll ask for it!' Mab snapped. 'He thinks he can defeat me – Merlin – but he's wrong. He'll use his magic – I'll force him to!'

There was no safe answer to make to Queen Mab when she was in this mood, but for the first time, Frik really began to doubt her superior leadership. She'd plotted and planned for as long as Frik could remember and every single one of her plans had come to nothing – including the creation of Merlin, the champion of the Old Ways for whom she'd had such hopes. Even the least suspicious-minded person might begin to wonder whether Mab actually *deserved* to succeed after so many failures, all of which were at least partially caused by herself.

Mab's head whipped around and she glared at Frik as though she could hear his thoughts. Frik assumed his most servile posture. This constant abuse had got to be very wearing, and he found that now that the boy was gone he missed Merlin's company more than he would have expected. Even when the lad was in a temper, he'd never taken it out on Frik. Now Merlin had defied Mab to her face – and about time, too, after all she'd put the lad through, if you asked him – and of course Mab wasn't taking it at all well.

'What are you going to do, madam?' he asked nervously.

'Come and see!'

She vanished, leaving Frik to guess where she'd gone and find his own way there.

The gnome squared his shoulders self-consciously.

It was too much to hope for that the worst was over. Whatever was about to happen, it wasn't going to be pleasant.

Mab barely acknowledged the arrival of her servant when Frik reached her Sanctum Sanctorum. She was gazing into her scrying crystal, fury fuelling her power.

How dare Merlin place his petty concerns ahead of her own! She was fighting for the survival of an entire *race* – what could one old woman's life matter against that? Selfish, cruel, obstinate . . . the boy was a catalogue of the worst human traits! She'd been a fool to hope that a creature like Frik could rouse in him a proper appreciation of fairy virtues or make him understand the nobility of the battle Mab fought. No, Merlin took after his mortal half, short-sighted and petty.

If you want something done right, do it yourself, Mab fumed bitterly. She'd paid too much attention to Ambrosia's prattling about love and compassion – she'd tried to be *kind* to Merlin, and only see how well that had worked out! The fairyfolk were not kind. Kindness was not part of Mab's nature. It shouldn't be part of Merlin's, either.

Now she would do what she should have done from the very beginning. She would show Merlin the full extent of her power, prove to him that his rebellion was foolish – and more than foolish: impossible. She would make him understand that the human world held nothing for him, that she, Queen Mab, was his natural ally, and the reinstatement of the Old Ways was his ultimate destiny.

Uther – Vortigern – she would sweep them both away and bring Merlin back to serve her if she had to drown all of Britain in mortal blood.

She gazed into the crystal. It showed her the image of the Great Dragon: Draco Magnus Maleficarum, the last of its kind. It had been born and bred for war, and today at last she would awaken it. She had been tapping the power of her realm for months, siphoning it into its inert body, and now her labours would bear fruit.

Mab clutched a fresh and potent crystal in each hand, willing all the chthonic power of the earth into Maleficarum's sleeping body. The great form reflected in her crystal began to shudder, its ribs rising as it took first one labouring breath, then another.

'Madam, are you quite certain this is wise?' Frik asked, very softly.

'Oh, yes . . .' Mab hissed.

Suddenly, within the crystal, Maleficarum raised its head. The ancient yellow eyes snapped open, blazing with fury, and the long triangular head on its snakelike neck whipped around as it gazed about its cave. It tried to rise to its feet, only to be balked by the walls of the cave. For an instant it seemed baffled by its confinement, then suddenly it gave a furious roar, a sound that echoed from the sides of the cavern with force enough to dislodge stalactites from the ceiling.

But Maleficarum was not done. It roared again, and this time the sound was accompanied by a rush of corrosive flame. The stream of fire met the wall of the grotto, and the rock seemed to shrivel out of its path, leaving a smoking blackened passage through the rock.

Determinedly, Maleficarum began to worm its serpentine body through the tunnel, toward freedom ... and prey.

It had slept for a long time, and it was hungry.

'The Great Dragon will ravage the land,' Mab gloated. 'Vortigern will build strongholds against its power in vain – Uther will think him weak and distracted, and plan his own attack in turn. And Merlin will be caught between them, a pawn that each side will claim as its own weapon. He will not be content to pretend to be a mere mortal – not when he can be a wizard . . .'

Frik regarded the crystal-sent image of the monster burrowing through the rock with professional distaste. There was no illusion to it, no subtlety – nothing but a brute hunger for destruction.

Frik's artistic soul rebelled against the very notion. Where was the challenge, the skill in winning through brute force?

It didn't seem fair, somehow.

Not that he would be foolish enough to say any such thing to Mab.

After a few hours of work Merlin realized that there was little he could do to repair Mab's damage to the forest cottage in a single day or even a single week. And there were more pressing priorities before him than tidying up his home.

At last he steeled himself to search through the debris until he found a spade. The winter air was biting as he left the cottage, and the friendly forest around the cottage, trees and woodlands that he had known all his life, now somehow looked oppressive and alien. He tried to shut out the *lostness* he felt, searching for the landmarks that would lead him to his destination.

He'd first stumbled over Elissa's grave as a child, long before he'd understood that Ambrosia somehow wasn't his real mother. When he'd asked Ambrosia about the grave, she'd explained about Elissa and why his real mother had to go away. She'd done the best she could, but the child Merlin hadn't been able to grasp the idea of death: for weeks afterwards he'd come here to sit upon the grave-mound and tell Elissa the things he did with his day, imagining her living just as he did, only in a house far beneath the surface of the earth. Eventually he'd lost interest, as children do, in what had been little more than a new game to him, but the idea of Elissa had always retained a sort of determined reality in his imagination, as though she were present and living but just out of reach.

Later, when Merlin better understood what death was, Elissa had not lost that kind of material existence in his imagination, for even before his training as a wizard and his visit to Anoeth, Merlin had known that death was simply another land to which everyone emigrated in the end.

And now both his dearest loved ones would be there.

After a short walk he reached the forest clearing where Elissa was buried, and for a moment he simply gazed at her grave, sobered by the enormity of what he must do. Then he marked out the dimensions of Ambrosia's grave beside Elissa's, scoring the snow-dusted earth with the edge of his spade, and began to dig.

Magic would have made everything easy, but Merlin had sworn to renounce all the magic he'd learned in Mab's kingdom and he meant to keep his vow. He knew he had been created to become Mab's champion. He wished he could forget it. Her blood ran in his veins, and each time he gave in to the temptation to use the magic he'd learned, Merlin knew he would become a little more like Queen Mab, until in the end there would be no difference between them and he would do everything she wanted without a single qualm. He had not chosen to be born a child of the Old Ways, his bloodline was no fault of his, but still the knowledge of his heritage gnawed at him as if it were a guilty secret, something wicked of which he should be ashamed.

At last the grave was dug, and his hands and shoulders ached from the labour of digging in the half-frozen ground. Now all that remained was to lay Ambrosia to rest. He knew that her friends would wish to be there when she was placed in the earth, and he went in search of them.

He knew somehow before he reached the hermit's hut that it would be empty, but Merlin went to see what was there anyway. An early storm had carried away many of the twigs that had made up its walls, and Merlin could see inside to the one tiny room. It was empty of all possessions, even Blaise's few beloved books.

The whole area had an air of long desertion. The clearing was full of windblown rubbish, the firepit filled with autumn leaves. No one had lived here for a long time.

Merlin shook his head, unable to believe it. Where

had the old hermit gone – and when? Had Blaise been forced to leave the forest against his will? How long had Merlin been absent from the mortal world, learning Mab's tainted magic?

There were no answers to his questions, and Merlin knew there never would be.

With a growing sense of despair, he went off in search of Herne. Though he did not know where the huntsman lived, he knew that Herne would never abandon his beloved forest, nor any of his favourite places in it. But though Merlin searched until the light became too dim for him to see his way, he could not find Herne either.

A terrible suspicion began to grow in his mind, that somehow with a wave of her hand Mab had erased everyone Merlin had ever known, so that he would be utterly alone and lonely.

I won't let you defeat me, Merlin vowed silently.

Wearily he returned to the cottage in the forest that he'd shared with his foster-mother.

The next day, when the sun rose, he laid Ambrosia to rest beside his true mother, Elissa.

There was a small cross such as the Christians used over his birth-mother's grave, but over Ambrosia's grave Merlin set no marker, only a border of white stones around the carefully smoothed and snowy earth.

In death as in life, Ambrosia would pay homage to no god.

The forest around him was stark and still with winter. Snow had fallen again the night before, and now there was a light sprinkling of white upon the bare black branches. Spring would not come for many months, and for Merlin they would be cold and hungry months, with Ambrosia's larder gone and her supplies scattered by Mab's attack.

But he would survive. The forest was his home.

If Mab thought that either hunger or cold would drive Merlin back to her, she was wrong. There was one last piece of magic he would perform, to seal his decision for all time.

He knelt at the head of the twin graves, and took a small flint knife from the pocket of his coat. He'd found it in the ruin of the hut, and recognized it as the one Ambrosia used in gathering herbs for her magic, for iron disrupted the life energies that gave many plants their magical virtue. It would serve as well for this purpose as it had for hers.

He held out his right hand over the fresh grave-earth, and with the knife in his left hand, cut a deep wound in the palm of his right hand. The pain burned harder than frostbite, but Merlin did not flinch. Blood was magic, words were magic: to swear in blood was a binding thing, that even the Old Ones must listen to.

'I swear,' Merlin said in a level voice, as his blood dripped to the earth, 'I swear on Ambrosia's grave and on the grave of my mother, that I will only ever use my powers to defeat Queen Mab. This I swear.'

He swept his hand outward, sprinkling the earth with drops of blood.

At the place where each drop of blood had fallen, tiny scarlet pimpernels sprang up out of season, blooming for a moment before they withered away again with the cold.

So. The earth accepts my vow.

And Mab, Merlin knew, had heard him, and he knew that she would do anything to reclaim his loyalty, try any trick, take any hostage.

That was why no action was safe.

Once he'd dreamed of being a knight, doing good works and winning the love of fair ladies through his heroism. Today, Merlin put those dreams aside forever. His only safety from Mab lay in being more cunning than she was, more clever. He would not follow the path she had set out for him. Instead he would follow the way the Lady of the Lake had unfolded to him. He would learn wisdom, not magic. He would gather knowledge from every source in the natural world to surpass Mab's cunning, and he would win the war he fought against her, because in the end he had to do nothing at all to triumph. He simply had to remain here, safe in his forest, and let the world pass him by.

That was all.

CHAPTER NINE

THE
COURTS OF
CRUELTY

*H*ow terrible can it be?

Lady Nimue told herself that going to see the king could not be very terrible at all, and tried to make herself believe it. She paced between table and chair and brazier, ignoring the wine-jug and goblets set out on the table and the warm bed filled with eiderdowns in the inner chamber. Though it was late, she could not sleep when tomorrow would bring an audience with Vortigern.

Outside, the wind of the moors wuthered against the sturdy canvas walls of Lord Ardent's campaigning tent. Inside, the thick woven tapestries hanging from the heavy ashwood tentframe hardly moved, and Nimue was as warm as if she were still home in her father's northern castle . . . though she wasn't nearly as safe. For Lord Ardent's tent was pitched on the vast open heaths of Cornwall, and over everyone in the camp towered the great granite ridge upon which Vortigern meant to build his castle, the natural barrier whose broad flat top had been used as a thoroughfare by invading armies from the Tuatha de Danaan to the Saxon usurpers.

On top of its sturdy length Vortigern was building a great castle, so that no one after him would be able to use this route to conquer Britain, and the construction was not going well. It was autumn once again; the building of Pendragon Castle had begun years before, and no architect in all of Britain had been able to make the walls stand upon their foundations. The heads of the failed architects were on spikes surrounding the ruined foundations; her father said that rumour had it that Gwennius, the latest one, would be joining his predecessors soon.

For Gwennius's sake Nimue hoped that rumour lied. She had talked with the worried little man a few times since Ardent had been commanded to bring her to court. All the good architects were dead, and Gwennius was the unluckiest of those who were left; a thin, fussy, grey-haired man who drank too much and who had been afflicted with a perpetual stammer since he'd taken this new job. It was no sinecure being Vortigern's architect, and no long-lasting position either. Nimue only hoped her own future would be brighter than Gwennius's. She did not know what the king wanted of her, and neither did Lord Ardent. Both of them would have to wait and see, as Nimue had waited these past several years for her future to begin.

Nothing in Nimue's life had gone as she had antici-pated on that last night she had spent within Avalon Abbey's walls. Her father had not married her off to the son of a fellow noble as she had feared and expected – though years had passed, the king had refused to give his permission for any marriage, for Nimue's marriage would bring an alliance between Ardent, one of Vortigern's most powerful barons, and whomever Nimue married. And – as anyone who had spent any time at court realized – even after so many years on the throne of Britain, Vortigern still saw enemies in every shadow and planned accordingly.

In one way he was right, as he was universally hated. But in another he was wrong, for Vortigern had long since crushed the rebellion from every heart but one.

Prince Uther's.

Constant's golden crown sat easily upon the long blond hair of the man who sat in the main room of the elaborate campaign tent, and his red cape was lined in costly ermine, but beneath these regal trappings King Vortigern wore full battle armour, his great sword belted at his hip. Even now, at night, safe in his tent, ringed around by guards who were either loyal or watching one another too closely to dare any treason, Vortigern did not feel secure.

He'd come from holding court in Londinium – another

round of dissidents to execute, the only thing that Britain apparently had an endless supply of – to see how the building of his castle was progressing. If he did not have sons to leave behind him when he died, at least he would leave monuments. The people would remember him, whether they liked it or not.

Unfortunately, Gwennius was doing no better than his predecessors; he'd have to execute the man soon, Vortigern thought. Not so much because of his string of repeated failures, but simply because he was tired of looking at him.

It's more work being a tyrannical despot than most people think.

The years that had passed since he'd seized Britain for his own had not been kind to him. The leonine young king had been replaced by an ageing and suspicious ruler; a king without an heir, whose lands were not at peace.

Let Uther be my heir, Vortigern thought sullenly.

If only the boy would meet him on the field. Vortigern yearned for a proper war instead of the endless skirmishes that had plagued every day of the last fifteen years of his rule. Things had not worked out the way he'd expected them to on that night so long ago in Saxony, when somehow he had realized that the Romans were gone and Britain was ripe for plunder. His body ached with the scars of many battles, but the British continued to defy him, no matter how many of them he killed. He couldn't even trust his friends.

A king has no friends, he thought to himself. *No. Instead, a king has . . . opportunities.*

And one of them had just arrived.

Vortigern settled himself more comfortably in the high-backed chair of state – there was a plate of painted iron between the wood and the cushion, placed there expressly to discourage daggers in the back – and regarded the man who had slunk through the formidable protection of his army specifically to meet him.

Yvain the Fox regarded the King of Britain just as warily. He was a slender nondescript man wearing dark clothes of very good quality that had yet seen better days. The only jewellery he wore was a thick gold hoop in his left ear and a signet of grey agate set in yellow gold on the first finger of his right hand, the ring that served as his pass through Vortigern's army. He wore a narrow beard, well-barbered, after the fashion of Prince Uther's court. There was grey in the beard, as in the curls of the short dark hair, yet Yvain did not appear to be an old man. Neither was he young; he simply *was*: an ordinary-looking, common-place man who could be forgotten the moment he passed from sight.

It was a highly desirable trait for a spy to possess.

Yvain had just come from France. By ship to Dover, by fast horse over three days to a stronghold of Vortigern's some way east of here, and then by much inferior horse here to this camp in the hours between moonset and dawn – the wolf's hour, when treason was plotted and murder done.

Now he awaited Vortigern's signal to begin his report. There was a silver-chased glass decanter that had come all the way from Byzantium on the table between them, filled with the finest Cyprian wine, but neither man made a move toward it.

Vortigern, because he did not rule out the possibility that it was poisoned. His visitor, because to take such a liberty in the presence of his master would be to sign his death-warrant. The king's temper was widely known to be increasingly erratic, and Yvain feared to overstep its bounds.

'Tell me the news, and don't pretty it up,' Vortigern said at last.

'Uther is coming,' Yvain said.

Vortigern snorted and reached for the decanter. He

poured two goblets full – blue glass, to match the decanter, set with opals and the cloudy green emeralds that came from the far east – and pushed one toward Yvain.

'I heard that last year and the year before. Uther's always coming, but he never quite gets around to launching his ships,' Vortigern sneered.

'This time he will. Lionors died last spring. Without the Old Queen to urge caution on him, Uther is hot for battle. He's bought mercenaries and ships, and he'll sail soon from Normandy. I have heard that he plans to summon the countryfolk to the Red Dragon standard when he lands, and then take whichever of the old Roman walled cities – Winchester, York – will open to him for his headquarters. He'll winter there, consolidating his gains, and attack your strongholds with the spring.'

'Because nobody fights in winter,' Vortigern said, as if to himself. He sighed, as if giving up a cherished plan. 'And neither do I. The weather's uncertain . . . supplies run low. I can't push the men that far without a good reason, not with a fire-breathing dragon raiding the countryside from Londinium to the Wall. Sooner or later the peasants are going to get tired of placating the beast with virgins, and then I'll have to come up with something else. Where is Uther landing?'

Yvain shook his head, unfazed by the rapid change of subject. 'I don't know, Your Majesty. If I waited to find that out, I would have been sailing with the prince, instead of bringing you this warning.'

'It might have been better if you had,' grumbled Vortigern. 'You could have brought me facts instead of another cycle of rumours. What's wrong with the wine?'

'Nothing, sire,' Yvain said bravely, and drained the cup.

There was a moment's pause, while both men decided the wine was not poisoned, then Vortigern emptied his own cup.

'I can return to them as soon as Uther lands, infiltrate his camp, and bring you fresh news,' Yvain suggested. 'No one notices me. They'll think I sailed with them, like as not.'

'Never mind that,' Vortigern said irritably, pouring himself more wine. 'I need you here. When Uther lands, who will remain loyal to the White Dragon – and who will go skulking off to join Uther? I need to know so I can take precautions.'

Yvain thought for a moment. 'I shall see what I can

discover. But Your Majesty might simply ask himself who among his army fought for King Constant. There aren't many lords from those days left.'

'Ah . . .' Vortigern stared unseeing past Yvain, toward the hangings of the tent and the night outside. 'I thought that would be your answer. Now go – and seek me out again when Uther lands his ships.'

Morning. The sky was white with high cloud and a thin monotonous wind blew, lofting the pennants of the tents in a brave display. In all directions away from the towering spine of rock upon which the masons toiled fruitlessly to build his castle, the land swept flatly toward the sea. The wind off the sea was cold and damp, so far as Vortigern had ever been able to tell. The salt tainted the air with the faint scent of blood.

It would have been warmer inside the tent. The side facing the construction was pegged open, revealing a large table spread with building plans and leaving one side open to the mercy of the elements, but Vortigern preferred to study the view rather than huddle beneath oil lamps conferring with Gwennius. On top of the ridge in the middle distance, workmen crawled, tiny as ants, over the scaffolding that half-concealed the curtain wall of Vortigern's new castle. After six years of building, they were no closer to completing their work than they had been on the first day of construction. He turned his head and spoke.

'How goes the building of my stronghold?'

He watched, pleased, as all the colour faded from Gwennius's face, leaving it a sickly greenish white. By now Vortigern knew that it was not the architects' fault that the building continued to fail, but executing them was one of his few remaining pleasures.

Lailoken effaced himself at the back of the tent as the king spoke to Gwennius, trying to stay as far away from Vortigern as possible without actually leaving the vicinity, something that was sure to be noticed.

Lailoken was the Royal Soothsayer. He was an old man, and he concealed his inadequacy beneath a facade of sheer terror. He had been in Vortigern's service for the last six weeks, ever since the king had run his predecessor through with a handy spear. He was the third Royal Soothsayer since the spring, and would have been happy to give up the job if he could think of any way to leave it alive.

Lailoken couldn't actually imagine what Vortigern wanted with a Royal Soothsayer, since the king never took anyone's advice but his own. As far as he could tell, Vortigern wanted to be agreed with, and this the aged soothsayer did as vehemently as possible on every occasion. It didn't bother him that his behaviour was undignified. He'd lost all pretence to dignity years ago.

Once he'd been a Druid, a priest of the Sacred Groves. But Constant had cut down his holy oaks, and then Vortigern had cut down *everybody*. Bitterly, Lailoken remembered the day at the sacred well of the priestess Ambrosia, when Vortigern's riders had come to slaughter the refugees from his tyranny, so that none would remain to sow discontent against the king. He'd run for his life, but it hadn't been flight that had saved him, but the luck to have tumbled into a midden heap, there to lie hidden from sight until the killing was done. When he'd finally dared to creep out of hiding, he'd seen no other survivors of the carnage. He'd never even seen Ambrosia's body among the dead.

Luck. That's one name for it, I suppose.

After the massacre, Lailoken had drifted from place to place, doing his best to hide what was left of his priestly powers, but even that hadn't helped him in the end. In the last few years, Vortigern had started rounding up the old and useless, executing them so that the food that would have gone to feed them could feed his army instead. Caught in such a round-up and faced with his immediate execution, the old Druid had been willing to claim magical powers in order to win a reprieve from death. He'd never dreamed that the claim would get him employment as the king's new sooth-sayer, for exactly as long as he remained amusing.

However long that might be.

Nimue had not slept, but despite her wakefulness, morning had come all too soon, and with it, her appointment to meet the king. She'd taken as long as she could over her bathing and dressing that morning, but Nimue dared not delay her father too much with her preparations. Vortigern was known to be impatient with late arrivals – Vortigern was known to be impa-tient with *everything* – and her father was so frightened these days . . .

Resolutely Nimue turned back to her mirror, and set the golden coronet of her rank upon her shining brown hair. She was wearing her finest gown, a dress of rich brocade, and looked every inch the noble lady that she was. Now she and Lord Ardent would go to answer Vortigern's summons, and she would discover that all her fears had been moondust and nonsense. What could Vortigern do to her without angering her father?

And Vortigern still needed Lord Ardent, and his troops.

'Father? I'm ready,' Nimue said, rising from her dressing table.

The day was cold and inclement, whipping her long hair into a tangle the moment Nimue stepped from the tent. A few yards away she could see the tent that Vortigern had set up for his architect's use. The king's black banner with its White Dragon fluttered like a pirate's flag from the roof-spire.

That's all that he is – just an old pirate! Nimue thought stormily, but she did not say the words aloud. The lines of care in her father's face were enough reason not to do so.

She studied the king curiously as they approached him, for Ardent had kept her away from him when she had been brought to court, and Nimue had never seen him. The Saxon had much the look of an ageing lion, she thought, the gold of his youthful good looks faded to the dross of age. The pale eyes glittered with suspicion, and perhaps even with madness, and the smile he turned upon her father was false and feral.

'It's a fine position for a new castle, don't you think, Lord Ardent?' Vortigern asked dulcetly.

'It will be impregnable, Your Majesty,' Ardent said quickly. 'No army could take it.'

'Not even Uther's?' Vortigern returned cannily.

He saw Ardent hesitate. The girl beside him must be Ardent's daughter, Nimue. She was a beautiful creature, and once more Vortigern toyed with the notion of marrying her. But he was through with marrying – it was bad luck for him.

'My spies tell me he's raising an army and getting ready to sail for England,' Vortigern added, watching Ardent's face. 'He wants to kill me. I can't blame him. I killed his father, King Constant.'

And I would have killed the whelp at the same time, if I'd got my hands on him. But he escaped. Was that your doing, Ardent?

'King Constant was a tyrant,' Ardent choked out.

'Not unlike myself,' Vortigern pointed out helpfully.

'Yes, sire,' Ardent said.

Vortigern saw his face change as he thought better of the remark.

'No, sire, no –'

'You don't sound very convincing, Ardent. What I'm interested in is – in case we have to fight – whose side will you be on? Mine or his?'

Vortigern didn't trust Ardent, but he needed him.

The question was, how could he ensure Ardent's loyalty – or at least compliance – without seeming weak?

'I've always been loyal to Your Majesty!' Ardent said, mustering as much conviction as he could manage.

'True, true,' Vortigern said agreeably. 'Up until now. The trouble is, I don't trust anyone any more. I want guarantees.'

'You have my word on it,' Ardent quavered, baffled and beginning to be afraid.

'Not enough,' Vortigern said shortly. 'I'm keeping your daughter as surety. Guards!'

He raised his voice and half a dozen men in the White Dragon livery stepped forward to take Nimue into custody. Ardent fell back before them, but the old warrior wasn't quite cowed.

'This is outrageous . . . sire,' he protested.

'I'm sorry,' Vortigern said, though not as if he meant it.

The guards marched past him, thrusting Ardent out of their way.

'My father will do what is right!' Nimue said as they approached.

Her voice held all the defiance that her father dared not show.

Vortigern smiled – a surprising, genuine smile.

'I hope he will; he never has before.' He spoke directly to the princess. When their gazes locked it was like a clash of swords between equals. 'If your father stays loyal to me, you'll be safe. If he betrays me, I will kill you.'

She glared into his eyes defiantly, but for all her bravery, she was still only a young woman, and when the soldiers seized her, Nimue's nerve broke.

'Father!' she cried as she was dragged away.

Vortigern watched Ardent's face carefully. Its expression never changed. The strategy had worked, then. Ardent was Vortigern's man.

For now.

In the Palace Under Hill, Mab watched events unfold in her scrying crystal. The image showed her the windy plains of Britain, and Vortigern's guards dragging a struggling screaming girl – Nimue – away to imprisonment. She could see Vortigern, Ardent, Lailoken . . . all threads in her weaving, little though they knew it.

Merlin thought he'd defeated her, years ago when Ambrosia died, but the boy had no idea what true patience was. Let him think himself free. The last tool that she needed to force him to use his magic was about to fall into her hand.

With no more than a thought, Mab transported herself to the architect's tent.

No one would be able to see her unless she wished it, and upon this occasion the Mistress of Magic did not wish to be seen. As she had in causing Queen Ganeida to die on her wedding night many years before, she would work behind the scenes to achieve her ends.

Now that he had settled Lord Argent, Vortigern turned his attention back to the architect.

'How does it go?'

He glanced toward the top of the ridge. The walls of the castle tower were obscured by a lattice of scaffolding, but all the timber in Britain could not conceal the fact that each time Gwennius's masons raised the walls of Vortigern's castle higher than six courses, their work toppled like blocks pushed over by a giant's impatient hand. There was no reason for it, but there was also nothing anyone could do could stop it, Gwennius included.

'Are you making any progress?' Vortigern asked, turning his back to the scene of the construction.

Even he could see that no progress had been made since the spring. He knew it, Gwennius knew it, and Gwennius knew he knew it, but still the man tried frantically to bluff, mispronouncing the terms of his craft in his haste.

'Fine, sire, fine. The linnets on the west side need bolstering –'

Vortigern found such desperate persistence vaguely charming; he made a pact with himself that if the walls managed to stay up for the next ten minutes, he would spare Gwennius's life.

At that moment a familiar rumbling began behind him. Vortigern did not need to turn around to see that once again the walls were falling. The scaffolding flew apart like straws in a windstorm. Men screamed desperately as they were crushed beneath an avalanche of tumbling blocks of stone.

Vortigern's face did not change.

'Please tell me exactly what happened,' he said mildly, as if requesting a report on the weather.

Gwennius stared into the king's eyes with the mute entreaty of a drowning man. 'I don't know, sire,' he answered, too stunned to be anything but completely honest.

So every one of Vortigern's architects had said in the end.

'Guards,' Vortigern said without raising his voice. 'Take him away.'

As the guards approached, Gwennius seemed to discover some last spark of self-preservation. He clutched at the rolls of plans, holding them against his chest as if vellum and ink could save him.

'It shouldn't have done that!' he cried as the guards reached him. As they dragged him away, Vortigern could hear him, still shouting: 'It's the linnets! I'm sure it's the linnets!'

Vortigern looked over his shoulder, toward his castle and away from its latest builder. Dust was still rising from the site of the latest disaster, and those who had not been caught in the collapse ran back and forth trying to help their buried fellows.

'And get me a different architect,' the king added, almost as an afterthought.

Invisible, Mab inspected her handiwork from beside the king. Since that long-ago day when he had decided to build here, she had toppled every single castle Vortigern had raised on this site, waiting patiently for him to despair. But not to give up – Vortigern never gave up, Mab knew that, from all the years of watching him turn against her plans to further his own. But he could certainly be driven beyond common sense.

'Why won't the tower stand?' Vortigern demanded.

And at last the moment Mab had been waiting for came: Vortigern consulted his soothsayer.

It had been years since Mab had managed to put into the king's mind the notion that he should have a soothsayer, but even the Queen of the Old Ways could not influence Vortigern to consult him. But what magic could not do, desperation could, providing you had enough patience.

And Mab had patience.

'I'm a soothsayer, Your Majesty. Not an architect,' Lailoken quavered. His eyes darted desperately from side to side, searching for an escape that didn't exist.

Mab smiled, awaiting her moment.

'So tell me,' Vortigern growled, taking a step closer to the old man, 'why is it that every time I try to build this tower it collapses?'

Lailoken wrung his hands in terror. 'Ah well. Yes, indeed. Hmmm . . .'

None of these delaying tactics worked.

'You think I should know that?' he asked tentatively.

'*Yes!*' Vortigern roared.

Goaded beyond patience, the king grabbed his seer by the throat, dragging the man up on his toes. The king's face was purple with rage; a terrifying sight for a brave man, let alone for a lifelong coward like Lailoken. Mab stepped up behind the old Druid and put an invisible hand on his shoulder.

Tell him you'll read the runestones, she whispered in his ear. *If you don't say something to placate him he'll kill you now, just as he did Gwennius. Come to me at Sarum, old man – call upon Queen Mab to save you . . .*

'Ah –!' Lailoken choked and struggled against the crushing grip upon his throat. His mind spun frantically, searching for the words that would save his life, and suddenly he found them.

'I'll – I'll read the stones!' he burst out. 'I will,' he added, as if he were convincing himself. 'That's something I do well.'

Vortigern released him with a shove that sent the old man sprawling. 'Then read them!' he shouted.

Several people turned to look, then turned away quickly lest the king catch them looking at him. Lailoken felt himself all over as if to convince himself that he was still alive, then turned and began to shuffle as fast as he could from Vortigern's sight.

Mab smiled and wished herself back to her underground palace. Her work here was finished. And the trap to catch Merlin was about to be sprung.

*   *   *

Vortigern gazed around himself – from the ruin on the hill, to the retreating figure of the soothsayer, to the figures of all the people trying so very hard not to catch his attention. A great weariness possessed him. Everything he touched turned to discord and destruction.

'Why? Why?' He stared into the heavens, as if he could call old King Constant's god to account. '*Why* am I surrounded by incompetent fools?'

He might be incompetent and ineffectual, but he was no fool. Lailoken hurried to his tent and hid himself inside.

The Royal Soothsayer's tent was much smaller than the king's – a single room with thick walls of double-hung canvas. It smelled strongly of herbs and incense and was filled with everything his predecessors had thought might placate the king or gain themselves a longer life – amulets, talismans, carved totems, and several trunks full of ornate costumes and other odds and ends. There were a compass, an astrolabe, and a half-finished horoscope spread out upon the table, and a stuffed owl looked down glassily from the centre-pole of the tent.

Lailoken ignored the gaudy clutter of the tent's

interior with the ease of long practice, flinging open the lid of the nearest trunk and rooting through it hastily. Almost the first thing his hand touched was a sack of runestones, but he tossed it aside without heed. Runes wouldn't save him now – he needed a hooded cloak and his secret horde of gold coins, and then to get out of the king's camp unnoticed as quickly as possible. He had no intention of trying any divination – he didn't need to read the future to know that the only thing that could guarantee Vortigern's soothsayer a long life was a great deal of distance from Vortigern.

Of course he knew *how* to tell fortunes. Every aspirant to the Druid's Grove was taught several forms of magic and divination – but it had been years since he'd done any magic. Read the stones? Where had that idea come from? And what if Vortigern didn't like the answer?

Finally Lailoken found the items he was searching for. He swirled the thick black cloak around himself and tucked his coins into a sack around his neck. It wasn't much, but it would have to do. He certainly didn't dare take any of the costly artifacts strewn about the tent. They could be easily traced, and the last thing Lailoken wanted was to be accused of theft and brought back to face the king's justice.

It was the king's justice he was trying to escape in the first place.

He picked up a knife – its purpose was to sacrifice animals, so that omens could be read in their entrails, but it would serve his purpose equally well – and carefully slit the fabric at the back of his tent. All he needed was a few hours' head start, and no one would ever find him . . .

'Going somewhere?' the captain of Vortigern's guard said from the doorway of the tent.

Lailoken jumped back from his labour and dropped the knife. He turned around, looking up into the stony countenance of Vortigern's chief enforcer and swallowed painfully. Sir Rhys was built like a granite cliff and was just as compassionate. The captain's well-used armour – and well-used weapons – gleamed in the pale autumn sunlight that shone in over his shoulder.

'Sarum,' Lailoken croaked, driven to invention by sheer panic. 'Sacred stones. Place of power. Very magical.'

'Your eagerness to be about the king's business does you credit,' Sir Rhys said, gazing from the cloaked soothsayer to the new slit in the back wall of the tent. 'But the king isn't going to make you walk all the way to Sarum all by yourself. No, he's sending me and a dozen soldiers with you, just to make sure nothing happens to you. We wouldn't want you to get lost and not find your way back here, now, would we? Now, let me help you pack for your journey, soothsayer.'

Sir Rhys smiled.

The followers of the Old Ways had called this the last day of the old year and the first day of the new: Samhain, the night on which the gate between the worlds was flung open and the spirits of living and dead, past and future, mingled together.

Lailoken shivered in the autumn cold. Sir Rhys's campfire was a small and lonely speck half a mile away. Lailoken had said he needed privacy for his devotions, and Vortigern's soldiers weren't any too eager to involve themselves with the spirits he might conjure, but Lailoken didn't fool himself into believing this meant he would be able to escape. Sir Rhys would have guards patrolling every escape route.

No, his only hope of help lay in the Old Ones, little help though they'd ever been to him yet. He gazed apprehensively about him at the towering stones of Sarum. It had been a long time since Lailoken had come here. The ancient sarcen stones brought back too many sorrowful memories. Ambrosia and all the others who had shared his faith – dead.

As he would be dead, if he did not find some way to divert Vortigern's anger and make Pendragon's walls stand.

Quickly he made his preparations: the white bull's hide laid out upon the ground, the libations of milk and beer poured at the four cardinal points, the bale-fire kindled of the nine sacred woods. It was amazing how easily the Old Ways came back to him, though he'd tried his best to forget them in the course of a lifetime's persecution. Though he'd tried to skimp on his preparations – who would ever see them? – a strange reluctance had held him back, and so to make his petition this Samhain night Lailoken was barefoot and crowned in mistletoe, wearing a robe of pure new wool that had been worked without any seam, cinched with a pony-skin girdle dyed with scarlet cochineal and studded with gold – the immemorial trappings of an observance that was vanishing in his own lifetime.

He knelt upon the bullhide and took the runestones in his hand. He did not know where his predecessor had got them from, but they were very old. The ivory they were carved of was yellowed almost to the colour of amber by time, and the stark angular symbols incised into each were worn nearly smooth with uncounted decades of handling.

'Oh, Mab – *dear* Mab –'

Lailoken closed his eyes and muttered almost to himself as he flung out the runestones upon the white bull's hide.

'I've been a worshipper of the Old Ways all my life, and now that life is in danger – and it's a precious life; it's mine – Oh, Mab, I've never had any real help – no, never – oh, what am I going to do? I don't know why his blasted tower keeps falling down!' He didn't really expect an answer, but he got one.

'The land is cursed!' Mab hissed, stepping out from behind a stone. Her black finery glittered in the firelight.

Lailoken fell back with a yell of terror, his eyes fixed on the apparition before him. His eyes glittered with tears, and unfamiliar emotions lifted his heart as he gazed at her.

Hope. Grief.

'You've appeared,' he said in a trembling voice. 'You've appeared after all these years! It *is* Queen Mab?'

The woman nodded regally. 'Yes, old man,' she said.

When she looked up again, the old Druid could see

that her eyes glowed in the dark like a wolf's or an owl's – proof that she was what she said she was.

Not that he'd doubted. No, not him. Never.

'The land is cursed!' Mab said again, her voice like the hissing of wind through winter branches. 'Neither tower nor castle will stand.'

Mab saw the old man's eyes fill with despair at her pronouncement, and waited for the emotion to run its course. Of course he would not simply accept that answer. He wanted to live far too much. She'd chosen him for just that fact, preserved him from untimely execution, kept her eye on him through all the long years of watching and waiting, as Merlin grew to manhood in his forest, thinking himself safe.

'So what do we do?' the old man said at last.

'We.' How arrogant these mortals are!

'You must find a man with no mortal father and mix his blood with the mortar,' Mab said oracularly. *I have him, I have him,* she gloated inside. *Merlin will never deny such an accusation when they question him – he has too much taste for the truth. And he wants to live too much to let Vortigern slit his throat. He'll use his magic to escape. He must!*

She watched as Lailoken digested her words.

'Ooh, ah . . . splendid,' the old seer said doubtfully.

Bumbling old fool! He was cowardly and half-senile, but senile old cowards had uses to which brave young men could not be put. And they could defeat brave young men in the end – with her help.

Say it, you old fool! Ask the question I have waited to hear for longer than you can imagine!

'But . . . a man who has no mortal father?' Lailoken asked grovellingly, torn between hope and despair. 'Er, where can I find a man like that?'

Mab smiled and came close enough to lay her hand atop his head. 'I'll show you . . .'

THE
COURTS OF
THE MOON

Years had passed as Merlin learned to live the lessons of the Lady of the Lake, trying to live always in the stillness that was the mystic centre of all things, to become a focus for the loving power that came from being and not from doing. Each day that he passed following her path, and not Mab's, made him stronger and more at peace, until even thoughts of Nimue and what might have been between them did not trouble him very often.

He lived quietly in the forest as the magic of trickery and illusion that he had learned from Mab and Frik dropped from his mind, unused, and in its place the Lady's gift – the knowledge of prophecy – grew. The seasons turned, and Merlin was content to wait, dreaming his dreams, for he knew that Mab was not finished with him nor with Britain, and that his greatest battles still lay ahead.

In his dreams he saw the future of Britain – battles he did not understand, kings who were still unborn. He was content to forget each of these dreams when he woke, for there was no one to tell them to yet. The dreams Merlin remembered, and acted upon, were simple homely ones, a farmer's plough slipping and injuring him, a ewe needing help to give birth. And from these small kindnesses his reputation grew, until all the north knew that deep in the wild forest lived a great wizard. Soon, Merlin knew, that fame would call him into battle, but he did not yet know how dearly that fight would cost him, or how soon it would begin. The day, it seemed, came far too soon.

As soon as he woke in the morning, he knew his fate would find him that day. Samhain had fallen a few weeks previously, and Merlin had expected the trouble to come then. When it had not, he had let his guard down a little, thinking that in the dark half of the year, when even kings stayed close to their own hearth sides, he would have a certain amount of shelter. But this morning, his senses, that had told him even in childhood when strangers trespassed in his beloved forest, told him there was danger afoot.

Merlin awaited it calmly. He went about his usual morning routine, preparing his simple breakfast of herbal tea and acorn bread, and then went to the clearing in the forest. Around him a circle of young trees stood like the pillars of a cathedral — a cathedral of the Old Ways, growing from the living earth, not made of dead stone as the Christians built. As soon as the thought came to him, Merlin pushed it away. To think in terms of the Old Ways versus the new religion was to fall into the same trap that Queen Mab had, a trap made of hatred and distrust. Merlin chose to walk a third path, neither of black magic nor white light, a path as grey as mist, where everything was judged on its own merits. He would not hate the new religion; neither would he follow the Old Ways. He would simply be as he had always been: Merlin the Wizard.

At midday he finally heard them – a troop of mounted soldiers crashing through the winter-killed underbrush. They wore the white dragon of King Vortigern on their surcoats, and riding at their head was an old man dressed as a Druid, though the reigns of two draconian kings had managed to nearly wipe the priesthood from the face of Britain.

So Vortigern has discovered he now has some use for magic? Merlin thought to himself. *This should be interesting.* He got to his feet and turned to face the soldiers just as they entered the clearing.

'Seize that man!' the old Druid blustered, pointing an accusing finger at Merlin.

Merlin tried his most disarming smile. 'Welcome to my home, sir,' he said mildly. 'How can I help you?' To live in perfect trust was the first lesson that magic taught. As the years had passed in his forest home,

Merlin had learned to live and act as if he expected goodness from all men, and such was the power of expectation that he had rarely been disappointed. Even now such humble sorcery worked its subtle magic: the old Druid dismounted from his horse, and when he spoke again, his tone was very different.

'The king wants to see you,' he said in more apologetic tones.

Now that he had come closer, Merlin could see how the old man's face was marked by lines of care and worry – though who didn't have such distress with Vortigern on the throne? At least, living here in the north, Merlin had been spared most of the concerns that ordinary people faced in their daily lives. But now the king was asking for him, and Merlin knew that somewhere, somehow, Queen Mab must be involved.

'You have only to ask,' he said gently.

'You'll come voluntarily?' The old Druid did his best to conceal his surprise. 'Ah, that's good. Most people are reluctant to meet King Vortigern. In fact, they're usually dragged in screaming. Not that I blame them,' he added. The last pretence of command seemed to leave him now as he sighed, shoulders drooping, and he suddenly looked like what he was: a frail, frightened old man.

'I'm the King's Soothsayer,' he admitted. Even Merlin in his isolation had heard of Lailoken. The poor man was hated by the Christians for his supposed wizardry and despised by the pagans for serving Vortigern. No wonder the old man looked so weary. It was a hard life when you fit in nowhere, and no one knew that better than Merlin, himself half-fay, half-mortal.

By now the rest of the soldiers had spread out around the clearing, surrounding him. Merlin saw that they had come well-prepared: all armed to the teeth, and, more to the point, they'd brought a spare horse.

'An important position?' he asked Lailoken.

'And a fragile one,' the old man said. 'I'm the third Royal Soothsayer this year.'

Merlin frowned to himself. His visions had promised him great danger ahead, but he could not believe that this frail old man meant him any harm.

'He must get through them at an alarming speed,' Merlin said politely.

'He gets through everything at an alarming speed,' Lailoken said sadly. He glanced at the ring of soldiers surrounding them, and then, as if remembering his duty, said, 'You are Merlin, the man without a mortal father?'

'Yes,' Merlin answered. There was no point in denying it. He was only a thread in a pattern that forces greater than himself were weaving, and long ago Merlin had learned to save his strength for the more important battles.

'I'm afraid the king wants you urgently,' Lailoken sighed.

Without being asked, one of the soldiers led forth the riderless horse. His expression said clearly – though silently – that Merlin would mount the animal one way or another. Bowing to the inevitable, Merlin vaulted gracefully into the saddle, and from that vantage point took a last look around his forest home. Something within him told him that it would be a very long time before he saw it again.

Before he was finished looking, the soldier who had brought him the horse mounted his own animal and began leading Merlin's charger away. In moments, Merlin and Lailoken were surrounded by soldiers, whose horses moved at a brisk trot along the road that led out of the forest, the road that led west . . . toward Pendragon, and the King.

THE STORY CONTINUES IN *MERLIN: THE KING'S WIZARD*

About the author

James Mallory attended schools in California and the midwest to study completely irrelevant subjects before moving to New York to pursue a career in writing. From an early age he has been fascinated both with the Arthurian legends and their historical evolution, an avocation which also triggered a lifelong interest in classic fantasy literature. His other interests include hiking, comparative religion, and cinema.

THE
MERLIN
MYSTERY

Jonathan Gunson & Marten Coombe

The Secret Lies Inside . . .

The Puzzle – hidden in the enchanting illustrations and story of Merlin and the water-sprite Nimue is the most intricate puzzle ever created.

The Prize – is Merlin's Wand, an alchemist's staff crafted from gold, silver, bronze, crystal and lapis lazuli, and also an accumulating prize fund. *For every book wherever sold will produce an extra grain of gold.* THE MERLIN MYSTERY will be published simultaneously all over the world and for every copy of the book sold 20p will be put into a prize fund which will grow and grow until the puzzle is solved.

All you need to solve THE MERLIN MYSTERY is in the book, and the solution is as likely to be found by a bright and determined child as by an expert puzzler.

WHO ON EARTH WILL WIN?

ISBN 0 00 224675 9

THE LORD OF THE RINGS
J. R. R. Tolkien

Part 1: The Fellowship of the Ring
Part 2: The Two Towers
Part 3: The Return of the King

The Lord of the Rings cannot be described in a few words. J. R. R. Tolkien's great work of imaginative fiction has been labelled both a heroic romance and a classic of science fiction. It is, however, impossible to convey to the new reader all of the book's qualities, and the range of its creation. By turns comic, homely, epic, monstrous and diabolic, the narrative moves through countless changes of scenes and character in an imaginary world which is totally convincing in its detail. Tolkien created a new mythology in an invented world which has proved timeless in its appeal.

'An extraordinary book. It deals with a stupendous theme. It leads us through a succession of strange and astonishing episodes, some of them magnificent, in a region where everything is invented, forest, moor, river, wilderness, town, and the races which inhabit them. As the story goes on the world of the Ring grows more vast and mysterious and crowded with curious figures, horrible, delightful or comic. The story itself is superb.'
                                                     – *The Observer*

'Among the greatest works of imaginative fiction of the twentieth century.'   – *Sunday Telegraph*

'The English-speaking world is divided into those who have read *The Hobbit* and *The Lord of the Rings* and those who are going to read them.'   – *Sunday Times*

The Lord of the Rings is available as a three book paperback edition and also in one volume.

The Last Raven
Craig Thomas

In the aftermath of the Cold War, the world is a less dangerous place . . . except for Patrick Hyde.

When he witnesses the shooting down of a Soviet airliner near the Afghan border, he has only one option – to reach London and Kenneth Aubrey. His enemies, American and Russian, have no alternative but to silence him . . .

To stay alive means killing and running – from Afghanistan to Delhi to California, Hyde pursues the truth as his enemies pursue him.

Can Aubrey save Patrick Hyde – can he even save himself?

The era of *glasnost* and *perestroika* is the most dangerous time for the last raven . . .

In *The Last Raven*, Craig Thomas reaches new heights of tension, suspense and action, to prove himself once again the master of the modern adventure story.

0 00 617918 5

Magician
Raymond E. Feist

New Revised Edition

Raymond E. Feist has prepared a new, revised edition, to incorporate over 15,000 words of text omitted from previous editions so that, in his own words, 'it is essentially the book I would have written had I the skills I possess today'.

At Crydee, a frontier outpost in the tranquil Kingdom of the Isles, an orphan boy, Pug is apprenticed to a master magician – and the destinies of two worlds are changed forever. Suddenly the peace of the Kingdom is destroyed as mysterious alien invaders swarm through the land. Pug is swept up into the conflict but for him and his warrior friend, Tomas, an odyssey into the unknown has only just begun. Tomas will inherit a legacy of savage power from an ancient civilisation. Pug's destiny is to lead him through a rift in the fabric of space and time to the mastery of the unimaginable powers of a strange new magic. . .

'Epic scope . . . fast-moving action . . . vivid imagination'
Washington Post

'Tons of intrigue and action'   *Publishers Weekly*

ISBN 0 586 21783 3

The Thief of Always
Clive Barker

*A disturbing fable exploring childhood fears
and delights from the maestro of dark fantasy.*

Mr Hood's Holiday House has stood for a thousand years, welcoming countless children into its embrace. It is a place of miracles, a blissful round of treats and seasons, where every childish whim may be satisfied.

There is a price to be paid, of course, but young Harvey Swick, bored with his life and beguiled by Mr Hood's wonders, does not stop to consider the consequences. It is only when the House shows its darker face – when Harvey discovers the pitiful creatures that dwell in its shadow – that he comes to doubt Mr Hood's philanthropy.

The House and its mysterious architect are not about to release their captive without a battle, however. Mr Hood has ambitions for his new guest, for Harvey's soul burns brighter than any soul he has encountered in a thousand years . . .

'A dashingly produced fantasy with powerful drawings by the author'
Daily Telegraph

'Barker puts the dark side back into childhood fantasy . . . A welcome modern-day return to classic form, this fable lives up to the publishers' billing as a tale for all ages'
Publishers Weekly

ISBN 0 00 647311 3

That Way Lies Camelot
Janny Wurts

Journey through time and space to alternate worlds
and the near future in a superb collection of
interconnected stories

The title story is a poignant and moving tale which deals
sensitively with the eternal blight of humankind - cancer.
Sandy is in the last throes of life and has one final wish. A
wish that, sadly, cannot possibly be fulfilled. For Sandy would
like to visit the Round Table of King Arthur - an impossible
task, but one which is about to be realised.

In *Dreambridge*, the last tree which links this world to the
world of the feys has been brutally attacked. Kirelle, apprentice healer, has been chosen to seek revenge on the humans
who have so thoughtlessly attempted to destroy this sacred
link. Can they be made to understand the gravity of their
actions?

And in Janny Wurts' brilliant *Fleet* stories we follow the
fortunes and misfortunes of Michael Christopher Jensen Jr.
and his numerous encounters with the space-pirate
MacKenzie James. Theirs is a relationship that will captivate
all readers and leave you wondering who the villain really is.

By turns sensitive, witty and imaginative Janny Wurts has
produced an unrivalled collection of short stories that will
hold readers enthralled by her all-round skill and creativity.

'It ought to be illegal for one person to have so much talent'
Stephen R. Donaldson

ISBN 0 00 648003 9

The
No 1 BESTSELLER

David and Leigh Eddings

Belgarath the Sorcerer

'This sixth volume in the Belgariad tells the full story of the legendary sorcerer Belgarath with all the verve and pace we've come to expect from these authors'

The Dark Side

Eagerly awaited for a decade, here at last is the full epic story of Belgarath, the great sorcerer learned in the Will and the Word on whom the fate of the world depends. Only Belgarath can tell of those near-forgotten times when Gods still walked the land: he is the Ancient One, the Old Wolf, his God Aldur's first and most-favoured disciple. Using powers learned over the centuries Belgarath himself records the story of conflict between two mortally opposed Destinies that split the world asunder.

A hugely entertaining work of great daring, wit, grandeur and excitement that confirms the role of Belgarath the Sorcerer as one of the mightiest fantasy creations of the century.

'Nobody writes modern fantasy like Eddings or as well . . . Eddings is at the top with the very best' *Vector*

ISBN 0 586 21315 5

The
No 1 BESTSELLER

David and Leigh Eddings

Polgara the Sorceress

The queen of truth, love, rage and destiny reveals all

Polgara the Sorceress is the crowning achievement of the great fantasy epic which began with The Belgariad and continued with The Malloreon. Once again David and Leigh Eddings display the epic imagination, humour and storytelling power which have made this series the most popular fantasy of modern times. It is a story of wizardry and politics, doom and evil, love and magic. Above all, it is the story of Polgara, a beautiful woman whose constancy and inner power have been the foundation of all the luck and love that have saved the world. At last, the full truth of The Belgariad is revealed.

'All the verve and pace we've come to expect'

The Dark Side

'Nobody writes modern fantasy like Eddings or as well . . . Eddings is at the top with the very best' *Vector*

'I wished *Polgara the Sorceress* was longer . . . the characters are vivid and genuinely likeable, and there's an easy lilt to the prose which makes reading it pure pleasure. It's a wonderful book' *SFX*

ISBN 0 586 21314 7